"Tell me something, Lea—do you offer yourself to every man who is granted entry through your gates?"

The instant the words left his mouth, Jared knew he'd be wise to protect his back. Before releasing her hand, he turned to face her.

He wasn't the least bit surprised to see the tight line of her lips, flushed cheeks, or the glittering rage in her eyes. What did amaze him was the heavy pounding in his chest. She was stunning, nearly robbing him of breath along with the ability to think clearly.

"Or was that display only for me?"

"Jared, don't." She pushed at his arms. "Let me go."

"I thought we were betrothed?" He lowered his head and tasted the soft expanse of her neck. The familiar scent of lavender enveloped him, making him only want more.

"Please." She trembled against him. "Please don't do this."

By the breathless tone of her voice, he knew she wasn't as immune to his attentions as she claimed. "Isn't this what you wanted last night?"

He trailed a line of kisses up to her ear, smiling as a shiver rippled through her. "Isn't this what you offered?"

* * *

Pregnant by the Warrior
Harlequin® Historical #978—January 2010

PREGNANT BY THE WARRIOR

DENISE LYNN

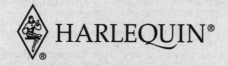

HARLEQUIN®

TORONTO • NEW YORK • LONDON
AMSTERDAM • PARIS • SYDNEY • HAMBURG
STOCKHOLM • ATHENS • TOKYO • MILAN • MADRID
PRAGUE • WARSAW • BUDAPEST • AUCKLAND

Recycling programs
for this product may
not exist in your area.

ISBN-13: 978-0-373-29578-4

PREGNANT BY THE WARRIOR

www.eHarlequin.com

Printed in U.S.A.

Available from Harlequin® Historical and
DENISE LYNN

Falcon's Desire #645
Falcon's Honor #744
Falcon's Love #761
Falcon's Heart #833
Commanded to His Bed #845
Bedded by Her Lord #874
Hallowe'en Husbands #917
"Wedding at Warehaven"
Bedded by the Warrior #950
Pregnant by the Warrior #978

Other Works include:

Silhouette Nocturne

Dragon's Lair

Chapter One

⁓⁓⁓⁓⁓

Montreau Keep—Spring 1142

Silent as North Sea raiders of old, the three longships slipped on to the sandy beach of Montreau Bay.

Lord Jared of Warehaven leapt from the centre boat, his booted feet splashing in the shallow water. Sword raised, he pressed forwards, leading his men into the cover of the tall grasses.

He glanced back towards the beach that had once been so familiar, but a thick cloud covered the moon, and hid his vessels from sight. Only in his mind's eye could he see the great dragon heads guarding the prows, each fierce beast nearly identical except for the colour of their jewel-toned eyes.

Jared turned to the task at hand. Anticipation rippled through his muscles. Smoothing his lips into a grim line, he headed for the cliff tops.

Situated between King Stephen's supporter, the Earl of York, to the south and the Empress Matilda's maternal uncle, King David of Scotland, to the north, Montreau was a choice bit of property. Especially now that its lord was dead, leaving only a lady in charge.

The same lady who had once promised to become his wife. Jared pushed the wayward thought aside. He had no time for reminiscing. The task at hand needed his complete attention.

After seven long years of a seemingly never-ending war for the crown, Empress Matilda, his deceased father's half-sister, had had an uncharacteristic change of heart. Her first order had been to take Montreau by force and hold it as her northern base.

But for a reason Jared could barely fathom, she'd changed her mind. While he was still to take the keep by force if necessary, he was ordered to retain Montreau's neutral position in the war and see to the safety of its lady and people.

The only true differences between the orders was that now lives would not be lost if the people didn't resist. And the Lady of Montreau would not be stripped of her holding. Instead, she would remain as a guiding hand—one that reported to him. A position he would relish until Matilda decided otherwise.

In an odd way Matilda's decision did make some sense. If nothing else the move would keep King David's men from gaining more ground in England, which in turn would keep Matilda from having to evict him once she attained the throne that rightfully belonged to her.

While his aunt disliked warring against family, she would do so if backed far enough against a wall. Jared well remembered his father's hasty exit from England.

Once Matilda decided to fight Stephen, Randall of Warehaven had chosen the safest option for himself and his family—he'd agreed to take charge of his wife's lands in Wales. That had left Jared in control of Warehaven and the task of choosing a liege.

An easy choice for Jared to make, considering King Stephen had wanted control of Jared's ships, whereas Matilda had vowed she'd do nothing so foolish. Thus far she'd stood by her word.

It would be interesting to see what Stephen would do once he discovered a small part of Warehaven's fleet in Montreau Bay and Jared in control of his runaway betrothed's keep.

At the top of the cliff separating the beach from the demesne land, he stared across the distance toward his target. The wavering light of numerous torches lining the walls showed that the messenger's description hadn't been exaggerated.

While Montreau was little more than a partially lit outline in the night, gone was the wooden tower keep with its timber pales encompassing the bailey. Now, even a fool could see it was more royal castle than keep. Larger than most stone keeps, it would not be easily taken.

What kind of reception would be waiting for him? He narrowed his eyes and smiled with wicked mirth. The lady would be shocked and outraged at his arrival. Jared tapped his weapon against his leg, ready for the confrontation to begin.

Soon, all would know if Montreau would remain neutral. And soon, he would know the sweet taste of revenge. He motioned the first group of ten men forwards.

* * *

A red-faced guard bolted through the double doors to the Great Hall. He dropped to one knee before the armed chair on the raised dais. 'My lady.' His head still bowed, he paused, gasping for breath, then he continued, 'The ships have beached.'

Lady Lea of Montreau pulled her sapphire-hued cloak tighter around her shoulders before once again glancing at the crinkled, well-read missives in her hand.

She'd known this moment would come. Three days ago a messenger from the Empress Matilda had delivered one missive announcing that a man would soon arrive to protect her and Montreau's future.

Lea had read between the lines more times than she could count. This unnamed man was being sent not just as a defender of the land, but as a prospective husband.

Five days ago, King Stephen had also sent a missive. His note had been more to the point. If Lea wished to retain control of Montreau, she had but a few months to deliver Montreau a son, or else wed one of Stephen's men.

She'd been widowed just over two weeks. Her husband had chosen a fine time to drown. He could have at least waited until she was with child. She shivered at the thought. It had been hard enough to be in the same room with Charles, let alone in his bedchamber—or bed.

The one time they'd tried to share a marriage bed had ended badly. Thankfully, in their four years of marriage, Charles hadn't found the desire to repeat the event.

If either royal liege thought she'd meekly accept another husband, they would be wrong. She'd had one husband and as far as she was concerned, that had been one too many.

She'd given her heart away many years ago, only to have it trampled beneath duty and honour. Thankfully Charles hadn't expected, or wanted, her love. By the time they'd wed she had learned to live with her broken heart and shattered dreams.

'My lady?'

Lea pushed away the thoughts and attended to the guard. 'How many ships?'

'Three dragon prows.'

The room spun and the floor beneath her chair tilted. Lea swallowed her gasp and closed her eyes, forcing herself to remain calm enough to think. After receiving the king's missive, she'd frantically summoned Montreau's midwife, knowing there was no man on her land who would fulfil her need of getting with child. Besides, she didn't want the man around afterwards to claim the child as his. Everyone needed to believe the babe was Charles's, conceived just before his death.

Uncertain how to find such a man on extremely short notice, she'd requested that the old woman create a charm that would quickly draw someone to her.

She had no use of a husband. In fact, she was much better off without one. The happiest days of her marriage had been the ones when Charles had been away from the keep. She and marriage simply did not suit. Her parents had made her aware at an early age that husbands and wives were little more than bitter enemies living beneath the same roof.

However, she did have need of a man.

The midwife had created many charms for her, some so malodorous that she'd not subject the pigs to the stench.

Lea had chosen a dream charm—one that would enable her to dream of the man who would best serve her needs.

While the charm had filled her dreams with visions of the man, unfortunately, he'd not appeared fully formed. He'd been nothing more than a vaporous warrior disembarking from a dragon prow before leading his men to her keep.

But Lea hadn't needed to see his face to know his identity. She'd yet to say his name out loud, because she had feared giving it voice would make it true. She had prayed hard and long that it would not prove true, that *he* would not come to Montreau and would remain only a wispy dream of the past.

Her prayer had been in vain.

What would she do now? She desperately needed a child, but not by *him*. Dear Lord, not like this. Her stomach knotted. She longed to run away, to hide, to simply vanish from Montreau. Anything, so that she didn't have to face the past.

But that wasn't going to happen. Whether Empress Matilda had sent him on purpose or not made little difference, her fate had been sealed. If she wanted to retain possession of Montreau, she had to produce a child.

Agatha, once her nursemaid and now her lady's maid, stepped closer to ask in a whisper, 'Lady Lea, what are you thinking?'

'You know what I must do.'

Agatha rested an age-gnarled hand on her arm. 'Nay, this is a choice you need not yet make.'

Lea shivered, wishing it could be otherwise. But there was no heir for Montreau and Lea would rather take her own life than pledge herself to one of Stephen's men.

She never should have taken Agatha into her confidence. But what was done was done. She ignored the maid to once again address the waiting guard. 'Tell the men to pull back into the courtyard.'

He said nothing, only rose and rapped his fisted hand to his chest before leaving to do her bidding.

'You will give yourself to the Empress Matilda's man simply to create a child?' Agatha's tone of censure said more than her question had.

Lea glared at the woman. 'Not just a child. An heir for Montreau.'

Her words had been clipped and steady. But her insides were a-quiver, trembling like a child frightened of a storm.

After a quick glance around the hall to make certain none was within hearing, Agatha queried, 'Is this stone keep worth more than your virtue, is it more important than your honour?'

Lea gripped the arms of her chair and leaned forwards. 'Yes. It is.' Until she could sort out her feelings and fears, she had to brave this through. 'What would you have me do? You know as well as I that if Stephen or Matilda controls this keep, our men will be forced into this war. How many lives should I sacrifice?'

Why did Agatha not understand? Montreau had been her entire life. As their only daughter, Lea had been groomed with the same goal in mind that they had had for her brother—until his death—and that was to retain control of Montreau. That was the only thing her parents had ever agreed upon.

They had raised her like the queen of a small country. Just like her brother Phillip, she'd been educated at great cost. They'd made certain she could read, write, speak French, Latin and English and understand mathematics. She'd not let their sacrifices and training be for naught.

Her family held this keep by the grace of King William I. The sealed writs were in a trunk at the foot of her bed. She would not permit Stephen or Matilda to drag Montreau into their war. Her men would not die in vain.

'But, my lady—'

'No!' Lea lowered her voice. 'Stephen offers nothing but war. Matilda offers neutrality—for a time.' She was well aware that the Empress could and did change her mind as often as the barons changed their allegiance. 'We will welcome her man into this keep.' Lea pinned her maid with a hard stare. 'Somehow, I must see to it Montreau gains an heir.'

'Lady Lea, you cannot place all your faith in dreams.'

Because she hadn't wanted to speak his name, she hadn't told Agatha the man's identity. As far as the woman knew, Lea had dreamed of a faceless man.

'I don't place all my faith in dreams.' Lea reached into her cloak to pull a small sachet free. Holding the yarrow dream charm in her hand, she mused, 'But sometimes dreams and fate are all that's left.'

Her gaze lingered a moment on the sachet before she lifted her head to once again face Agatha. 'You have always placed your trust and sometimes my well-being in midwife Berta's hands. Should I now turn my back on what you have taught me not just by word, but by deed?'

Agatha's face crumpled as she lowered her gaze to the floor. 'No. I only ask you to have a care for your own safety and give a thought to your virtue.'

'Would that I had the opportunity to do so.' Yet deep inside, she knew time was of the essence.

But her thoughts at the moment were focused on more than just her virtue. The man who had so ruthlessly tossed her love aside had come back. Not to—or for— her, but because he'd been ordered to guard Montreau.

And Jared of Warehaven always followed his liege lady's orders.

She should be outraged—and Lea knew that she would be—later. Right now, though, she risked becoming lost in memories and thoughts of what might have been.

No.

She couldn't allow that to happen. If she didn't want to relive the pain of loss—and she didn't—then she needed to act as if the past had never happened.

If she treated him like a stranger perhaps then she'd be able to see her plan through—somehow.

Her other worry—the one that should be at the forefront of her concerns—was about Montreau's men. If they thought her life was in danger, they would defend her and the keep to the death.

It was imperative that she keep her wits about her. She'd not have unnecessary bloodshed on her hands, nor on her soul—not when it was within her power to prevent it.

Lea rose and lifted her face to the cool draught ever present in the Great Hall. 'Do you not feel it, Agatha? Can you not sense the change in the air?'

She folded her hands and stared at the doors. 'I may stain my virtue in your eyes, but in the end Montreau will remain safely in my hands.'

'My lady.' Agatha rested a hand on Lea's shoulder.

She patted the maid's hand, hoping to alleviate the woman's worry without divulging how familiar this man was to her. 'I do not fear what need be done. Have I not dreamed of this warrior? His arrival in a dragon prow only confirms the rightness of this decision.'

The maid sighed, then lowered her hand. 'What would you have me do?'

'Take yourself from the hall. Be safe and keep well until I have need of you.' Lea glanced at Agatha, adding, 'I would not rest, knowing you were in harm's way.'

Once the maid exited the hall, Lea debated whether to meet him here, on the wall, or in the bailey. Her experience with men was limited to having her heart broken by one man and being wed to another who had proved how much he despised being married to her at every turn.

No. She'd not think of failure. She could do this. But how was she to set her plan in action without her lack of experience proving her downfall?

She had to forget how well they knew each other and treat Jared like any other man. After all, it had been years since she'd stared so adoringly into his emerald gaze. Years since she'd made such a fool of herself.

She needed to catch him off guard. That should help her gain the upper hand.

She left the Great Hall and castle without a backwards glance.

'Lord Jared.' His weapon still drawn, a guard skidded to a rocking halt before his liege.

Jared forced the man's sword aside with the back of his gloved hand. 'What news have you?'

While sheathing his weapon, the man answered, 'The gates are open. A lone figure awaits between the towers.'

Jared could hardly believe what he'd heard. 'Where are the guards?'

'We went as close as we could without being detected and from what we could see, they appear to have gathered along the walls—unarmed.'

While Matilda had sent word of his arrival, there'd been no time to wait for a reply. He had no way of knowing what sort of reception they would receive.

The lady of this keep held little liking for him—even though more than once she'd professed her undying love. He didn't have the leisure of trusting her—she'd destroyed that long ago. This could be a trick. He could be leading his men into a well-laid trap. 'One man, you say?'

'Aye. The bailey is ablaze with torchlight, but we saw only one man in the gate entrance.'

Jared frowned. Thus far Montreau had remained neutral. But there was no telling what Lea would do if she felt threatened. He'd not risk the souls he'd brought with him. He had not amassed his own small army by being careless with his men's lives.

'Rolfe.' He beckoned his second-in-command to join him a distance away from the gathered men.

'My lord, what are you planning?'

'Are the men ready?'

'Yes. Everyone is accounted for, and more than eager for the battle to begin.'

Jared was well aware his decision would not be welcome. 'It seems we may not need to wage a battle after all. Montreau's gates are open and the men appear unarmed.'

Not surprisingly, a sour look of disappointment crossed Rolfe's face. 'Did I overhear the guard correctly? A lone figure awaits?'

'That's what he said.'

'How do you plan to proceed?'

Jared frowned. 'If I order the men forwards, Montreau's troops might take up arms when we are in the open.'

'The losses could be great.'

'There is no way of knowing for certain. Since the Empress sent word, the lady may welcome our arrival.' He knew better than that, but had only said so for his man's benefit. If the lady had the desire to shed blood, Jared knew she'd be more than happy to shed his. He decided, 'I will approach alone.'

'No.' Rolfe jerked to attention as if slapped. 'You can't do that. I will go.'

'Your loyalty is appreciated, but you are not in a position to make terms if need be. If anything goes wrong, you will need to lead the men.'

Rolfe nearly growled at his statement. 'If anything goes wrong, Montreau will be naught but ashes and memories.'

Jared knew his man's vow was not a vain boast. Regardless of his aunt's orders, Warehaven's men would brutally raze the castle and everyone within if his life was endangered.

He stepped out of the protection of the sparse woodland ringing the castle. The sense of peril creeping along his spine made his hand itch to draw his sword. But he pushed the urge aside and strode toward the castle's gates.

Halfway across the barren field, the force of the wind increased, buffeting him with an odd sense of foreboding. He glanced at the stars dotting the sky and at the full moon. Its pale light spread across the field, and washed over the gate towers.

Drawing nearer the keep, Jared realised his guard had been partly correct. A solitary figure did stand in the open entry way. But the light from the torches illuminated not a man, but a woman.

Her long, unbound hair whipped about her in the wind. Would the raven tresses still feel like silk beneath his touch? Would they curl around his wrist like chains as if to hold him near?

Jared gritted his teeth against the unwarranted memories.

Less than a dozen feet away, he stopped and glanced up at the walls. The *brave* men of Montreau stood at attention, holding their helmets on the wall before them, their empty hands in full view. They seemed content to permit a lone woman to welcome what could potentially be an enemy.

He drew his gaze back to Lea. Even if he hadn't known her, he would guess her to be Montreau's lady by her proud stance. Jared couldn't decide if he thought her brave, or senseless.

To his chagrin, she grew more striking with each step that brought him closer. Her regal-like, straight posture belied her height. He knew from experience that the top of her head would barely reach his shoulder when her cheek rested against his chest.

The long sapphire cloak bunched on the ground around her feet. From the way it didn't move in the wind, she apparently stood on the extra length.

The familiar frame of ebony hair set off the paleness of her heart-shaped face.

She looked fragile—vulnerable. He wanted nothing more than to care for her, protect her. Jared swallowed his instincts, knowing that was the image she'd intended to portray. He'd fallen for that hoax once before.

Determined to keep their former relationship nothing more than a distant memory and from making a spectacle in public, he focused on the business at hand. He stopped an arm's length before her. 'I come to protect this keep in the name of the Empress Matilda.'

She nodded. 'I have been apprised of your arrival.' She motioned to her men. 'We have no quarrel with this visit by Empress Matilda's men.'

Visit? Jared raised an eyebrow at her statement. 'Lady Lea, perhaps you misunderstood. This is not a simple visit. My men and I are to secure Montreau from all.'

'All?' Her brows furrowed in question. 'Surely not from its own inhabitants?'

'From all.' Jared wasn't backing down on this. The empress had ordered him to take and hold Montreau.

'But…' Her voice trailed off as if uncertain how to respond.

Jared motioned towards the keep. 'We can discuss the details inside.'

'Details?' She shook her head. 'Details of what?'

'The details of you surrendering the control of Montreau to me.'

Lea straightened her back and lifted her chin a notch. She met his gaze with a hard stare. 'This is *my* keep, Warehaven. I will surrender control to no one—not even you.'

Jared's fingers instinctively tightened around the hilt of his sword. 'Then I will take it from you.'

She drew in a deep breath at his brusque tone. Jared wasn't making an idle threat. He would indeed use force to take her keep if he felt the need.

She'd not expected this to happen. The empress's missive had only hinted at giving control of Montreau to him. Her actual words had stated that he would merely protect her and the keep.

Apparently, her orders to him had been somewhat different. Empress Matilda was a woman not to be trusted. Lea silently cursed herself. Like a simpering nit she'd ordered her men not to fight and had opened her gates, permitting Warehaven free access.

She glanced past him, scouring the field and beyond for signs of his men. Could she summon enough courage and strength to shove him out of the gate and call her men to arms?

'Rest assured, Lea, there are enough men out there to raze this castle.'

Lea dragged her attention back to Jared. She needed to stall for time to figure out what to do now. 'And what are the terms of Montreau's surrender?'

'Terms? There are no terms. You and your men will not be harmed. Your keep will remain intact. For all appearances nothing will change.' He leaned closer. 'Except all orders will come from me.'

His voice had lowered to a deeper, more gravelly tone—one he normally reserved for issuing a warning. Lea stared up at him. His eyes darkened as his pupils enlarged. Granted, she had little experience with other men, but she knew this one well and recognised that look. He might be here to take control of her keep, but he couldn't hide the fact he still found her desirable.

A fact she could bend to her needs—if she was careful.

Lea willed herself to move just the barest breath closer and asked in her most sultry whisper, 'And I am to remain your—hostage—during your possession of my lands?'

Jared's gut tightened. Her voice sang across his ears like a siren's song, inviting him to taste the rose-tinted lips that formed the words she spoke.

But he'd tasted those lips before, and while they'd been yielding and sweet beneath his kiss, they'd told nothing but lies.

'The Empress requires no hostages.'

She rested a hand on his chest. 'Then what am I?'

Her cloak fell open with her movement. The thin gown she wore beneath appeared nearly transparent in the flickering torchlight.

Jared ignored the heat of her touch and swallowed past the sudden dryness in his mouth. He narrowed his eyes. He'd wondered before if she had set a trap for him and his men. Obviously she had. And he was in grave danger of becoming her victim.

He warned, 'All I know for certain is that you foolishly play with fire. We are done talking. This keep is now under my command. There are no hostages. And no terms.'

Without backing away from his warning, she stared up at him. Her lips parted to draw in breath; unblinking sapphire eyes, rimmed by thick, black eyelashes, held his rapt attention.

'I cannot change your mind?'

Jared's heart slammed against his chest. He inhaled, and hoped the act would keep his mouth from falling open at her brazenly unspoken offer. Any man with a shred of honour would order her inside. They would demand she cloak herself and leave the courtyard.

Sometimes honour was for fools.

Any man with half a wit would tear his gaze from her lush form and look around for the trap she'd so obviously set.

Sometimes wit was a useless weapon.

Jared stepped forwards and, unmindful of his mailled tunic, pulled her hard against his chest. Other than a brief flinch, she was pliant in his arms. He lowered his head to her ear and hotly warned, 'Lock yourself inside your chamber, Lea, or this time I will claim what you so boldly offer.'

She turned her head to brush her lips against his, whispering, 'Are you not here to assume complete control?'

Chapter Two

Lea's heart raced as she ran up the winding stairwell to her chamber. She slammed the door behind her and leaned breathless against the rough-hewn wood.

He'd pushed her away, but not before she'd seen the lust flare to life in his hungry gaze. She'd felt his heart pound beneath his maille. He knew exactly what she'd been offering.

Jared of Warehaven might still be angry she'd jilted him in such a cowardly manner, sending her father to do the deed because she'd been too hurt to face him. He might be a warrior hardened by these last seven years of battle, but he was still a man. A man who still desired her.

She could hardly believe what she'd just done in the bailey. A sliver of guilt washed over her. What would her parents think of her brazenness?

She quickly pushed aside the self-reproach. Neither her father nor her mother would fault her for doing everything she could to retain Montreau. They might not agree with her method, but they would applaud the end result.

But what about her? How was she to live with herself if she did become pregnant?

Lea crossed the chamber, dropping her cloak on to the bed as she strolled toward the narrow window opening. The courtyard was ablaze with light and quickly filling with the Empress's men.

She easily spotted him. Her heart tripped before settling to a more normal rhythm. Jared of Warehaven was a fine specimen of a man, more appealing now than before.

Tall enough, and muscular enough to make a woman feel protected—safe. His dark sandy-blond hair was shot through with newer strands of silver that glittered like metal in the torchlight.

Jared ordered everyone about. By the time he finished, there were as many of his own men on the walls as those from Montreau.

Hard to believe, but he'd grown even more confident with age. It showed in the way he immediately took charge as if he'd been commanding Montreau for years. Only one of her men dared to show displeasure at the orders. And he'd been soundly knocked to the ground. Still the fool thought to fight back. His rebelliousness faded instantly when the tip of a sword was pressed against his neck.

The guard's act of outright rebellion had been foolhardy. Thankfully Jared had generously spared his life where another might not have been as kind-hearted.

When all was in order, he headed towards the keep. Lea lingered a moment or two longer at the window, then turned to don something more suitable—more demur— before she went down to meet him in the Great Hall.

The thin, finely woven chainse had served its purpose. Wearing it beneath her full cloak without an over-dress had been extreme, but she'd wanted to see his reaction. Her test had proven successful—he still desired her. Anger, rage had done nothing to negate their physical attraction to each other.

Shared passion had never been a problem between them. From the moment she'd first seen him at King Henry's court she'd been drawn to him.

Nine years ago, barely out of childhood, she was fifteen and desperately in love for the first time. At three years older Jared of Warehaven was a man in her eyes.

And when he'd shown up here at Montreau a few months later, Lea thought her father would have an apoplectic fit. He was outraged that anyone would dare to even consider courting his *baby*. Jared had stood up to her father and eventually, to her amazement, her sire had relented.

She loosened the side laces of her gown and pulled the garment over her head. The chilled air of the chamber cooled her body, making her realise how warm she'd become thinking of Jared.

The door to her chamber banged against the wall. With the gown in her hands, she stared at the intruder.

Jared froze in the doorway; he'd been expecting the chamber to be empty. What was she doing in here instead of the lord's chamber? Hearing footsteps in the hallway, he kicked the door closed behind him.

'I knocked. No one answered.'

She dropped the gown, gasped, and then quickly retrieved it to hold against her body. Surely she didn't think that mist of cloth would protect her.

It had only taken a moment, but he'd seen enough of

her to whet his appetite. The urge to turn away warred with the need to crush her soft curves to his chest.

'What do you want?' Her voice nothing more than a breathless whisper, Lea coughed, then asked, 'What are you doing in here?' Her tone had turned icy.

'I knocked.'

'You said that.'

He cursed his sudden distraction. 'When no one answered, I thought the chamber was empty.'

'So?' She looked at the leather saddlebags and blanket roll in his hands. 'You thought to make this chamber your own?'

'Yes.'

'The men sleep in the hall.'

Jared dropped his possessions to the floor. 'The lord doesn't.'

'The lord is dead.'

He certainly didn't feel dead. His blood rushed too hot and far too fast for him to be deceased. 'I am not sleeping in the hall on a pallet when there are plenty of bedchambers available.'

'As you will. But you need find another one. This chamber is not available.'

Her dismissive tone was new to him and it grated. He took a step towards her. 'A short time ago you made it plain you were very available. It stands to reason this chamber would be, too.'

Lea held her ground, one inky brow lifting as she steadily said, 'I've changed my mind.'

'Yes, you've always been quite good at that.'

'What's done is done, Jared. I have no wish to discuss the past.'

Neither did he, not right at this moment. But some day, some day soon, he would demand an accounting of her actions the day of their wedding ceremony.

She turned away, giving him a full view of her back and lovely rounded—Jared tore his attention from the sight.

With a glare over her shoulder, she ordered, 'Go.'

Jared cleared the distance between them in three strides. He pulled her against his chest, revelling in the warmth of her body against his, even as his mind flinched at the idea of holding this traitorous woman so close. 'You don't give the orders here any more.'

He felt her tremble in his hold. Yet, she shrugged as if nothing of any importance threatened her. 'As you will. Please, my lord, leave me be, so I may dress.'

Jared gritted his teeth at her attitude. He could do with her what he willed and none would stop him.

He tapped the bed with the side of his booted foot. 'You play a foolish game, Lea.'

'You will do nothing I don't permit.'

For a heartbeat he wondered what had happened to rob her of the ability to reason. 'You of all people can't be sure of that.'

'Yes, I can. While I cannot fathom why Matilda sent you in particular, she would never have sent a crude barbarian to hold Montreau. Not if she wanted to avoid a battle with York.' She tipped her head to glance up at him. 'Do you have enough men at hand to defeat the Earl of York?'

He had to admit that she still had plenty of reasoning ability. Too much, perhaps. 'I have enough men at hand to protect Montreau from any who attack.'

She laughed softly. 'So you say.'

'Perhaps you forget. King David is near at hand.

Whatever I may, or may not, lack in manpower, he more than compensates. And since he is Matilda's uncle, I do not think he would ignore a summons for help.'

'Perhaps. But I do not believe King David would attack Montreau.'

'And what leads you to believe that?'

'He likes our apple tarts far too much.'

Jared lifted his gaze briefly to the ceiling, then released her and stepped back. 'Apple tarts?'

She swung away, out of his reach. 'Did not your aunt tell you? Montreau is the peacekeeper in this war.' She leaned towards him as if prepared to tell him a great secret. 'We do it with food. King David is partial to sweets—especially the cook's apple tarts.'

He might have lost this dispute, but he refused to acknowledge her win. Instead, he headed for the door, pausing to retrieve his possessions and to order, 'Get dressed…' Jared drew a long, heated stare down her body '…in something more appropriate to your station and meet me downstairs.'

She said nothing until he was nearly out the door. Then she called out, 'In due time, my lord.'

Jared slammed the door behind him. He rubbed his forehead. When his aunt had given him the orders to come here, why hadn't he argued more fiercely?

What had he been thinking to come to Montreau? He'd known from the start that dealing with Lea would not be easy.

He'd fully expected to have his mind beset by memories best left locked securely away. But he hadn't expected his body, or his wilful desire, to so easily remember how she felt in his arms.

Worse, she knew it. He could tell by Lea's easy manner that she'd recognised the blaze of desire. What worried him was that she didn't try to push him away, or to cry out in fear. The woman who absolutely refused to wed the son of a bastard was not afraid of his anger at her rejection, nor did she seem to fear his lust.

Lea of Montreau was up to something.

How had he let himself be tricked into this task so easily?

Lea reluctantly opened her eyes as sunlight blazed across her bed. She groaned and rolled over to escape the brightness of the day.

'Agatha, please. Close the bed curtains and let me sleep.'

'Don't tell me you are tired.'

Lea jumped at the deep male tone. Grabbing her covers tightly, she rolled on to her back. 'Are you lost again?'

'No, but you are.'

She glanced around him at her chamber. 'You are mistaken. This is my chamber. Where is my maid?'

'I am here, my lady,' Agatha called from across the room.

'And she'll stay right there until I say otherwise.'

'As you will.' Lea did her best not to smile as his jaw tightened. He obviously hated that phrase. She'd have to remember to use it often.

'I waited for you in the hall last night.'

'Did you?' She yawned. 'I found that I needed sleep.'

He muttered something she couldn't quite hear before grabbing the edge of her covers. 'Get up. Get dressed. Get down to the hall.'

Lea clung to the covers. 'I will. Just as soon as you leave.'

'I think not.' He tugged at the covers.

Tightening her own hold, she replied, 'Excuse me?'

'It's apparent you still don't know how to follow orders. So, this time, I'm going to teach you.'

That's what he thought. She was no longer the same naïve young woman he'd known before. Heartache and marriage had seen to that. 'You are upsetting my maid.'

On cue Agatha started wailing and wringing her hands as she paced the chamber. With any luck half the castle would arrive within minutes to see what caused such a ruckus.

Jared released her covers and moved away from the bed. 'I will await you below. But if you do not hurry, I will return.'

'As you will.'

Once again his jaw tightened and he muttered something, but thankfully headed for the door without further comment.

Lea flew from the bed and hugged Agatha, laughing. 'Thank you.'

The woman patted her back before pushing her gently aside. 'Just like a trained dog I am.' The maid pinned her with a hard stare. 'Did you know Lord Warehaven had been sent?'

'No.' Lea shook her head. 'Not until the guard said the ships had beached and then I knew it could only be him.'

'And you let me believe some stranger was coming to claim Montreau.'

'To be honest, I thought a stranger would worry you less.'

Agatha snorted, then turned to retrieve a chemise and gown from the bench. 'I'd been laying these out when his lordship burst in.'

Lea glanced at the door and the locking bar across the top. 'We'll have one of the men lower that bar to a level we can reach.'

Agatha's eyebrows shot up. 'And you think that will keep him out if he's of a mind to get in here?'

Obviously her maid remembered Jared's rash temper, too. 'Maybe not, but at least the splintering wood will give us some warning.'

'You are sorely testing him, child.'

'I know. But it is no less than what he deserves.'

'After all this time you still think to make him pay for something he couldn't help?'

'Something he couldn't help?' Lea disagreed. 'He had a choice and he didn't choose me.'

'You forced him into a corner. Did you truly believe he would choose you over the Empress's orders? Lady Lea, choosing you over his liege would have stripped him of his honour, not to mention his self-worth.'

'Others have refused to follow Matilda and Stephen into war. Jared's own father refused to become embroiled in this senseless battle for the crown.'

Agatha nodded. 'And where is he now? Sitting comfortably in his own keep?'

No. Jared's parents were living amongst the wild Welsh. She doubted if they had many comforts at all. 'I would have lived anywhere as long as Jared was by my side.'

Even as she said the words she knew they weren't

true. 'We could have lived here at Montreau. My father took neither side and we were not turned out of our home.'

Agatha briefly touched her cheek. 'And you know why that happened as well as anyone.'

Lea's throat tightened at the memory. Her brother, Phillip, had been hunting near a village to the north when it had come under attack by Stephen's men. Since the battle had been waged as a warning to King David, the men had killed everyone before burning the village and the fields.

Phillip hadn't known what was happening and when he tried to help a villager, he'd been murdered for his trouble.

In retribution against Stephen, Matilda's men had razed two villages in the south.

Lea would never forget the night her brother's body was returned to them. One of Stephen's men had recognised the Montreau seal on Phillip's ring and brought him to the keep.

Her mother had been inconsolable for many months afterwards. Her father had bitterly voiced his disgust of both Stephen and Matilda.

For weeks men from the king and the empress had tried to gain her father's support. He had refused them all. Only when Stephen himself had come to Montreau did her father strike a deal.

Montreau would take neither side. They would remain steadfastly neutral, giving neither support nor gold to either of the combatants.

Stephen had sent word to Matilda and she'd sent her uncle to Montreau in her stead. That was when they'd discovered King David liked apple tarts. In truth, Lea was fairly certain what he actually liked was the cook. But that had always remained nothing more than a rumour.

Whether that was true or not didn't matter. What did matter was that there were signed documents granting Montreau's status of neutrality.

So, yes, she knew why her father hadn't chosen a side. What she could never understand was why Jared felt compelled to do so.

For seven long years the land was in turmoil. Brother fought brother. Father fought son. Innocent people died. Crops were wasted. Buildings and land destroyed.

How could Jared have cared so little about her that he put senseless killings and destruction above what they could have shared?

How could anyone have expected her to live with a man who so obviously enjoyed the bloodshed?

'Yes, Agatha, I know why Montreau has remained safe thus far.'

'And yet you still insist on testing the patience of the Empress's man?'

'Yes. Yes, I do.'

The maid slipped the chemise over Lea's head. 'You are playing where you have no experience.'

'He's no different from any other man.'

'Oh? And a lot you know about men.' Agatha adjusted the skirt of Lea's gown. 'Besides Lord Jared, you have only Charles to use as a comparison. And, child, where Charles was merely unappealing, this man is dangerous.'

'Unpredictable at times, perhaps. But I don't think he's dangerous.' Lea believed what she'd told him last night. He wasn't going to do anything she'd not permit.

'Do you still intend to follow through with your plan?'

Agatha's question gave Lea pause. She wasn't certain she could. The idea of seducing Jared overwhelmed her with all the implications it carried. She knew him—quite well. If he ever caught wind that she'd had a baby, he wouldn't be as accepting of the child's parentage as others.

No, she wouldn't put it past him to come back to Montreau to investigate the claim himself. Besides, she didn't know how long he would be here to begin with. If he remained long enough to witness her pregnancy, she'd never get rid of him.

At one time she had loved him so much that having his children had been one of her goals. In her dreams they'd had three or four children—all of them conceived and raised in love.

Knowing Agatha was studying her closely while waiting for an answer, Lea admitted, 'I'm not certain. I need time to think about what to do. But in the meantime it can't hurt if I gain his interest and ensure it remains until I do decide.'

'I am warning you, Lady Lea, Jared is no longer a young man inexperienced with life. He will play this game of yours for only so long. Then he will take matters into his own hands. Be careful you don't get more than you bargained for.'

She didn't agree, but to appease her maid she promised, 'Fear not. I will be careful.'

Jared stepped out into the bailey with Lea at his side. He squinted against the sunshine.

The problem with a clear, blue sky and calm spring

breeze was that such perfection cried out for something to go horribly wrong.

He stole a glance at the vision of loveliness beside him. At least she hadn't kept him waiting. And, to his grateful relief, she'd chosen a gown suitable to wear in public.

While the idea of seeing her body through the sheerness of that misty fabric she'd worn last night would actually please him, the idea that others would be looking, too, oddly bothered him.

In fact, to be honest, it bothered him far too much. And it shouldn't. She was no longer his betrothed, so what did he care if she displayed her wares for all to see?

He'd been played for a fool once. He wasn't about to let her worm her way into his heart again. He needed to remember that she was nothing more to him than a charge to oversee until further orders arrived.

Jared clenched and unclenched a hand. Hopefully, those orders would arrive soon. He'd vowed to protect Montreau and its lady.

A lady he'd once desired above all others. One who had propositioned him at the gates last night. While it would be easy enough to protect the keep and people from an outside enemy, who would protect the lady from him?

Especially since she now had a body that begged for a man's touch. The years had been more than kind to Lea. She had always been lovely, but now the slimness had softened into curves.

Curves he'd like to caress.

It was all he could do to remember she was a lady and deserved the same care and consideration he'd extend to his sisters. But his mind laughed at that—Lea was most definitely *not* one of his sisters.

He was jarred out of his thoughts by her laughter as she called out to a passing man, 'Behave yourself, Simon. I might need to talk with Alyce.'

'Who is Alyce?' That she bantered with everyone they encountered set him on edge even more, making his voice harsher than he'd intended.

She looked up at him, surprise evident on her face. 'Simon's wife. He was flirting with one of the girls.'

'And how is that any of your business?'

'Everything that happens at Montreau is my business.'

'Not any more it isn't.'

'You will not be here for ever—my lord.'

'Do not count on that. You might be calling me lord for a long time to come.'

It took him a few steps before he realised she was no longer at his side. With a curse, Jared turned around to see her heading back to the keep.

He quickly caught up with her and grasped her arm. 'Where do you think you're going?'

She shook free. 'As far away from you as possible.'

'What's wrong? You are free to loosen your tongue on me, but as soon as I return the favour you run away to pout?'

'I am not pouting and I am most certainly not running away from you.'

'Since I am familiar with your running away, I'd have to disagree. What would you call it?'

'Nothing.' She lifted her face to the sun. 'I call it nothing. It is simply too glorious a day to be ruined by a foul mood.'

Not that he would admit it, but she had a point. 'Let us call a temporary truce. Show me around Montreau.'

She shrugged. 'You know your way around Montreau, I've no need to show it to you.'

'Perhaps, but a lot has changed since I was last here.'

'What do you wish to see?'

Jared nodded across the bailey. 'The newer additions. Start with the stables—'

'My lord!' One of his men stationed on the wall shouted at the same time one of Montreau's men called out, 'My lady, riders approach!'

'Riders?' She started for the wall.

Jared lengthened his stride and stopped in front of her. 'What are you doing?'

She looked at him as if he'd lost his wits. 'Going to see who approaches.'

'No.' He beckoned to one of his men. 'Escort the lady back inside the keep.'

She stepped away from the guard. 'If he lays one hand on me, I'll see it severed from his arm.'

The guard's eyes widened.

Jared glared at her. 'You will do as I say, or I swear, Lea, I will have you locked in a cell.'

The look she gave him spoke louder than any words. At this moment it was apparent she hated him fiercely. But he didn't care—she couldn't despise him any more than he'd hated her for so long. Right now, it was his duty to see she was safe and he'd be damned if he'd fail in that.

'Just last night you permitted an army into your keep.'

'I had been advised of your arrival.'

'You weren't told exactly who was coming, only that a man from the empress would be arriving.'

'I knew it was you—'

'No.' He cut her off. 'You only guessed. Had you

guessed incorrectly, had I been a stranger walking through your open gates, I could have razed Montreau and killed everyone, including you.'

She paled, but said nothing in her defence. How could she, when as far as he was concerned there was no defence for such an unthinking action?

'Don't test me on this, Lea. You will not win.'

To his relief, she turned towards the keep. 'I expect a full report on my visitors.'

Jared motioned the guard to follow her, then called out, 'My visitors, Lea.'

She stopped and faced him. 'I expect a full report.'

He nodded, wondering why, when she tilted her head at that arrogant angle, did her mouth look so kissable?

Once she was safely back inside the keep, he mounted the wall and waited for the three riders to come close enough to hail.

Instead of granting them entry, he ordered, 'State your business.'

One of the men, dressed a bit finer than the other two, urged his horse closer. 'I am Markam Villaire, here to see my brother's widow. Who are you?'

'I am Lord Jared of Warehaven and Montreau. What business have you with Lady Lea?'

'Lord of Montreau?' Confusion was evident by his deepening frown. 'As Lord Charles's only surviving relative I am here to ensure Montreau's safety. Am I arrived too late?'

'My lord, a moment.' One of Montreau's men stepped closer. 'While he is Lord Charles's brother, he does not have the lady's best interest at heart.'

Jared had already gathered that by the man's statement. He'd not come to protect Lea, but instead to see to her property.

'Too late? For what?'

'I need not answer to you. You are a stranger to me.'

Jared wrapped a hand around his sword hilt. 'I am in control of this keep.'

'By whose orders?'

Since Jared had not the slightest clue to whom this man was loyal, he drew his sword, answering, 'By my orders.' He pointedly stared at each of the three men. 'Do you think to challenge me?'

Not surprisingly they all shook their head. 'No. There is no need for such rashness. May I at least speak to the lady before going on my way?'

Something Jared couldn't name twisted at his gut. He'd permit the man in, but he'd not take his attention off him for one heartbeat. He nodded towards the gate tower, ordering, 'Let them through.'

Chapter Three

Frustrated, Lea prowled the Great Hall. Anger bubbled near the surface, making her feel trapped. Not just by her tightly reined temper, but by the over-watchful eyes of Warehaven's guards. She was confined like a prisoner in her own hall, unable to escape with them at the doors.

Yes, she had left the gates open—she'd known they were coming. Not only had the empress sent word, but Lea had dreamed of the longships and him. Who else would have arrived by dragon-prow longships?

Besides, it wasn't as if she lacked the ability to reason. Had she felt even the slightest qualm for Montreau, she'd have ordered the gates closed and her men to take up arms.

She wanted to rail aloud at his high-handed treatment of her, but knew it would be a waste of her time and energy. And while she had every right to resent being ordered inside the keep, she was certain he would see any grievance as nothing more than a woman's complaint.

The oversized double doors groaned open. Lea swung around to berate Jared, only to swallow her words before she could utter a sound. She stared at the men walking into her keep.

What were Markam Villaire and his men doing here? After sending him news of his brother's drowning, she'd expected him days ago. He hadn't responded to her missive, or bothered to attend the memorial mass held for Charles.

Not that his lack of response had surprised her. She and Markam had little liking for each other. At their initial meeting he had considered her a weak, timid woman he could manipulate at will. She'd instantly recognised him as an overbearing tyrant.

What he lacked in height—Markam was the only man she could literally look down on—he more than made up for in arrogance and browbeating.

While Charles had taken his brother's tactics in his stride, she had taken great pleasure in showing Markam she'd not be so easily intimidated. An act that had done little to endear her to her husband or brother-by-marriage.

But in truth, since he hadn't shown up for the mass, Lea had thought—and hoped—she'd seen the last of him.

So what did he want now?

The moment Villaire spotted her, he waved his men aside, dropped a mask of concern over his face and hurried towards her with his arms outstretched. 'Dear sister Lea, I came as quickly as I could.'

Lea had to fight the urge to flee. Not that she feared him, but when a Villaire displayed any semblance of human emotion, she knew they were up to something.

Something that would not bode well for her.

Just before he could put his arms around her, Lea

sidestepped away to turn towards a servant. 'Bring our guest food and drink.' She then nodded to one of Warehaven's men, suggesting, 'See if your lord is hungry.'

Certain she'd made her disdain clear, she turned back to Villaire. Lea motioned him towards the raised dais at the far end of the Great Hall and asked, 'Why are you here?'

'Did you not send for me?' He dropped on to the high-backed chair before she could take her seat.

Lea wanted to point out that she was the Lady of Montreau and that he was in her chair. But she didn't want to raise a commotion in front of Warehaven's men. Instead, she leaned against a wooden support beam a few feet from the chair, forcing Markam to turn towards her.

'Send for you? No. I only informed you of your brother's passing.'

'His body has washed up?'

Being crass and unthinking was something both of the Villaires had mastered. 'Not yet.'

'Then unless you know something you aren't sharing—' Villaire's eyes narrowed '—you can't be certain he is dead.'

Was he accusing her of something? 'The men in the other boat saw his vessel overturn. They looked for him and the other four men well into the next morning.'

She had stood on the shore all night, waiting, watching, freezing in the sea-swept wind while the men took turns diving into the frigid water. They'd used weighted fishing nets, dragging the water for Charles and the others. They would have continued for ever had she not called a halt. By mid-morning the waves had increased, tossing the anchored boats nearly into each other. She'd seen no reason to lose more men to the sea.

Lea added, 'Besides, were Charles alive, he would have come home. Or at least sent word of his whereabouts.' Her husband hadn't been the sort of man to live without his comforts for long.

It had been one of the reasons her father first thought Charles a suitable match. He knew Villaire would never be the type of man to go off to war, endangering the neutrality of Montreau. The mere idea of Charles sleeping on the hard ground, or even on a pallet, was laughable.

'What if my brother is injured? He could be hurt so badly that he is unable to return to your side, or send you word.'

The sense that Markam was up to something only increased with his insistence that Charles could still be alive. She refused to believe that was possible.

'No. We searched the shoreline for miles in either direction. The men went to each village along the way to make certain all knew what had happened. So, even if he were unable to send us word, one of the villagers would have seen to the task.'

Markam turned away from her, and folded his hands on top of the table as if in prayer. 'I cannot believe—I refuse to believe he is dead. Not until someone can show me proof.'

His voice trembled and cracked with emotion. Lea stepped away from the beam, frowning. Charles and Markam had never been close. Of what benefit was this overt display?

'What type of proof do you require?'

Lea jumped at Jared's question. She'd not seen or

heard him enter the hall, let alone approach the dais. How long had he been standing there, listening?

Markam lifted his head and turned the saddest, most grieving look towards Jared that Lea had ever seen, before lowering his head nearly to the table. His shoulders trembled. The lout was enacting this charade for Jared's benefit.

She opened her mouth, only to snap it shut when Jared shook his head once and raised his hand, commanding her silently to be quiet. Before she could gather her wits, he moved her aside and took a seat on the bench running the length of the table.

'I will have the men do another search for your brother. Until then, you are welcome to stay at Montreau.'

Markam cleared his throat and sat up. Lea watched speechless as his feigned expression of grief changed to one of gratitude. Jared didn't know this man. He wouldn't recognise the shimmer of devious plotting in the slightly narrowed gaze. Charles's brother would trick him, manipulate him into something distasteful.

'My Lord Warehaven, thank you. You are too kind.'

She tapped Jared's shoulder. 'A word?'

He ignored her and kept his focus on Markam. 'I am sure that, with your assistance, the men will be successful this time around.'

Markam's eyes widened. 'My assistance?'

It was all Lea could do not to laugh at the horror etched on the man's face. Perhaps she'd misjudged Jared. It was possible he'd seen Villaire for the weasel he was.

Even so, there was one thing wrong with the plan. If Markam were underfoot, how was she going to seduce Jared if she decided that was the path to follow?

Certain Markam was in capable hands, Lea left the men alone. She needed some air and time to think of her next move.

Jared watched Lea slowly leave the hall. He'd expected her to storm away, angry that he'd taken over lordship of Montreau and invited Villaire to stay.

Instead of appearing outraged, she acted more thoughtful, as if her mind were elsewhere. He'd have preferred the anger—at least then he'd know what to expect. Jared feared her contemplative mood would only spell trouble—for him.

'My sister-by-marriage is a very attractive woman, is she not?'

Unwilling to give away any information about his prior relationship with Lea, Jared said, 'I suppose.' He backed up the lie by saying, 'I haven't yet had the time to notice.' He turned his attention to Villaire. He didn't like the man in the least, but it might prove interesting to see where this conversation led. If nothing else, it would pass the time.

'It is too bad she is still wed to another.'

Jared paused before replying. While Villaire wasn't to be trusted, he was the dead man's brother. Perhaps it was still difficult for him to accept the death. So, he countered, 'You truly believe that your brother is still alive?'

'Perhaps, or perhaps not. Without a body, who is to say?'

It wasn't so much the man's words, as it was the tone. Villaire sounded—smug—all knowing. The slight smirk when he glanced away served only to make Jared trust him less. 'We should know in a day or so.'

'Even if we do not discover Charles's remains, I have already petitioned the king.'

'For what?'

Villaire sat back in the chair. He rubbed his hands along the wooden arms as if they belonged to a woman and announced, 'Guardianship of Montreau.'

The only response that statement deserved was an outright laugh. But Jared wanted to know the workings behind this man's illogical ideas. He turned away to summon one of the maids for something to drink. At this point in time he didn't care what. He'd drink vinegar if it would keep him from choking on his suppressed mirth.

When the young woman placed a pitcher and goblets on the table, Jared waved her away before pouring two goblets of ale. He swallowed half the contents of one, then offered the other one to Villaire, saying, 'Montreau has a guardian. Me.'

'Yes, but you have no rights to Montreau.'

Had things turned out differently seven years ago, that would not be true and none of this would be happening. But the exchange of vows had never happened. And he'd still been too angry with her to protest her betrothal to Villaire the next year.

From what Jared remembered of their betrothal agreement, the only person who had any rights to this castle was Lady Lea. Even he was here only until Matilda had need of him elsewhere. 'And what rights do you claim to Montreau?'

Villaire eased further down into the chair as if prepared to make himself a nest in the ornate seat. 'She is wed to my brother. However, if rumours of his death should prove true, I am her only surviving kin.' He took a long drink, then continued, 'It is my duty to see that she and Montreau are cared for properly.'

Jared stared at a flea scurrying across Villaire's forehead, wondering idly if a quick dagger strike would kill the flea. If someone didn't see this man for a conniving opportunist, they might believe the cur's explanation.

Unfortunately for Markam, he recognised the gleam of prospective gain in his eyes. Since the church would never permit Villaire to wed his deceased brother's wife, he would most likely wed her to someone of his choosing—someone of the same ilk as he, albeit weaker—someone Villaire could easily control. Then he would milk every ounce of profit from the keep and land.

Jared frowned. Lea obviously disliked, or distrusted, her brother-by-marriage. Otherwise she wouldn't have sent a guard to find him.

What would happen when she protested Villaire's plans? There was no doubt she would fight him at every turn. How well would the man care for her then?

No. Jared was here to protect her and Montreau. Nothing was going to happen to either.

Markam asked, 'Did you say you were from Warehaven?'

'Yes.' Even though he knew the answer, Jared asked, 'Why do you ask?'

'Aren't you the Empress Matilda's man?'

'Yes.' Jared had no reason to deny his loyalty.

Villaire's lips thinned. 'In fact, aren't you the son of her bastard brother?'

Jared smiled, intentionally flashing his teeth like a hungry predator. 'That I am.'

He leaned closer, satisfied when Villaire flinched away. 'I suggest you keep a civil tongue in your head when speaking of my family, lest I take offence.'

'Does Lady Lea know who you are?'

'Of course she does.'

'And she permitted you entry to Montreau?'

'She had no choice.'

'You forced your way into my brother's keep?' Villaire's eyes widened. 'But—but you, sir, are the enemy.'

Enemy? At a neutral keep? 'No. Lady Lea knew I was coming.' He couldn't help adding, 'But force would have been an option had she not permitted me entry.'

Now Villaire's face paled. He rose. 'I need speak to Lady Lea about this. I cannot let this pass.'

'Let what pass?' Jared rose and glared down at the man. 'This is neutral territory. It always has been. I am here to ensure it remains that way.'

'But King—' Villaire clamped his mouth shut as if he'd been about to say too much.

Jared's hand twitched toward his sword. 'Stephen will find a warm welcome should he decide to declare Montreau for himself.'

Backing away, the other man kept his blinking stare trained on Jared's weapon. 'I will take this up with the king myself.'

'You do that.'

'My lord?' Lady Lea's woman, Agatha, approached the table. She pointedly ignored Villaire and instead addressed Jared, 'It is almost time for the meal. Will you be much longer?'

Jared shook his head. 'No. We're done here.'

Villaire turned on his heels and headed for the doors. He would most likely take his anger straight to Lea.

Certain the lady could hold her own for a time, Jared followed at a slower pace.

Even Villaire wasn't fool enough to physically harm Lea. But nobody could know how far, or hard, she would push her brother-by-marriage.

Jared rolled the tension from his shoulders. It might prove interesting to discover which one of them would need to be protected.

The sound of heavy, belaboured breathing and foot-steps behind her made Lea aware she was no longer alone. She didn't need to turn around to see who thought to disturb the quiet she'd found in this tower.

The walk up here wouldn't have caused Jared's breathing to be so hard. Agatha's footsteps wouldn't be as heavy. That left only Villaire. Now what did he want?

'What—were you thinking—to give that—man entry to Montreau?' Markam gasped without greeting.

'I don't answer to you.'

Markam joined her at the wall and to her surprise he laughed before informing her, 'That will change soon enough.'

A scheming Villaire was nothing new to her. However, to be the object of this Villaire's scheme unsettled her more than she'd admit.

Lea couldn't decide what bothered her more—his comment, or his ominous tone. Where Charles had been petty, at least he'd been easy to read. Something dark and unreadable lurked behind Markam's words.

Knowing he expected the question, she kept her voice steady and asked the obvious, 'And why is that?'

'Since you can do nothing to change things, I see no reason not to prepare you.'

He turned to face her, leaning his shoulder against the

wall. 'I have petitioned the king. Soon Montreau will be under my control.'

Lea's first impulse was to tell him how insane his idea sounded. But the sick, sinking cold dread settling in the pit of her stomach froze the words in her throat.

What if King Stephen decided to ignore the royal writs stowed away in her chamber?

With Charles and both of her parents dead, Markam would be considered her sole living relative. Even if the relationship existed only through marriage, it would stand up to any royal or ecclesiastical test.

Her second impulse was to throw him over the side of the tower. But he wouldn't fit through the cut-outs in the crenellated stone and she doubted if she could lift him over the wall.

Instead, she shrugged nonchalantly, before saying, 'You might want to discuss that with my betrothed first.'

Markam's eyes widened until they appeared ready to bulge from his head. He finally sputtered, 'Betrothed? My brother may not even be dead and you are already involved with another man?'

'Your brother is dead.' Of that she was certain. 'Besides, the betrothal wasn't my choice.'

'Who's made this decision?'

'Empress Matilda sent word a few days ago.'

Markam's frown drew his eyebrows together. 'And the man?'

'Lord Jared of Warehaven.'

Chapter Four

Disbelief deepened Markam's frown. He stepped closer to Lea. 'Warehaven said nothing about a betrothal to me when I told him of my plans.'

That was because Jared didn't know about it. This fabricated betrothal had been the only thing she could think of quickly. Of course now she had to explain it to him.

It would just be temporary, until Villaire left. It wasn't as if she expected Jared to take it seriously. In fact, she was fairly certain he'd be outraged at the claim.

Before she could respond to Markam, strong fingers curled over her shoulder, making her flinch in surprise.

'I said nothing because we'd hoped to finalise our arrangement before making it known.' Jared's deep voice floated over her shoulder.

Obviously he'd heard enough of the conversation to realise what she was doing and for some reason had decided to play along, although she didn't expect that to last more than a short time. Eventually, she would still have to explain.

While she was grateful for his help, Jared's warm

touch and closeness made her nervous. An attempt to put a little more distance between them resulted in him moving close enough to bring the hard plane of his chest against her back.

The heat, and just the mere thought of his tall, strong form against hers was—distracting. The nearly forgotten warmth made her remember things best left in the past.

His frown easing, Villaire asked, 'So, no plans are set for a quick exchange of vows?'

'No.' Lea shook her head.

'That is good.' He stepped away from her and headed toward the stairs, pausing at the door long enough to add, 'It would be a shame if you were to commit bigamy because of a marriage made in haste.'

She tried to move away, but Jared held her in place. After Villaire's footsteps faded away, he demanded, 'Explain yourself.'

His breath raced hot against her ear. Shivering, Lea swallowed, giving herself a moment to clear her head of the sudden dizziness threatening to overtake her. 'He is planning to take Montreau.'

'And you think to lessen his greed by lying to him?'

'It wasn't exactly a lie.'

'Are you suffering from some malady of the mind?'

'No. Not at all.' The only malady she was suffering from at the moment was the warmth of his body against her back and the feel of his unyielding hold on her shoulder.

'What makes you think this fabrication about a betrothal isn't exactly a lie?'

'The note from the empress.'

He released her shoulder long enough to spin her around to face him. 'What note?'

For a moment, no longer than a heartbeat, she missed the warmth of his body. But when she looked up at him, she quickly stepped back from the anger simmering in his emerald glare. 'The one she sent telling me you'd be arriving.'

'She sent you a note explaining that I was coming to protect you and Montreau. There was nothing else in the missive.'

He was wrong, but she wasn't going to argue with him. 'As you will.'

His jaw tightened. A small pulse along the side of his stubble-covered cheek jumped. 'Don't.'

Lea glanced briefly over the edge of the wall and held her tongue. It was a long way to the ground from here. Baiting Jared alone, on the tower-wall walk, most likely wasn't the wisest move on her part.

'You do still have this missive?'

'Yes, of course I do. In my chamber.'

Before she could offer to retrieve it for him, he was tugging her toward the stairs. 'I want to see it. Now.'

He didn't believe her. She followed along, asking, 'What reason would I have to lie to you?'

Jared made a sound that sounded suspiciously like a snort of derision. Without releasing her hand, he led her down the steps. 'You never needed a reason before. Why would now be any different?'

'I beg your pardon?'

'Don't play the simpleton with me, Lea. You know exactly what I'm talking about. Do you really want to discuss this now?'

'No. We have nothing to discuss. Nothing, Jared. Not today, or ever.'

He didn't need to turn around and look at her to know she was answering through clenched teeth. The angry edge to her voice was unmistakable. Good. She deserved to be angry. In fact, the angrier the better. It was time she experienced just a little of what he'd felt at her betrayal.

Arriving at the door to her chamber, he asked, 'Tell me something, Lea, do you offer yourself to every man who is granted entry through your gates?'

The instant the words left his mouth, Jared knew he'd be wise to protect his back. Before releasing her hand, he turned to face her.

He wasn't the least bit surprised to see the tight line of her lips, flushed cheeks, or the glittering rage in her eyes. What did amaze him was the heavy pounding in his chest. She was stunning, nearly robbing him of breath along with the ability to think clearly.

Jared stepped round her and pulled Lea into the chamber. Holding her against his chest with one arm, he slammed the door closed behind them and dropped the locking bar into place.

'Or was that display only for me?'

'Jared, don't.' She pushed at his arms. 'Let me go.'

'I thought we were betrothed?' He lowered his head and tasted the soft expanse of her neck. The familiar scent of lavender enveloped him, making him only want more.

'Please.' She trembled against him. 'Please don't do this.'

By the breathless tone of her voice, he knew she

wasn't as immune to his attentions as she claimed. 'Isn't this what you wanted last night?'

He trailed a line of kisses up to her ear, smiling as a shiver rippled through her. 'Isn't this what you offered?'

'I…I…' She lowered her arms and leaned against him. 'It was a mistake.'

Jared caressed her hair; the silken strands did indeed still wrap around his hand as if fighting to hold him close. 'A mistake? So your claim that you knew I had come to protect Montreau was nothing more than yet another lie?'

'No. I—'

He tugged her hair, forcing her head back, and covered her lips with his own to stop her words. Jared didn't want her to talk, he had no need to hear her lies and half-truths.

The only thing he wanted from her was her anger, her outrage and this. The feel of her soft, yielding lips against his and the sweet taste of her returned kiss.

He wanted to punish her for the hell she'd put him through. He had loved her. There had been no one else for him. She was his.

And mere hours before exchanging their vows she'd sent her father to call off the ceremony.

She'd done more than just wound his pride. He had gone off to battle not caring if he lived or died. The foolish risks he'd taken those first few months fighting Stephen's forces had cost him not his own life, but the lives of loyal men who had followed him into war.

He blamed himself for being witless enough to fall prey to her charms. And he blamed her for caring so little. He would never forgive either of them.

Lea stiffened. She struggled against his embrace, jerking her head to break their kiss. 'Please, Jared, not like this.'

Her voice broke and he stared at the tears gathering in her eyes. Releasing her, he stepped away. 'You didn't expect kind words and a soft touch, did you?'

'No.' She didn't expect him to be gentle. It wasn't the harshness of his words, the force of his kiss or the strength of his embrace that frightened her. It was the rage she sensed swirling around him.

If they made love now it would be their first time together. While they'd enjoyed each other's bodies before, it had never gone further than touching and kissing.

She wanted nothing more than to be naked beneath him. Charles had found her revolting. He had hurt her, berated her for his lack of enjoyment and left her crying in their marriage bed, never to return.

Lea knew it would not be that way with Jared. But she didn't want him to take her out of spite. As much as she wanted—needed—a child, she would not risk conceiving one from an act filled with hate and anger.

'Then what do you want?' Jared's hard glare sliced into her heart.

She tore her gaze away. Staring at the floor, she answered, 'A little less hatred.'

He remained silent a moment, then cursed softly before asking, 'Where is my aunt's missive?'

Lea sighed. It was so like Jared to bring a complete halt to something by focusing on another task. They had never been able to have a serious conversation, because as soon as it became uncomfortable for him, he cut it off.

She opened the trunk at the foot of her bed and handed him the crumpled message. 'Here. You tell me what she meant.'

She followed him across the chamber. Jared sat on a stool by the window opening to read the note. When he leaned forwards, resting his elbows on his knees, his hair fell across his face.

Lea reached out instinctively to push it back. As if sensing her movement Jared glanced up at her, his brows arched in silent question of her action. She stopped herself mere inches before touching the burnished strands.

'Forgive me.' She turned to look out over the bailey while he went back to reading Matilda's missive without comment.

'There is nothing in here about a betrothal. What exactly did you think she meant?' he asked, waving the note in the air. 'She states that she's heard about your recent loss and that she's sending a man to protect you and Montreau from any who might see this as an opportunity to take unfair advantage of you.' He paused, then added, 'Her intent was to offer aid.'

Lea refrained from rolling her eyes. The empress would be the last person to offer aid.

Especially if she could gain something instead. Both Stephen and Matilda would strip this keep from her possession if they thought they could get away with the deed and not suffer loss of life or gold.

There was no doubt in Lea's mind that Matilda was up to something that would not bode well for her. Of course she'd not tell Jared her thoughts about his aunt. She'd tried that once before and all it had gained her was a tongue-lashing and more proof that battle and honour were more important than anything else—including her.

So, instead she agreed, 'Yes, I realise that.' Lea turned around to look at him. 'Read the last part again, Jared.'

He shook his head, but did as she bid. His frown alerted her that his second reading gave him cause for concern.

The sudden tightening of his jaw let her know that she hadn't imagined things. He apparently came to the same conclusion she had upon rereading it the third time.

Jared sat up straighter. The wide-eyed look of disbelief on his face might have been humorous if the subject didn't so involve her.

At his prolonged silence, Lea prompted, 'Well?'

'So, my aunt thinks this man she's sending might prove useful to you in more ways than one—if you so decide this time.'

He spoke the words 'this time' from between clenched teeth, meaning his reaction was almost the same as hers—first shock, then horror.

Lea said, 'At first I thought nothing of it, until I reread the missive a couple times. Even then, while it seemed rather cryptic, it made little sense to me until I realised the man she was sending might be you.'

Jared stood up and handed the missive back to her. 'I am not going to wed you, Lea.'

She stepped back at his bluntness, answering in the same manner, 'Thank God for that, because I have no intention of marrying anyone.'

'Seems to me that your brother-by-marriage might have other plans on his mind.'

Now they were back to the reason for this charade she'd begun. 'That's why I concocted a betrothal.'

'Of all people, why to me?'

She really had no good answer for him. 'The betrothal was all I could think of that quickly. Why you? Because I know you and you were available.' She didn't add it was because she was certain it would never happen so he was also a safe choice.

'I am not available to you.'

Was he going to expose her lie? 'Jared, please, I know you have every reason to despise me, but I beg of you, don't tell Villaire the truth.'

His silence sent a cold shiver down her spine. He headed for the door without comment, making her even more wary.

Lea knew full well that this would be her only chance to convince him to help her, so she grasped at the one thing she thought might work. 'Matilda sent you here to protect me and my keep.'

Jared came to an instant halt. He turned to look at her. 'I find it amazing that you would suddenly place honour and duty above all else. You can't have it both ways, Lea.'

Just as he reached up to remove the bar from across the door, someone knocked on the other side.

Lea groaned. That's what she didn't need—someone finding her and Jared together in her chamber alone.

'Lady Lea, are you in there?'

Relieved at the sound of Agatha's voice, Lea replied, 'Yes. Just a moment.'

Jared opened the door and brushed by the open-mouthed maid.

'What are you thinking?' Agatha bustled into the room. 'Rumours of the lady's betrothal are flitting through Montreau faster than an arrow flies.'

'That didn't take long.' Obviously Villaire had opened his mouth the minute he left the tower.

'You know how tongues wag, yet you ensconce yourself in your bedchamber with Lord Jared? That will have the keep buzzing for months.'

'He wanted to see the missive from the empress. It's not as though we were doing anything other than talking.'

'Spoken with all the surety of a child.' Agatha crossed her arms against her chest. 'You know better. It won't matter what you were or weren't doing, people will talk.'

'Let them talk.' It wouldn't be the first—or last— time someone talked about the lady of a keep.

'And when word makes its way back to King Stephen?'

Oh, good heaven. Lea's stomach clenched. She hadn't thought about that. If somehow she did manage to conceive a child and the king heard the slightest rumour that the child might be a bastard, she'd end up with a husband she didn't want.

The older woman dropped down on to a bench, asking, 'And what about this betrothal? Is there any truth to it?'

Lea stuck her head out of the door and checked to make certain nobody lurked in the corridor before she sat down next to Agatha. 'No. Villaire is planning something, so I lied about already being betrothed.'

'And Lord Jared played along?' Agatha's whispered question belied the shock on her face.

'I don't know why, but for that moment he did.'

'For that moment?'

'I can't be certain he'll not tell Villaire the truth.'

'You mustn't let him do that.'

Lea sighed. 'And how do I stop Jared from doing anything?'

'Make the betrothal real.'

If she hadn't been sitting down, Lea knew she'd have fallen at Agatha's suggestion. 'The man despises me.' And other than the physical attraction, she wasn't too sure she didn't feel the same towards him. Neither of them was about to become united in marriage—at least not to each other.

'You could do worse.'

Charles was proof enough of that. 'I am not going to take another husband.'

'Soon it will be apparent that you are not carrying Charles's baby. When that is discovered, you won't be given a choice in the matter. So, why not take advantage of the choosing while you still can?'

While there was some merit in Agatha's idea, Jared would be the last person Lea would choose. 'If Warehaven were in full control of this keep, Montreau's men would find themselves embroiled in this senseless war. I'll not have it, Agatha.'

'Montreau is neutral. Surely Lord Jared wouldn't change that status.'

'War is in his blood—it is his duty. Lord Jared had intended to wed me, then leave for battle the next morning. If he was willing to risk making his wife a widow so quickly, what makes you think he would give a second thought to Montreau?'

'Lady Lea, you were still overwrought about Phillip's death at the time. Did you ever ask Lord Jared what he'd intended for Montreau?'

Lea shook with remembered anger and fear. She'd asked him. His response had enraged and frightened her. 'Of course I did. His not-so-friendly reply was that it was his responsibility to follow orders—regardless of whether I liked them or not.'

Before Agatha could say a word, Lea added, 'There was no sense to be gained from Phillip's death. My father would not send Montreau's men into battle for Stephen or Matilda. Neither will I. He fought to remain neutral and won. Enough lives have been lost. Enough crops have been ruined. People are starving to death for lack of food. Innocent women and children are dying because they've been left without someone to defend them. Montreau and its people are my responsibility. I could never marry a man who did not feel same. I will not jeopardise my men or their families for anything—not even love.'

Agatha patted her shoulder. 'Child, I know how passionate you are about Montreau. But what will you do now?'

Lea took a deep breath, seeking a measure of calm. 'I can only hope that Jared doesn't tell Villaire the truth and that the men find Charles's body quickly. After that, I don't know. I need a little time to think of what to do next.'

The older woman rose. 'At least you have given up the idea of conceiving a child.'

Not wanting to irritate herself, or her maid, further, Lea remained silent. She hadn't given up on the idea, because it was a perfect solution. She just wasn't altogether certain Jared was the right man. Her feelings towards him were too volatile, too jumbled with Phillip's death, Montreau and their past.

There would be too many emotions tearing at her if she became involved with Jared again. Emotions, feelings he'd never share.

Chapter Five

Jared stood on the windswept beach, trying to ignore the cold mist slowly drenching him with each blast of the wind.

For three days now he and the men had combed the rocks and reeds lining Montreau's bay, searching for the body of Charles Villaire.

Each day he'd had to shame, or browbeat, Markam Villaire into helping find his brother's body. Jared wasn't about to force his or Montreau's men into doing a task Villaire wouldn't perform.

Not when the task had already been done. According to Lea, and her men, they'd combed the shoreline for miles in either direction and dragged the bay more times than they could remember. He had no reason to doubt their word.

Ellison, the captain of Montreau's guard, said the lady herself had overseen every hour of the search, braving the cold, biting wind and spray longer than some of the men.

Jared glanced down the beach and saw that, just as

she had yesterday and the day before, Lea stood at the water's edge. She pulled her wool ermine-lined mantle tighter about her shoulders, tucking her chin into the fur lining at the neck.

What was she looking for so intently? Did she not trust him or his men to do the task correctly? Or did concern for her missing husband keep her on the beach? What would she do if they found the body?

One of his men stopped beating the reeds to stretch. Catching Jared's line of vision, he said, 'She must have loved him dearly.'

Two of Montreau's men working nearby snorted until they nearly choked, then paused to catch their breath. The older one shook his head. 'No one had cause to love that man, least of all his wife.'

After agreeing, the younger man added, 'She probably only wishes to make certain the devil isn't coming back from the dead.'

When the men went back to work, Jared walked towards Lea. Upon hearing of her betrothal to Villaire, he'd often wondered it if had been a love match.

In his darkest wishes he had hoped not. He hadn't wanted her to be happy—only to suffer pain and heartache. Had she? Had his wishes been granted at her expense? Suddenly the idea sickened him.

Yes, she'd broken his trusting heart. She'd dashed his hopes for a love match.

But heartbreaks did heal, although the scar remained, sometimes pricking at him mercilessly—especially of late. But the loss had eventually become bearable.

Did he forgive her for the betrayal? No. He didn't know if he ever would. But he had learned a valuable lesson. Claims of love were not to be believed. When he decided to wed—if he ever decided to wed—it would be a match made for convenience and gain. There'd be no emotional attachment involved.

As he drew closer she turned to look at him. Jared slowed his steps, surprised by the dark circles beneath her eyes and the paleness of her face.

'You need to return to the keep.' He stopped alongside her to gaze out over the water.

'No…' Shivering, she paused. When the shaking lessened, she continued, 'If my men can stand the cold, so can I.'

'You are not a man, Lea, and you look sick.'

'Thank you for such a prettily worded compliment.'

He ignored her sarcasm. 'It will be rather difficult to thwart Villaire if you are confined to bed with an illness brought on by your own stubbornness.'

'I look sick and I'm stubborn, too. You create such a lovely description of me.'

She was obviously looking for an argument. She'd not get one from him—not now, at least. He'd gain no enjoyment from arguing with someone not up to the challenge.

'I don't need to tell you how lovely you are. But apparently I do need to tell you to get out of the cold and mist before you take a fever.'

She snuggled deeper into her full-length cloak. 'I'm fine. Just tired.'

Tired? She looked exhausted. 'When was the last time you slept?'

'What do you care?'

'I don't,' he answered honestly. 'But Matilda will have my head if anything befalls you.'

Another shiver racked her body. 'Ah, yes, orders above all.'

'What else is there?'

'Go back to your men, Jared. I have no need of your honour to duty.'

'Enough.' He draped an arm across her shoulders and turned her away from the bay. 'Your teeth are chattering and your temper is showing. Neither is attractive.'

She pulled away from him. 'I'm not out here to be attractive.'

'Why are you out here?'

Lea turned back to look at the bay. 'To make certain I didn't miss something when we searched for the body before.'

Something chipping away at his heart urged him to ask, 'Will you be upset if we find nothing?'

She looked up at him. The haunted look in her eyes gave him a moment's pause.

'No.'

While her expression had caught him off guard, her whispered answer had sent a chill down his spine. Montreau's men had been correct—the lady obviously had little love for her deceased husband. But was it something more than just a lack of love? Did she have a reason to fear his return from the grave?

Gently grasping her shoulder, Jared redirected her away from the water. Without giving her a choice, he led her towards the path up to the keep.

She tried to move away from his hold. 'Leave me alone, Jared.'

'No, Lea.' He tightened his grasp on her shoulder in warning. 'You'll either come along like a lady, or I'll carry you like a petulant child. It makes no difference to me because, either way, you are returning to the keep.'

To his relief she didn't offer further resistance. Instead, she quickened her pace to walk ahead of him so that his arm no longer rested across her shoulders.

'I know my way back.'

'Since it's your land, I'm glad to hear that.'

'You don't need to follow me.'

She wasn't going to be rid of him that easily. 'Pretend I'm not here.'

'If only it was that easy.'

Since there wasn't anything he could say that she wouldn't construe as snide or nasty, he said nothing. Instead, he silently followed her up the hill. The climb seemed almost too much for her at times. She would take a step forwards only to wobble backwards two.

Finally, when he was certain Lea was about to fall to the ground, he swept her into his arms, ordering, 'Hush. Don't say a word.'

Her exhaustion was evident from the fact that she didn't struggle at all. She held herself as stiffly as she could, but thankfully, she didn't fight him.

Once inside, she claimed, 'You've carried me far enough. Put me down, I can walk on my own.'

Jared doubted it, but he understood Lea's desire not to be carried to her bedchamber—especially by him. He lowered her legs to the floor and released her.

As she turned to climb the steps, he said, 'I expect Agatha to come tell me you are in bed beneath a pile of warm covers before I return to the bay.'

The man was insufferable. Lea spun around to tell him so, only to lose her balance. She grasped at the wooden railing, but missed. The next thing she knew she was right back in his arms.

Mortified, she pushed against his chest. 'Put me down.'

'I didn't carry you this far only to have you break your neck on the stairs.' Without releasing her, Jared headed up towards her bedchamber.

'I just tripped.' She tried to swing her legs over his arm, but the weight of her heavy cloak hampered her movements. 'I can walk.'

He tightened his hold. 'Stop it before you kill us both.'

To only add to her humiliation, Lea burst into unwanted tears. 'Please, put me down.'

His eyes widened. 'Good God, Lea, have you slept at all these last few nights?'

She shook her head. No, she hadn't been able to sleep. Fear that he'd tell Villaire the truth, and worry that Villaire would succeed in his quest to gain control of Montreau, had kept her awake pacing the floor in her chamber.

How was she supposed to sleep when everything she held dear was in danger of being taken from her?

Jared kicked the door of her chamber open and set her on her feet next to the bed. He undid the clasp at the top of her mantle and tossed the sodden cloak to the floor.

'My lady, what is—?' Agatha hurried into the chamber, coming to a halt when she saw Jared.

'Get out.' Jared glared at the woman.

Agatha ignored him, rushing forwards instead. 'My lord, you shouldn't be in here.'

'Does everyone in this keep ignore orders?' He pointed at the door. 'I said get out.'

'But—' Agatha looked at Lea. 'My lady, are you unwell?'

Lea was too tired to answer or argue. She stared at the bed, wondering if it had ever looked more inviting. She'd explain things to Agatha and argue with him later. Right now, she just wanted a moment of silence and a few moments of sleep.

'She'll be fine. Get out.' He turned the maid around and pushed her towards the door. 'If I need you, I'll call.'

After closing the door behind her, he grabbed a blanket from a nearby bench, then returned to Lea. Sitting on the edge of the bed, he tugged her closer. 'Lift your arms.'

'I can get undressed.'

'I'm sure you can.' But that admission didn't stop him. Jared struggled with the damp laces for no more than a few heartbeats before retrieving a knife from the scabbard hanging from his belt and slicing up the seam on one side of the gown and sleeve.

Grasping the hem of her gowns, he pulled them both over her head, freed her arms and tossed the garments on top of her cloak.

Lea instantly crossed her arms over her breasts, gasping as the cool air of the chamber rushed against her skin. 'You can go now. Thank you.'

As if she hadn't said a word, Jared quickly and methodically dried the dampness from her body with the extra blanket, and then rose to push her down on to the bed. He made quick work of removing her soft boots and stockings before briskly rubbing heat into her feet and legs.

She was naked, shivering and unable to protect herself against anything he might do. She closed her eyes, praying he'd leave.

Her prayer went unanswered.

He pulled the covers back. 'Lie down.'

His tone was gruff and, without the strength to argue, she didn't question him. But once she was tucked in beneath the blankets, Lea asked from between chattering teeth, 'Are you going to leave now?'

Jared stood over her. A frown drew his brows together. He touched the side of her cheek with the back of his hand, then felt her forehead.

'No. Move over.' He pushed her across the bed and sat on the edge once again.

Confused, Lea struggled to stay awake. 'What?'

His boots hit the floor with a thud. 'I said move over.'

'You are not—getting into—this bed.' Lea marvelled at the sudden slurring of her words as she shivered hard enough to make her jaw hurt. She closed her eyes. 'So—cold.'

'I know.'

She heard the rustle of clothing being removed and felt a breeze as the edge of the blanket was lifted. The bed dipped and she knew she should stop him. But the warmth of the hard chest against her and the arms pulling her closer were far too welcome to reject.

Lea curled tightly against the warmth, pressing her nose into his chest with her hands folded between the two of them. 'Don't—'

'Go to sleep.' He pulled the covers up over her head, encasing her in a warm dark cocoon.

Jared closed his eyes. He had no idea what he was doing, or thinking. He only knew that he wasn't about to let her fall ill while under his protection. People would think the worst—they'd believe he'd exacted revenge by seeking her death. And, heaven forbid, if she did die, he would always wonder if he'd somehow let it happen on purpose.

He was angry at her, at times despised her, but he didn't wish her dead.

Certain Lea's maid would be just outside the door with her ear pressed against the wood, he called out her name.

As he'd suspected she would, Agatha came into the room almost immediately. 'My lord?'

She came to a gasping halt halfway to the bed. 'What are you doing?'

Moving faster than anyone would guess, she spun around to close the door to the chamber before coming to the side of the bed.

'My lord, I must ask you to leave.'

'You can ask. But I'm going nowhere.' Jared nodded toward the brazier. 'Build up the fire in this chamber.'

Agatha remained rooted in place. 'But—'

'But nothing. Your lady is exhausted and has taken a chill. She needs warmth and sleep.' Over the edge of the covers he glared at the maid. 'Does it look like I'm doing anything to her?'

'No.'

'Heat.' Jared nearly growled the word. To his relief the older woman jumped into action.

While she worked at building a fire, he asked, 'Why didn't you know she hasn't slept?'

'My lord?' Agatha rose from her task to stare at him. 'When I enquired about her health, Lea insisted she was _fine_.'

'And you believed her?' A near-sightless person could have seen she wasn't fine. 'Did you even look at her?'

'Yes, but—' Agatha shrugged. 'When I suggested

she rest, Lady Lea waved me away. She was bound and determined to be on the beach when Lord Charles's body was found.'

Jared stopped tormenting the maid. He knew better than anyone else that Lea wasn't going to do anything she didn't want to do.

Agatha approached the bed. 'Has she taken a fever?'

'I'm not certain.' He rested his cheek against the top of her head. 'I don't think so. But she was wet and freezing cold. She needed warmth—quickly.'

When the maid glanced towards the door, he suggested, 'Go down to the kitchen and bring up something for her to eat and drink when she awakens.'

'I'll do that.' She reached up to pull closed the curtains on the door side of the bed. If anyone should stick their head into the chamber, they'd not see him in the bed.

Agatha peered around the curtain to add, 'If you don't mind, I'll pass the word that the lady is ill.'

'Good. That should help keep the gossips at bay.' Since he'd so boldly carried Lea to her chamber and hadn't returned below stairs yet, he was certain tongues were already carrying tales through the keep.

The last thing he needed was for his aunt to catch wind of this. She'd have the two of them wedded before he could finish explaining what had happened.

He wasn't certain who would be more horrified— him, or Lea.

Asleep, Lea relaxed and uncurled against him, draping one arm over his chest. Jared tensed, trying desperately not to remember the feel of gentle swells and soft skin beneath his touch.

But his traitorous memories and body ignored him.

Instead of a nearly frozen, exhausted woman pressed against him for warmth, in his mind it was Lea—*his* Lea, not the woman next to him.

Her lips had met his hesitantly at first, but soon she had eagerly returned his kisses. She had tensed beneath his caress, but soon, very soon, sighs and tremors of desire had chased away her uncertainty.

His only problem had been making sure not to take their love play all the way. He'd promised her they would wait until the day they exchanged vows. Even though it had taken every ounce of willpower he possessed, he'd not broken that vow.

Sometimes, considering what she'd done to him, he wished he hadn't been so vigilant in keeping his promise.

Lea turned her head to rest her cheek against his chest, dragging a sigh from Jared. It was going to be a long night.

Warm. She was far too warm.

On the other hand, Lea was thankful for the heat. It was more welcome than the freezing cold. She burrowed into the warmth behind her, stopping at the feel of another body against her back.

Too tired yet to move way, she reached behind her, encountering the hard, tensed muscle of a man's naked thigh.

'Go back to sleep.' Jared's voice brushed against her ear, causing a shiver that didn't come from the cold.

She tried to roll away, but he tightened his arm round her waist, drawing her closer.

'Fear not. We've done nothing except sleep under Agatha's watchful eyes. She sleeps on her pallet.'

Even though her maid was no more than ten feet away, Lea knew she should vehemently protest this intimacy. She hadn't invited him to her bed and should order him from the chamber, or summon Montreau's guards to do so.

She'd be within her rights to scream, to have him confined to a cell until the empress could be informed. No one would blame her if she were to reach beneath her bed, grab the dagger concealed in the frame and use it to stab him.

If anyone discovered him here they would think— dear Lord, they would assume nothing but the worst!

Lea slowly inched her hand toward the edge of the bed—

'It's not there.' Jared sat up and grasped her wrist with one hand. With his free hand he reached beneath her pillow and slid something from beneath it.

'Here.' He slapped what felt oddly like a dagger into her hand before releasing her wrist to lay back down. 'Now will you go back to sleep?'

'Thank you.' She slid the weapon back beneath the pillow.

Jared did little more than grunt a response before once again wrapping his arm round her waist and pulling her close.

Her pulse raced. Drawing in breath was near impossible with him so close that she could feel his heart pounding against her back. She leaned as far away as his embrace would permit.

He grasped her hip, holding her still. 'You would do us both a great favour if you'd just stop moving.'

Lea tried to relax, but it proved nearly impossible. All

she could think of was the warmth of his chest against her, his arm wrapped so protectively round her, and the unmistakable hardness pressed against the backs of her thighs.

Mere days ago she would have taken advantage of this closeness. Conceiving a child would ensure Montreau's future.

Now that the opportunity was…at hand…she knew it would not be possible.

There was nothing sweeter in her memories than the stolen moments she and Jared had shared in darkened alcoves. He'd been the first man to kiss her, to touch her and the only man to give her fulfilment.

Her chest ached with longing. She hadn't realised until this moment how much she'd missed him, and missed his touches and kisses.

If she turned over to complete the act with Jared, it would not be simply for a child. Making love to him would break her heart—again. It would remind her of all the things that had been good between, and of all the things that had gone so wrong. She would once again remember all of the shattered dreams they'd held for their shared future.

Lea fought the gathering tears. Enough of them had been shed years ago; she'd waste no more of them now.

Chapter Six

Lea stretched, gasping at the pain lacing through her body. She tried again, but this time more slowly, still unable to locate a single muscle that didn't hurt. Reaching out, she swept the bed, relieved to find herself alone.

Alone? Lea blinked her eyes open. Of course she was alone. Why wouldn't she be? Last night had been nothing more than a dream—albeit an odd dream.

For some reason, she remembered waking up during the night next to a warm, muscular body. More to the point, Jared's warm, muscular body. Since that would never happen, it had to have been a dream.

After throwing back the covers, Lea sat up and groaned. What had happened to her? She felt like she'd been trampled beneath a dozen horses.

'My lady?' The bed curtains parted and Agatha stuck her head through the opening. 'Good, you're finally awake.'

'*Finally* awake?' She craned her neck, trying to stretch the stiffness away. 'How long have I been asleep?'

Agatha busied herself in the chamber, picking up

discarded clothing, and opening the shutters before returning to the side of the bed. 'Just under two days.'

She handed Lea a gown. 'It seems your lack of sleep took its toll while you were on the beach.'

She slid the gown over her head. Now she remembered—Jared had brought her back to Montreau. Then, when she'd tripped on the stairs, he'd carried her up here to her chamber, although she didn't remember anything after that except being grateful for the bed beneath her, the covers over her and the warmth beside her.

The warmth beside her?

'Agatha, was I...?' Not quite certain how to ask, Lea hesitated. 'Did Jared...?'

'Did he sleep with you? Yes.' The older woman took pity on her. 'But he did nothing more than warm your body. You were nearly freezing, Lea. We feared a fever might set in.'

'We?' She could understand Agatha's concern. But Jared's? 'Why would he care if I lived or died?'

'I don't.' Jared walked further into the chamber. 'But your people and Empress Matilda might not take kindly to you dying under my protection.'

Lea rose and shook the undergown down into place before turning to look at him. His intense gaze, hungry and hooded, sent her mind whirling. She swallowed, trying to regain her composure and a measure of common sense. 'Oh, yes, I forgot. I am your duty at the moment.'

The lout flashed a smile at her before he nodded. 'Good. I see you've regained your fighting form.'

Unwilling to prolong his unsettling presence in her chamber, Lea refused to be baited into arguing with him. 'Was Charles's body found?'

'No.' Jared took a seat on the bench nearest the door. 'I plan on calling off the search today if nothing is found.'

Lea frowned. That meant they'd been searching for five days now. It should never have gone on this long.

'You want them to keep looking?'

'No.' Lea realised he'd misinterpreted her frown. 'It's been far too long already. Call it off, bring them in.'

He nodded in agreement, but didn't seem eager to leave. She wanted him gone from her chamber before she said, or did, something that would give away how just his mere presence was making her notice things about him that she'd been able to ignore—until now.

Things like the breadth of his shoulders, the length of his legs, the way his hair fell across his face when he turned his head, or the crinkles that formed at the sides of his eyes when he smiled.

Like he was doing now. Even though it was only half a smile, it lightened the expression on his face, and oddly enough her mood.

She looked away. 'Don't you have something to do?'

Jared stretched out his legs. 'No.'

The tone of his voice, deep and steady, made her pulse tremble. Oh, yes, she desperately wanted—needed—him to leave.

Intentionally seeking to anger him into leaving, she asked, 'What about Montreau? Are you not avoiding your duty to the keep by sitting here where you aren't needed?'

'I'm certain Montreau is fine.'

Something about the tone of his voice set her senses on alert. That half-smile wasn't a smile—it was more of a gloat. What she had read as an easy manner was in truth…smugness.

He was doing a bad job of hiding some secret. If his badly hidden mirth was any indication, it was a secret she would most likely not find pleasing.

When he finally got around to revealing what he was hiding, Lea knew he'd expect her to show some emotion—shock, surprise, perhaps even disgust or horror.

No matter what he divulged, she refused to give him the satisfaction of watching her fall apart like some weak-kneed woman. She'd already displayed enough of that to him.

Of course the trick would be in getting him to tell her the secret now while she was prepared.

Grasping at straws, she asked, 'Since Charles's body wasn't found, is it safe to assume you'll be sending his brother on his way?'

Jared's smile broadened. Lea tensed. His reaction told her that this secret somehow involved Villaire. That knowledge made her ill.

'No. I'll not be able to do that just yet.'

Keeping her voice steady wouldn't be easy, but she took a breath, then asked, 'And why is that?'

Jared rose to head for the door. Lea refused to be kept hanging from the end of a string he held. 'Jared, stop. Why can't you ask him to leave?'

To her relief, he paused in the doorway and turned to look at her. 'Because he has acquired a new husband for you.'

Lea's brief moment of relief vanished, along with her determination not to show surprise. She raced after him. 'What?'

Jared didn't stop; he lifted an arm and waved at her over his shoulder.

'My lady, catch!' Agatha called out a warning to her.

A gown hit Lea on the shoulder, making her realise she hadn't finished dressing. Knowing he'd make good his escape before she could dress, she glanced out into the corridor, grabbed a mantle from a peg by the door and dashed after Jared while holding the front of the long cloak together.

'Jared!'

His curse drifted up from the stairs. But he came back upstairs, stopping before her to give her a long head-to-toe look. 'You spend two days in bed sick and now you run about the keep without shoes or a gown?'

'What do you mean Villaire has found me a *husband*?'

Jared hushed her before turning her around. 'Keep your voice down.' He pushed her towards her chamber.

Once inside, she spun round to confront him. 'Well?'

'Villaire found you a husband. What part of that statement do you fail to understand?'

He was enjoying this far too much. It was apparent by the twitch at the corner of his mouth. She longed to take her anger and frustration out on him, but retained enough sense to keep her fisted hands at her sides.

'He doesn't have the right.'

'I know that. You know that.' Jared shrugged. 'Obviously Villaire and King Stephen think otherwise.'

'Stephen? What does he have to do with this?'

'From what I've heard, this John—Blackstone—carries a writ stating that he has permission from the king to court you.'

Lea felt an unseen fist slam into her stomach. 'What?'

'You should be thankful he didn't arrive with outright permission to wed you.'

'I'd be more thankful had this man not arrived at all.'

'Come now, Lea. Montreau is too rich a prize for you to have assumed you'd not be wed again whether you wanted to or not.'

He was wrong. Actually, she had no intention of ever wedding again. She didn't care how rich a prize her keep was to anyone.

'I am *not* marrying this man.' If Villaire had found this prospective husband for her, the man was likely a dolt who could easily be controlled by her brother-by-marriage.

'Don't tell me.' Jared waved toward the door. 'Tell them. They await you below.'

He was going to send her to the wolves alone?

'I thought it was your responsibility—your duty—to protect me.'

Jared nodded at Agatha. And to Lea's shock the maid left the chamber, closing the door behind her.

'Agatha? What…where…' She turned on Jared. 'Now you order my maid about?'

'Agatha is part of Montreau. That makes her my responsibility.'

Lea couldn't believe what she was hearing.

'Oh, yes, all of Montreau is your responsibility— your *sacred duty*—yet you are going to leave me to fend for myself against Villaire.'

Jared closed the distance between them. 'Is it any less than what you deserve?'

This was how he planned to get even with her? She gazed up at him. 'Yes! It is far more than what I deserve. I am sorry I hurt your pride and embarrassed you. But

I didn't ruin your life. I didn't take all you possess from you.' Fear and pain shot up her spine. 'I didn't condemn you to a life of hell.'

She didn't think watching his men die wasn't his own version of hell? Jared grasped her upper arms. 'You have no idea what you did to me.'

The hoarseness of his own voice caught him by surprise. After all these years her betrayal was still a raw open wound. It shouldn't bother him so much. He no longer cared for her, so their past should have no effect on him.

'Did you tell him that I lied? That you and I are not betrothed?'

'No.' He wanted her to be present when that lie was exposed. 'I thought I'd leave that for you to explain.'

'Jared, please.' She grabbed the front of his tunic, bunching the fabric between her fisted hands. 'I will do anything—' Lea swallowed hard '—anything you ask to keep my secret.'

Certain she'd take offence, he winged an eyebrow as if mocking her, and asked, 'Anything?'

'Yes. Anything. Everything. All I have is yours—I will give it to you freely. Just please, Jared, please don't tell Villaire the truth.'

He stared down at her, amazed at the desperation of her tone. Yet, instead of seeing this as the perfect opportunity to savour a taste of revenge, he was struck with the sudden, illogical urge to help her.

What hold did this woman have over him? Her lower lip quivered, yet she held his stare—although her eyes appeared suspiciously bright.

Jared released her arms to pull her close. She needed

him and to his chagrin he could no longer deny how much he wanted her.

His lips a breath away from hers, he cursed her, 'Damn you, Lea.'

Even though she pushed against his chest, her lips were soft and pliant beneath his. In a matter of heartbeats, she parted them to return his kiss and snake her arms around his neck.

When Lea relaxed in his arms and moaned softly, every memory of her flooded his mind. The days they'd shared, the softness of her skin, the laughs and teasing, the sweetness of her kiss and the stolen moments.

He wanted more than stolen moments and kisses. Jared backed her towards the bed.

Lea didn't resist. She let him lead her across the chamber, ignoring the cloak as it fell from her shoulders to rustle on to the floor. In fact, she clung to him, inviting him to share her desire.

They fell on to the bed in each other's arms. When he broke their kiss, Lea whispered his name.

He recognised the hunger and longing in her breathless whisper. It matched his own. At one time he had dreamed of this moment—how could he ignore the heat setting his body afire with lust?

He traced a line of kisses along her jaw, pausing against the soft spot beneath her ear. 'Stop me now, Lea.'

She couldn't have stopped him had she wanted to. Not now. Lea didn't care if this was what he wanted in exchange for his silence. It didn't matter. She wanted him, needed him, longed to once again lose herself in the magic of his touch.

'No, Jared, don't stop.'

She moved beneath him, straining to get closer, to feel his touch upon her.

His ragged groan brushed across her ear. The longing it conveyed sent ripples of anticipation skittering the length of her body.

Lea tugged on his tunic, pulling one end free of his belt. She longed to stroke his flesh, wanted to feel the play of his muscles beneath her hands.

'Jared.'

He must have understood her frustration, because before she could be certain of his intention, their clothing lay in a pile on the floor. Now there was nothing to prevent her from running her hands over hard muscles, or stroking warm skin.

Before, their stolen moments had been fraught with the danger of discovery. And so there had been half-clothed, brief sessions of heavy breathing, deep kisses and near-frantic touches.

This would be their first time sharing the luxury of a bed. No longer did they need worry about the expectations of their parents. They no longer needed to restrain their desires. Instead, they could let lust and passion guide them.

Lea trembled at the thought of giving herself fully to Jared in ways she'd only imagined before now. She curled her fingers over his shoulders, holding on as he parted her lips.

His kiss demanded a response as his tongue swept along hers. She moaned softly against his mouth.

His lips left hers to trail a hot line to the soft spot beneath her ear. 'I want all of you.' The huskily spoken statement brushed a heated shiver down her spine.

She sighed as Jared caressed her breasts, teasing the already hardening nipples. She arched into his caress, more starved for his touch than she'd realized, and closed her eyes.

His lips trailed fire across her breast, over her collarbone and up the length of her neck.

The heat pooling between her legs begged for his attention. Lea slid her hand down his chest and stomach to rest against the length of his erection.

He brushed her hand away. Slowly trailing his fingertips along her collarbone, he paused to gently trace the outline of her breasts before chasing the shivers down her torso.

The first ragged sigh of anticipation hadn't even fully left her lips as his gentle touch skated along her leg, parting her thighs to stroke over her mons before slipping between the slick folds.

She gasped at how quickly her body responded to his touch. Jared's kisses, his caresses, tormented her until she begged breathlessly, 'Jared, please.'

He drew up over her, supporting his body on his elbows, cupping her face, and came into her with a sure, fluid stroke that drew a cry from her lips.

While his touch was gentle, his thrusts and kisses were not. She clutched him tightly to her, crying out his name as she fell headlong into fulfilment.

Jared covered her lips with his own and answered her cry with a deep ragged one of his own.

Spent, he fell alongside her, breathing hard. He gathered her into his embrace and kissed the top of her head. 'We were fools to wait.'

She couldn't disagree. Had she known making love

with Jared would be this…amazing…she would have ignored her parents' wishes. Perhaps then the past might have been different.

But it wasn't different and, to Lea's horror, guilt and shame threatened to overwhelm her. While she'd often wondered what it would be like if Jared made love to her, not once had she given a thought to the aftermath.

She felt like a whore. The only difference was that instead of gold, she'd offered her body in exchange for his silence. And there was nothing to assure her that he would keep his word. She'd been foolish to trust Jared, to permit herself to get so caught up in the moment that she'd temporarily forgotten how much he disliked her.

He sat up on the edge of the bed and gathered his clothing. Lea grazed her teeth across her bottom lip, trying to decide what to say—or do.

Finally, unable to stand it any longer, she blurted out, 'You won't tell Villaire the truth now, will you?'

Jared tensed, but said nothing as he pulled his shirt over his head.

Suddenly panicked, Lea cried, 'You promised!'

He shrugged into his surcoat, picked up the rest of his clothing and headed towards the door.

She calmed her tone. 'Jared, please.'

Without pausing on his way out of the chamber, he said, 'I promised you nothing, Lea.'

Chapter Seven

Lea stared at the door—again. The inanimate object had been the sole focus of her attention since Jared had left her in open-mouthed shock.

All through her bath and even now while she absently combed her hair dry, she'd gone over his action again and again.

She'd known he was angry about her untimely rejection. And she'd expected some type of revenge—maybe even deserved it. But she never would have imagined his revenge to be so brutal, cruel—or thorough.

He'd used her. Not just her body—after all, she'd made the offer and so had no one to blame for that except herself.

But Jared had known exactly how her body would respond to his touch and had used that against her. He'd made her mad with desire until she all but begged for more.

Then, just when she'd begun to believe their feelings toward each other could be more companionable, he'd tossed it back in her face.

If Jared told Villaire the truth about their imaginary betrothal, everything would fall apart around her. She was nearly out of time to conceive a child she could claim as Charles's. With both Jared and Villaire here it would impossible to even find a man, let alone conceive a child.

Her stomach knotted with the realisation that she'd taken a big risk with Jared. But it was doubtful their one time would result in a child—she prayed that would prove true.

It had been a mistake, a huge mistake. Jared made her feel things and think things she had put behind her years ago. She needed to make certain the opportunity to be alone with him never happened again.

'Lady Lea?' Agatha queried from the doorway. 'They await you below.'

'Villaire or Jared?'

'Both, along with Sir Blackstone.' Agatha made a sour face when mentioning Villaire's companion.

Lea set the comb down. Not anxious to see any of them, she said, 'They can either start the meal without me, or keep waiting. It is up to them.'

'Would you like my help?' Agatha asked as Lea swept her hair over her shoulder.

The woman would complete the task of braiding her hair too quickly and Lea was in no rush to join the men. She answered, 'No. I'm fine. I'll be down when I finish.'

Her presence wasn't required. Jared would only make her more nervous and sick to her stomach on purpose. Villaire would take advantage of every opportunity to belittle her. And this Blackstone only wished to size up his prospective bride.

Why couldn't they all just leave her alone? She and Montreau didn't need, or want their proffered help.

Jared stared at the men milling about the over-crowded Great Hall. He'd rather be with them, flirting with the women, sharing a drink, a laugh and a tale than sitting at the table on the raised dais with Villaire and Blackstone.

He glanced at Agatha; catching her attention he raised one brow in question. She shrugged in reply. He'd sent the woman above stairs to inform Lea they awaited her for the meal. She was taking her sweet time joining them.

This was probably his payment for leaving her chamber the way he had. What had she expected him to say? They'd just been intimate and all she could think of was if he was going to keep her secret or not.

That shouldn't have bothered him. It isn't as if they shared any feelings toward each other—at least not tender ones.

But it had sounded to him as if she were begging and that irritated him. He wasn't used to weak-willed women, and had not the slightest inkling of how to deal with them. Nor was it something he wanted to learn.

He would rather they argued or snarled at one another than try to figure out how to respond to whining or begging. Such instances always left him feeling…incompetent, and that did nothing except anger him.

Jared frowned. He needed to think about something else instead of Lea. Other than someone he needed to protect, she wasn't his concern. He'd need to be more careful in the future and stay out of her bed. As much as he enjoyed making love to her, it would only lead to problems later. Problems he wished to avoid.

Right now, the food was getting cold and the men had yet to eat. Just he started to rise to go see what was keeping her, Villaire said, 'We will eat without her.'

Jared sat back down and glared at the man. 'No. This is her keep. We will eat when the lady arrives.'

It certainly wasn't as if Villaire would perish from lack of food any time soon. The man ate enough for two men, all day long. Jared was amazed at the amount of food the short, squat man could shovel into his mouth.

He wondered how close Charles had been in appearance and action to his brother. If they were alike, in either circumstance, he would pity Lea if she hadn't so deserved such a man.

Villaire shifted, turning towards Jared, to ask, 'I am told you have called off the search?'

'Yes. Enough time has been spent searching for a body that is apparently there no longer.' Jared leaned back in his chair, adding, 'I think it would be safe to assume the sea has claimed him.'

The expression of deep sorrow, one that Jared had quickly recognised as false, fell over Villaire's face. If this man felt anything for his dead brother, it wasn't sadness. Greed for what he saw as a chance to grab control of Montreau, perhaps. The thrill of presumed power over Lea and her keep, through Blackstone, most definitely.

Villaire could wallow in his dreams all he liked— they would never come to fruition. Jared would gut the man first.

He'd sworn to protect her. So until the empress saw

fit to relieve him of this duty, or she remarried, he'd see to it that no one forced any unpleasantness upon her.

For the briefest moment, the hall fell quiet. Jared looked towards the stairs to see Lea approaching the table. Her bright green gown made her look overly pale, but he doubted if that was caused by any lingering illness. She was more likely still upset with him.

He glanced at Villaire. 'You need take another seat.'

'Why would I do that?' The man gripped the arms of the high-backed chair.

'Because you are in Lady Montreau's seat.' Jared toyed with his eating knife. 'You will move.'

Villaire shot him a dark, hate-filled look, but he did rise to wave Blackstone down a chair.

Lea signalled a start for the meal, then sat down between Jared and her brother-by-marriage without comment.

'Ah, yes, and a fine meal it will be.' Villaire glared at her, continuing, 'Congealed gravy, greasy cold meat and wine that tastes like verjuice. I never should have expected better since, under your control, Montreau never could set a decent table.'

Jared thought for certain Lea would throw a well-aimed dagger at Villaire's heart. To his surprise she merely looked down at the trencher they shared. He stared at her. Surely she wasn't going to let that swine get the better of her?

Finally, she suggested, 'Perhaps you would be happier if you were before your own fine table instead of mine.'

Villaire laughed before shaking his head. 'Oh, no, my dear sister, it is becoming more and more apparent that my brother let you slack far too much in your duties. If you are to wed Blackstone, you need to be taught how to manage a keep correctly.'

'Trust me, you can be certain that I am not going to wed this Blackstone.'

As if she'd said nothing, Villaire continued, 'You obviously require a firmer hand in your retraining. Thankfully, I am well experienced in seeing that it is applied correctly.'

Jared read far too much of a threat beneath those words. 'The first brigand that lays a hand on Lady Montreau will see it cut from his arm.'

Lea made a sound that sounded suspiciously like a choked laugh. Villaire paled, and was quick to say, 'My Lord Warehaven, you misunderstood. I never meant she needed a hand put to her physically, only that she obviously needs more detailed guidance on how to perform her duties so she brings no disgrace to her husband.'

'My husband is dead.'

Ignoring her statement, Villaire reached out to pat her hand. Lea jerked away from his touch. Nonplussed, he cajoled, 'We all understand how distressing Charles's passing has been for you. But rest assured that Sir Blackstone will help you through your grief.'

Lea glanced at Jared before leaning forwards to glance past Villaire to Blackstone, before once again addressing her brother-by-marriage. 'If you brought him here to wed me, you have wasted his time.'

'He comes with the king's permission. Besides, any other woman would show gratitude at having someone willing to care for them and properly run their keep. You are an oddity who disgraces your gender, dear sister.'

'And you are—'

Jared slid an arm across her stiff shoulders and interrupted, 'I should be insulted that the two of you seem to have forgotten one thing.' He paused, waiting until Villaire and Lea turned their attention towards him before continuing, 'Lea is already betrothed—to me.'

Lea relaxed beneath his touch. Her expression softened and she touched his shoulder.

Jared gritted his teeth. If she so much as mouthed one word of gratitude he would set everyone straight about this supposed betrothal.

She must have understood his glare because she quickly lowered her hand and looked down at the table.

Villaire's face turned red as he blustered, 'But King Stephen—'

Lea slammed a palm on the table, cutting off anything Villaire was about to say. 'Has nothing to say about what happens at Montreau.'

'That's where you're wrong, my lady.' Blackstone smiled slyly before suggesting, 'Before you turn down my suit, you may want to hear what I have to say.'

'It's doubtful anything you say will change my mind, but feel free to talk.'

Blackstone and Villaire exchanged a look, making Jared wonder if this had been planned beforehand.

After glancing around the Great Hall, Blackstone rose. 'Perhaps somewhere more…private?'

'No.' Jared hooked a foot around one leg of Lea's chair, preventing her from leaving. 'You can talk here, or not at all.'

Lea wanted to tell Jared to mind his own business, but she was indebted to him for keeping their betrothal alive. Besides, she really had no wish to be alone with Blackstone.

'No. Lord Jared is correct, you can talk here.'

It was petty and uncharitable of her, but she found him physically unappealing, thin with sloping shoulders, pale skin, thick lips and a weak chin that would one day soon fall into folds.

And his tiny ice-blue eyes made her nervous. Every time he looked at her she could easily envision a blue-eyed rat staring at her.

Of course, she also had to admit that even had the man been gorgeous it wouldn't have mattered—his association with Villaire alone made her distrust and dislike him.

The man's cold glare made her suddenly glad Jared had insisted they remain at the table.

Blackstone shook his head. 'I would think something as personal as a proposal deserves a little privacy.'

'Proposal?' Lea couldn't hide her shock. She thought he'd come to court her, not offer marriage within mere moments of seeing her for the first time.

'Did your maid not tell you?' Villaire sighed. 'Even the servants are sadly lacking in knowing their duty.'

Since he was only criticising Agatha to get under her skin, she ignored his comment. Instead she focused on the question. 'My maid told me Blackstone was here to court my favour.'

'With King Stephen's blessing,' Blackstone added as if she'd be impressed with the announcement.

'Since you are not courting Stephen, his blessing means nothing.'

'If you possessed any wisdom you would have

realised that King Stephen will soon be your liege lord. Montreau is surrounded by the king's supporters; once they send David running back to Scotland you will be alone.'

Villaire looked pointedly at Jared. 'The empress will be unable to raise an army large enough to stop Stephen.'

Lea feared he might be correct. After all, David was nearly encroaching on church property in Durham. The church didn't seem to care who won this war for the crown. They wouldn't lift a finger to defend either side.

Jared's laugh caught her by surprise. He didn't seem to be the least bit concerned by Villaire's dire scenario.

'For Stephen to beat Matilda his supporters would have to chose a side—and be loyal. A promise of gold, land, title, keep or a rich wife changes loyalties in less than a heartbeat. This war will never end—not until one of them dies.'

While his laugh had surprised her, the bitterness in his tone concerned her. A warrior that bitter had little hope in a successful outcome. And if he had no hope that his liege would prove victorious, how could he win on a field of battle?

She'd seen many of Jared's moods—from angry to overjoyed—but never had she seen him bitter or hopeless.

Villaire was adamant. 'One way or another Stephen will win. Eventually all of the barons will come to their senses. They will not give fealty to a woman, especially to one that is not their own.'

Jared countered, 'She is still of Norman blood— more than some of them.'

It wasn't Matilda's fault her father had wed her to a German emperor. Lea sympathised with Matilda's plight. A daughter of the royal house had less say in the choice of a husband than she did.

'It matters not.' Villaire's voice rose. 'No man of any integrity will answer to one who is perceived as lesser than he.'

'They lost their integrity when they turned their backs on their sworn oath to King Henry.'

Where Villaire's voice had risen, Jared's had deepened. Lea needed to stop them before a war broke out in her hall.

It was possible—near probable—that Jared would see through her attempt and ignore her, so she turned her focus on Villaire. 'What right have you to concern yourself with Montreau's loyalty? We are, and in this war always will be, neutral.'

'I have already told you that I intend to petition King Stephen for guardianship.'

Actually, he'd told her that he had already done so. Was he now telling so many lies that he was unable to keep track of them?

Lea motioned towards Blackstone. 'I assume the king is still contemplating your request since your friend only has permission to court me, not wed me.' She pursed her lips and frowned as if considering something important. 'I wonder why that is? Perhaps Stephen is not as trusting of you as you seem to think.'

Markam Villaire smiled, then took a long drink of wine before he shrugged and said, 'That matters little. I am rightfully your guardian and if the king does not agree, I'm certain the church will.'

'The church?' Lea laughed. 'With the speed they move, we could all be dead of old age before the church makes a decision.'

Markam's face once again reddened. 'You find this amusing?'

Yes, she did. And she most certainly didn't need Jared's leg pressing against hers to silently warn her not to say so. Didn't he realise that sort of contact would only serve to muddle her thoughts?

Lea gathered her wits about her before answering. 'Amusing? No. I find this whole plan of yours despicable.'

Blackstone leaned forwards to address her. 'Despicable? What sort of woman are you to so degrade help from your brother?'

'No one was talking to you.'

He jerked back as if she'd physically slapped him, but quickly recovered. 'You, my lady, need learn to guard your tongue else I change my mind.'

Lea nearly choked on the wine she was drinking. 'Change your mind? About what? Courting me? Trust me, Sir Blackstone, such a move on your part will not break my heart. I have no need of, nor do I desire, your courtship.'

Villaire glared at her, warning, 'You go too far.'

'I don't go far enough. I want you and your lack-witted—'

Jared rose quickly and pulled her chair away from the table. 'I need some air.'

Lea glanced up at him. 'You know where the door is located.'

Without asking permission, he assisted her up from her seat. 'I desire your company.'

'I'm honoured.'

Jared ignored her droll tone of voice. With his hand under her elbow, he led her across the hall.

Lea couldn't help but notice that nearly everyone stared at her. She wanted to groan. As usual, whenever Villaire was around, she'd managed to make a spectacle of herself. Why did she permit that man to goad her when she knew full well he did it on purpose?

Once outside, Jared released his hold. 'While I agree your brother-by-marriage is…irritating, he's nothing more than a bothersome flea you should ignore.'

'Thank you, my lord, for pointing that out.'

He walked away, saying. 'Don't be tiresome, Lea.'

'Tiresome?' Following him, she said, 'You tell me how I should behave, treating me like I'm a child, and then calling me tiresome?'

'A child? Hardly.' Jared turned around, but kept walking backwards. 'I know for a fact you aren't a child. You do realise what they'll do now, don't you?'

'Of course I do.' Since she'd antagonised them, they would make her life even more miserable.

'Good.' He presented his back to her, adding, 'Don't complain to me when Blackstone becomes your shadow and Villaire keeps a close eye on the courting progress.'

Unfortunately that's exactly what they would do. And since she was so against the idea, Villaire would also vigorously pursue his plea for guardianship.

She needed to get the two of them out of Montreau. She might not be able to do so, but she knew who could. 'Jared?'

He stopped and turned to look at her. 'What?'

Lea could see the wariness in his narrowed gaze. A trace of guilt almost made her change her mind. 'Now that the search for Charles's body is done, is there any reason for Villaire to remain?'

'No.'

She moved closer and looked up at him. 'So, there'd be nothing to prevent you from ordering him to leave.'

A cool night breeze ruffled her hair. Jared reached up and tucked the wayward strands behind her ear. 'Not if I was so inclined.'

The shiver rippling down her arms had little to do with the night air and more to do with the brush of his knuckles against her skin. Lea knew she was playing a dangerous game, but ignored the urge to step away. Instead she placed a hand on his chest. 'You don't like the man any more than I do. Isn't it time he returned to his own keep?'

Jared traced a fingertip against her cheek. 'Would that make you happy?'

She leaned into his touch. 'Very.'

His lips quirked into a half-smile before he bent to brush a kiss across her lips. 'Then I think he should stay a while longer.'

Lea froze. She lowered her arm and stepped back. Certain she'd not heard him correctly, she asked, 'What?'

'I think he should stay a while longer,' he repeated, the smug smile deepening. 'My task here is to protect you and Montreau. That doesn't necessarily mean I'm sworn to make you happy.'

He'd seen through her ploy. 'Why, you…' Uncertain what vile name to call him, she let her curse trail off.

'What, Lea? What am I? A bastard? A lout? You crook your finger and when I don't rush to do your bidding I'm the lowest of low?' He shrugged and walked away, adding, 'Save your wiles for someone else.'

Shaking with rage, Lea shouted, 'Damn you, Warehaven.'

He instantly returned to her, his anger as evident as her own. 'Oh, now it's Warehaven, is it? Not long ago it was "oh, Jared, please".'

Before she could respond, he pulled her against his chest. 'Fear not, Lea, I was damned the day I met you.'

His mouth covered hers. There was nothing gentle in his kiss, but when the heat in her veins flared to life, she suddenly didn't care.

Lea pressed tighter against his hard thighs and chest. She clung to his shoulders for support, wishing she could somehow get even closer.

Jared pulled his mouth from hers to trail hot kisses to her ear, then whispered, 'Stay away from me, Lea. For both our sakes, just stay away.'

Chapter Eight

From her chamber, Lea stared at the activity in the mud-churned bailey. Even though it had rained non-stop for the last ten days, Jared had the men training daily.

She'd followed his orders and stayed away from him, although she wasn't convinced it was best for both of them. They hadn't so much as exchanged a word in all that time. Instead, she'd watched him from afar—when she wasn't dodging Villaire and Blackstone.

The distance between them had done nothing to lessen the desire from flaring to life whenever she thought of him. It didn't cool the passion building as she watched him from across a room. Nor did it stop the tremors from rippling down her spine when she heard his voice as he spoke to someone else.

He was like some magical spell—or curse—hanging over her night and day. Not even in her sleep could she escape her longing for his touch. Over and over she'd dream of being in his arms, of his caress, or his kiss.

Lea bowed her head. She was pathetic. She was

hopelessly in lust with a warrior. A man who thought more of war than of her. A fact he'd proven once again.

Just over a week ago, Jared had gathered Montreau's men and started working on their defensive skills. At first she'd thought he'd been preparing them to go to war, but Agatha, acting as their intermediary, had explained that he wanted Montreau's men capable of defending the keep should the need ever arise.

She had no argument with his forethought to the safety of Montreau. Some day Jared would leave and it only made sense to make certain they could fend for themselves. They'd been lucky thus far, but who knew how long that would last? Especially now that a lone woman commanded the keep.

'My lady?' Agatha entered the chamber carrying a tray of food. 'Are you feeling any better?'

The aroma of highly spiced meat wafted across Lea's nose. She took one look at the tray and clamped an arm around her tumbling stomach. Waving at the tray, she said, 'I was. Please, take that from here.'

Agatha took the tray back out into the hallway. Leaving it there, she re-entered the chamber. 'Is there anything you'd like?'

'No. Thank you, I'm not hungry.'

The older woman placed her palm against Lea's forehead and cheeks. 'There's no fever to speak of. Should I summon the midwife?'

Lea shook her head. 'It'll pass.' At least it had for the last four mornings. By the time the sun was high in the sky she would feel better.

Besides, she had a sneaking suspicion a midwife

wouldn't be able to cure what was wrong with her. Lea forced the thought aside, refusing to give her fear life.

'Villaire and his shadow are asking for you.'

'That's nice.' Her voice dripped with sarcasm. 'What excuse did you use this time?' As she'd expected, the two men never gave her a moment of peace.

'The truth. I told them you were feeling poorly.'

Agatha busied herself about the chamber, while Lea turned back to the window. She glanced at the gathering storm clouds, wondering when the weather would finally break. Being cooped up in the keep and having to constantly dodge Villaire and Blackstone was getting on her nerves. Many more days of this and she'd be screaming like some crazed fishwife.

With a sigh, she turned her attention back to the bailey, only to meet Jared's stare. Her heart raced and her cheeks flamed. Yet she couldn't look away.

It had been such a mistake to be so intimate with him. Now she couldn't get him out of her mind. The harder she tried to forget what they'd shared, the more she wanted him. Of all the men in the world, why did she have to crave Jared of Warehaven's touch?

Somehow she'd have to set her desires aside. But when he cocked an eyebrow and shot her a seductive half-smile before turning away, Lea feared she'd still desire him long after he left Montreau.

Jared fended off a sword blow from the man with whom he parried blades, sending the less experienced man to his back in the mud. Montreau's men were sadly out of practice. If the keep were attacked, he wouldn't be able to depend on their assistance to any great degree.

They didn't complain about the training—in truth, they seemed relieved to have something constructive to do. However, they weren't quick enough on their feet to keep them from falling into the mud on a regular basis. He reached out and pulled the man to his feet.

'Simon!' he shouted at one of his guards standing on the sidelines. 'Make yourself useful.'

Stepping out of the small, makeshift mêlée, Jared glanced at the keep. She was looking at him—again. He could feel it as a tingle against his neck.

What the hell had he been thinking to take her to bed? Jared rolled his eyes at the witless question. Any fool knew that he hadn't been thinking.

He and Lea had waited so long—years—and unfortunately, the pleasure had far exceeded any of his wildest daydreams. Now, the feel and taste of her was in his blood. And it ate at him, filling him with a mindless, driving need that made him lash out in frustration.

He'd told her to stay away from him and so far, to his amazement, she'd done his bidding. It was safer that way. Safer not just for her, but for both of them.

Her presence made him long to ravish her, to lose himself in the softness of her hair, the scent of her skin and the intoxicating sound of her breathless sighs of pleasure. But the moment he touched her all of the anger and pain welled forth with an undeniable thirst for revenge.

While it was doubtful he would ever forgive her, he didn't want to hurt her. Doing so would only fill him with guilt and self-loathing.

Jared looked up at her. Lea was a beautiful, bewitching temptress—passionate, giving, untrustworthy and heartbreaking. He tightened his grip on his sword. If the empress didn't order him from here soon, he feared losing what little control he had left.

'This is taking far too long. She's making up excuses to avoid you intentionally.' Markam Villaire pounded a meaty fist on the arm of the chair.

'What do you suggest I do?' John Blackstone leaned against the alcove wall in the bedchamber he and Villaire shared. 'She's made it near impossible for me to court her.'

Not that he cared about the courting part. He was already betrothed to another. But the gold Villaire offered was too tempting to resist.

Once he wed Lea, he would move his love into Montreau. Berta wouldn't mind. After all, this keep was consideringly better than the hovel she resided in now. John was certain that, after some sweet words and love-making, Berta would readily accept the situation.

'The time for courting her is at an end. If the two of you don't wed, or at least announce your betrothal soon, Stephen will withdraw his support and I'll never gain control of Montreau.'

Once again, John asked, 'What do you suggest I do?'

'Do I have to instruct you on everything?'

'She's your sister-by-marriage. You know better how to deal with her than I.'

Markam tapped the arm of the chair. 'You need to force her hand.'

Shocked, John gasped. 'You can't mean I am to…?' He searched for the right word, praying it wasn't as he feared. 'You want me to…assault…the Lady of Montreau?'

'Not exactly. But if she fears that is a possibility, she might then be more amenable to your will.'

The man wasn't thinking clearly. 'Or she'll tell Warehaven and my head will be hanging from a gate post.'

'Then you need make certain she doesn't tell him.'

'Lord Villaire, you seem to be forgetting the lady is already betrothed to Warehaven.' A complication neither of them had expected.

Markam laughed. 'Do you have any common sense? If this betrothal of theirs held any merit, they would have made a public announcement. At the very least Warehaven would have requested permission to wed from the empress. I am fairly certain their betrothal is nothing but a ruse for my benefit.'

He might be correct. After all, Montreau was far too great a prize for a union with its lady to remain private. 'How do you know he hasn't requested permission to wed her?'

'My men keep their eyes and ears open. Warehaven hasn't sent any messenger to his aunt.' Markam frowned while taking a long swallow of wine. He set the goblet down. 'Something has happened. All isn't quite right between the two of them.'

John had noticed it too. Of late, Warehaven and Lady Lea seemed to go out of their way to avoid each other. They didn't speak, nor would they occupy the same room.

Villaire mused, 'If we could discover what occurred, perhaps we could use it to our advantage.'

'But that would require being able to speak to the lady.' A task that thus far had proven fruitless.

A door down the corridor closed. Seconds later Agatha, the lady's maid, walked by Villaire's open door.

Markam smiled. "I think I've found our solution to that problem.'

* * *

Lea closed her fingers around the cloth in her hand. 'What do you mean she's missing?' She stared at the guard, certain she'd not heard him correctly.

The young man shifted from one foot to the other, displaying his nervousness. 'My lady, we have looked everywhere and found nothing but that belt on the tower stairs.'

Her heart pounded with worry. 'Have you informed Lord Warehaven?'

'Not yet. We were waylaid by Lord Villaire before we could report to Warehaven.'

Certain that Villaire was somehow involved, Lea narrowed her eyes. She crushed the belt in her clenched fist. If he wanted her attention, he'd chosen the perfect way to gain it.

She waved the guard aside and stepped into the corridor. 'You go and report to Warehaven.' Knowing what she was about to do could prove risky, she added, 'Tell him I'm going to the south-west tower to deal with Villaire.'

After waiting for the guard to disappear down the stairs, Lea headed for the far end of the corridor and the stairs to the tower. Since that's where Agatha's belt was discovered, she assumed Villaire waited for her up there.

She pushed the door at the top of the stairs open and stepped out into the night. A cold stiff wind whipped her unbound hair across her face, forcing her to drag the wild mass from her eyes.

'My dear sister, if you would braid it like a lady should then you wouldn't have that problem.'

'What do you want, Markam?'

'Want? Nothing. I didn't send for you.'

His feigned look of innocence would be laughable were the situation not so dire. 'Where is Agatha?'

He leaned over the wall and waved to someone below, then turned back around to face her. 'You can rest assured that she is heading for the kitchens.'

'Good. Now if you'll excuse me.' Lea reached behind her for the door, only to find her way blocked by Blackstone.

'Not just yet, Lady Lea.' He quickly reached up and wound a hand through her wind-whipped hair. 'You and I need to talk.'

Lea tried to jerk away from his hold, only to have Blackstone tighten his grip on her hair until she winced. She clung to his wrist, hoping to lessen the pull against her scalp.

Villaire laughed. 'It seems you have a slight problem, sister dear. Perhaps it would be easier to relax.'

Tears of pain stung her eyes. Lea released Blackstone's wrist and stopped struggling. As Villaire had suggested, the hard tug lessened.

'Since you've seen fit to avoid John's courtship, perhaps that means you wish to skip the niceties and go straight to the betrothal…' he paused to smile and tip his head as if contemplating the two of them before adding '…or perhaps even the wedding.'

'There will be no wedding between us.' Angry, Lea nearly spat at him. 'I would sooner—' Blackstone cut off her words with another hard tug.

He pulled her head back until his lips were next to her ear. 'Surely you don't still believe you have a choice in the matter?'

Villaire sighed. 'Charles was wrong to give you so

much freedom. I told him more than once to curb your ways, but he wouldn't listen. So, now the task is left to me.'

Clinging once again to Blackstone's wrist, Lea shouted, 'I am already betrothed to Warehaven; he will have your heads.'

'By the time he discovers what has transpired it will be too late for him to do anything except fume.' Villaire added, 'Perhaps the next time he thinks to wed an heiress he won't be so slow about seeing the deed done.'

'I'm warning you, Markam, this is a mistake. If you do anything so foolish as force me to wed Blackstone, Warehaven will see I am widowed before the end of the ceremony.' She didn't know if that was true or not, but hoped it would give her brother-by-marriage something to think about.

'The only mistake I made was in letting my brother wed you instead of doing so myself.'

Had this cur been the last man on earth she would have taken her own life before becoming his wife. 'My father never would have permitted such a match.'

'Your sire was a spineless fool who would have done anything I told him to do as long as it meant his precious keep was spared from suffering in this war.'

Staying out of the war had nothing to do with Montreau. He had done it because of her brother. But she wasn't going to explain that to Villaire. However, she did disagree with his description. 'My father was not spineless, nor was he a fool. I can guarantee you that he never would have forced me to wed you. Never.'

Blackstone jerked on her hair. 'It matters little what he would, or wouldn't have done, since we are here to discuss your marriage to me, not Markam.'

Lea ground her teeth together to keep from crying out in pain. Catching her breath, she demanded, 'We aren't going to talk about anything unless you release me.'

'So you are finally ready to discuss the details?'

'Yes, yes, I am.' She would say anything to gain her freedom from his relentless hold.

He swung her around and slammed her against the wall before removing his grasp. Lea gasped for breath to clear her now blurry vision. Afraid the man would kill her before Jared arrived, she dodged to her right in an attempt to put at least an arm's distance between her and the men.

But Blackstone was quicker. He grabbed a handful of her gown and pushed her back against the wall, then pinned her in place with his body. 'You aren't going anywhere.'

Lea pushed against his chest. Unable to move him, she punched his shoulder. Blackstone only laughed. 'Did no one ever warn you about picking a fight with someone larger and stronger?'

He raised his fist. The blade of a sword sliced through the sleeve of his surcoat, pinning his arm to the wall alongside Lea's head. A dagger slid in front of his neck.

'Did no one ever warn you about abusing those smaller and weaker than you?'

Lea nearly fainted at Jared's deadly tone. She wanted to ask what had taken him so long, but couldn't get the words past the thickness in her throat.

He moved Blackstone away from her with the edge of his dagger. 'Agatha awaits you in your chamber. Go.'

As quickly as her shaking legs could move, she raced towards the door without a backward glance. She didn't care what Jared did to Villaire or Blackstone. All she wanted was to get as far away from them as quickly as possible.

Jared waited until Lea disappeared down the stairwell before turning his full attention to the man on the other side of his dagger blade. 'What did you think would happen when I discovered your plan?'

Blackstone swallowed hard enough to push his own neck more firmly against the weapon. With his free arm, he pointed at Villaire. 'It was his idea.'

Jared knew that already. He would deal with that cur later. For now it was enough to know that three of his men held Villaire captive.

'Placing blame on another doesn't answer my question.' He twisted his dagger a hair, wishing he could slice the man's throat. Unfortunately, killing one of Stephen's supporters would endanger Montreau's neutrality.

'Let's try again. What had you planned for the lady?'

Blackstone clamped his lips tightly together. But a little more pressure from the dagger, just enough to nick the man's flesh, had his eyes bulging and tongue wagging. 'My lord, please, I meant her no physical harm. I wasn't going to rape her, only make her think it was a possibility. We were hoping to frighten her enough to agree to a quick marriage.'

'Did you forget she already has a betrothed?'

Blackstone stuttered, but finally managed to say, 'We thought it was just a hoax to put off my suit.'

'You thought wrong. I should castrate you just for threatening her.'

The man paled. He shook like a frightened girl. His

eyes welled with tears borne of terror. 'Please, my lord, I beg you, spare me.'

The man deserved to be terrified—more so than he was already. Jared flashed his most evil smile. 'You wouldn't die. Not if a good physician could be found quick enough to stem the blood loss.' He jerked the tip of his sword from the mortar, hoping he hadn't ruined the weapon. Trailing the tip slowly down Blackstone's side, he mused, 'It would most certainly keep you from threatening to harm another woman.'

The man went limp. Jared removed the dagger edge from his throat and let him fall to his knees pleading for mercy. His mission with Blackstone completed, he turned to advance on Villaire.

Just as he assumed would happen, Villaire started blubbering before Jared got within arm's length. He didn't care. This coward needed to be put in his place for once—at least when it came to Lea. For nearly two weeks he'd watched and listened as Villaire had belittled and bullied her. Her brother-by-marriage had unjustly found fault with everything she said or did. From what Jared had heard from Montreau's men and women, her husband had done the same thing. She hadn't deserved that type of treatment, especially not from men who were greedy only for her property and cared nothing about her.

It would give him great satisfaction to simply ram his sword through Villaire's blackened heart. The cost of such an act might be war, but right at this moment it was a cost he'd pay gladly.

He stopped mere inches from Villaire. 'Give me one valid reason I should let you live.'

'Killing me will bring Stephen's wrath down on Montreau.'

'Stephen's wrath?' Jared shook his head at Villaire's pitiful attempt to save his useless life. 'Stephen wouldn't waste the time or energy on avenging your death. Were you that important to his reign, he would have given you guardianship of Montreau.'

'He's considering my petition.'

Jared shrugged. 'Then he wastes his time. I've made the decision for him. You will leave here immediately and do not return.'

He addressed his guards. 'See that Villaire and Blackstone gather their possessions and then escort them to Montreau's borders.' Before dismissing the men, he emphasised, 'Do not cross the border yourselves.'

He didn't want any of his men losing their lives because of Villaire.

Chapter Nine

Lea staggered into her chamber. The more she thought about what had just happened with Blackstone and Villaire, the more frightened and ill she became.

They could have harmed her greatly in their attempt to force her hand in marriage. She had the feeling they wouldn't have cared overmuch had they killed her.

'Lady Lea.' Agatha walked out of the small alcove off the side of the bedchamber. 'Did they hurt you?'

Fearing her voice would break if she spoke, Lea shook her head. When the older woman opened her arms, she went into them like she had as a child.

Agatha patted her head, whispering, 'Poor baby. Come, some sleep will do you good.'

Nerves stretched too tightly to sleep yet, Lea pulled out of the embrace. 'No. Not yet.' She sat down on the bench near the lit brazier. 'Tell me what happened. How did they get you out of the keep?'

Agatha sat next to her. 'Villaire told me you were in the village and had need of me. I had no reason not to believe him.'

'He didn't threaten you, or harm you?'

'Oh, no, my lady. When I realised they had lied and returned to the keep, Blackstone waylaid me, only to lock me up in an unused shed.'

She didn't need to add that since it had been raining most of the day, there would have been nobody near the sheds to hear her shouts.

Lea shivered. 'I am so sorry. I never thought anyone else would get caught up in Villaire's plots.'

'It wasn't your fault. I should have known better than to trust his word.'

'What were the two of you thinking?' Jared entered the chamber. 'You both could have been killed.'

Unable to disagree, Lea remained silent. Agatha wasn't as meek. 'We weren't, so what might have been matters little.'

'Since the safety of this keep and your lady is my responsibility, it does matter.' He frowned at Lea a moment, before ordering Agatha, 'Leave us.'

The maid hesitated, putting an arm around Lea, then asked, 'Will you be all right?'

'I am not the enemy.' Jared nearly growled. But he softened his tone slightly as he assured her, 'She will not be harmed.'

Lea nodded. 'I'll be fine, Agatha. Go, get something to eat, and rest. You've had a hard day, too.'

Jared folded his arms across his chest, staring down at her until Agatha left the chamber, closing the door behind her.

Then he asked, 'Well?'

Now he was going to badger her, too? She'd had

enough of men today—especially ones who wanted to treat her like a witless fool.

She rose and quickly walked to the window. 'Go away and just leave me be.'

He was behind her in an instant. 'Why did you think it necessary to confront Villaire and Blackstone alone? You knew they'd done something with your maid, yet you willingly put yourself in danger.'

His tone was harsh, clipped. He was angry…and something else that she couldn't quite put her finger on. Lea turned to look up at him. While his outraged frown drew his eyebrows nearly together and his tight lips formed a hard line, his jewel-toned eyes didn't sparkle like emeralds.

Her breath caught in her throat. He'd been more than just worried—frightened? Heaven above, if this man of war had feared for her safety she'd been in more danger than she'd imagined. No wonder he was now *badgering* her.

Lea's knees threatened to buckle. Her heart thudded anew. She threw herself against him, clinging to his shoulders for support, to whisper, 'Thank you.'

Jared wrapped his arms around her, holding her close. He buried his face in her hair, warning, 'Don't ever do anything so foolish again. Do you hear me?'

Relieved to be held in a safe embrace, she nodded against his chest. Jared's heart beat a riotous tempo beneath her cheek. Whether he would ever admit it or not, he *had* feared for her.

A shudder rippled through her at what could have happened; a strangled gasp escaped her lips.

Jared's warm breath brushed across her ear. 'Hush, they can't threaten you any more.'

Lea pressed tighter against him, seeking comfort in the safety of his arms. She turned her head, tilting her face towards his to whisper, 'Kiss me.'

Jared groaned, knowing a kiss would not be enough to satiate his growing hunger. He wanted more than just a kiss and the feel of her soft body against him.

He met her lips, brushing lightly against them. 'What is this, Lea? What do you want?'

She rose up on her toes, threading a hand through his hair, trailing her nails lightly along his scalp, stroking the rim of his ear. When he shivered in response, she answered, 'I want to feel alive.'

Jared passed his hands down her back, caressing her hips before cupping the full roundness to lift her up his body.

He wanted there to be no mistaking her request, so once again asked, 'What do you want, Lea?'

She hooked one leg around his and pressed her body tightly against the length of his erection. 'You. All of you.'

Her husky whisper nearly singed his ear, shattering his control.

Jared turned to cross the chamber with her still in his arms. He lowered her to the bed, her legs dangling over the edge, then knelt between them.

Wanting to savour the feel and taste of her soft flesh, he quickly removed her shoes and stockings.

He had little doubt that his aunt would soon recall him to court. This would likely be the last time he had the opportunity, the pleasure, of making love to Lea. And while it was wrong—doing this went against everything he believed—he wanted her, needed her more than he needed air to breathe and much more than he needed to cling to the ragged edges of his honour.

Pushing the skirt of her gown up, Jared trailed his fingertips along the length of her legs. He could no longer deny the simple fact that even though he would never forgive her, could never trust or love her, he would always crave her, would always desire her. And he would never forget her when he left. She moaned at the feel of his lips behind her knee and gasped with anticipation when he pressed hot kisses up the soft pale flesh of her inner thigh.

The sound of her ragged breaths, her breathless sighs, were like the finest wine to his senses. They inflamed him, begging him not to stop.

She offered no resistance when he pushed gently against her thighs, and he knew she was as eager for his intimate touch as he was to taste her.

She jumped at his first touch, and he held her steady, enjoying her passionate response to his teasing torment.

'Oh, Jared.' Straining for release, she curled her fingers into the bedcovers.

He laughed softly, knowing what she wanted, yet unwilling to end his play so soon.

Lea groaned at his laugh, cursing him in a breathless pant, 'Damn you, Warehaven.'

The familiar curse only tempted him to wrest a begging scream from her lips before giving in to her needs.

He dragged her closer to the edge of the bed. Without a pause in his wicked torment, he reached up to undo the laces of her gown.

Lea thought her heart would pound out of her chest.

She knew what he was going to do. And while the sweet torture would be pure heaven in the end, her submission would once again prove his complete domination over her body and her lust.

When he caressed her breast to tease the tip, at the same time sliding his touch into her warm depths, she knew without a doubt she would submit to his will. The only question was—how quickly would she beg him for release?

If it were possible, she would stay in this state of bliss for ever. It was the closest feeling to love she would ever experience. But when he stroked her, she knew her bliss would soon come to a shattering end.

Lea's breath hitched; her stomach clenched. The intensity of her building climax brought her off the bed. She curled her fingers into his shoulders, begging, nearly crying, 'Jared, please, please, now.'

To her relief, he answered her plea, holding her tightly as he took her over the edge of desire.

She fell back on to the bed with a sigh, wishing and longing for more, but accepting what he gave.

With a low growl he rose, tearing off his clothing at the same time.

But instead of coming over her, he grabbed her hips to flip her over and up on to her knees.

Lea lowered her forehead to the bed and moaned. The sweet torment was far from over. As if he'd read her mind and knew she'd longed for all of him, Jared would fulfil that wish.

He came into her hard and swift, dragging a gasp of welcome from her as he took his own pleasure, sought his own release while coaxing hers back to life.

He lifted her, pulling her back against his chest, giving him easy access to her body—an access he made full use of.

His lips against the soft flesh beneath her ear rippled shivers down her spine. The sensitive tips of her breasts pebbled, hardening beneath his touch. Her stomach quivered beneath the palm of his hand as it slid lower to cup, then to tease between her legs.

Lea clung to his forearms for support. No amount of begging would stop him this time. If his control was as strong as it was before, she would be limp as a rag before Jared stopped his caresses and found his own release. And that wouldn't happen until she voiced a surrender.

It was a game—one they both enjoyed. She could think of no pleasure greater than the times she'd been the one to make him lose his tight rein, shouting his surrender and pleading with her to cease.

Now—Lea sighed and leaned her head against his shoulder—now with him filling her, stretching her, she wasn't at all certain she'd be able to withhold a scream of surrender for long.

But until then, she would revel in his attention, because she doubted if she'd ever enjoy such pleasure again.

As her stomach clenched and thighs trembled uncontrollably, Lea dug her nails into Jared's arms. Much as she'd love to test his endurance, hers was nearly at an end. And she'd suddenly remembered they hadn't bolted the door.

With one final caress of her breast, he slid a hand over her mouth, whispering hoarsely, 'I've got you.' Unable to catch her cries with his own lips, he'd stop the entire keep from hearing her with his palm.

Fulfilment teased her, beckoning her to the edge, only to retreat, over and over until her heart pounded in her ears, and her body begged for air.

Then standing at the edge, when she thought it would once again dance away, a cry tore from her as she fell into its dizzying heat.

Jared held her tightly, his lips at her neck, his body working in rhythm with hers until she fell lax against him. Lowering his hand to caress her stomach, he asked, 'Enough?'

Lea laughed weakly. Unable to draw in enough air to speak, she nodded.

He let her upper body fall to the bed, and with a driving need found his own release.

Jared fell easily on top of her, threading his fingers through hers; he kissed the back of her neck before rolling to his side, dragging her along.

Lea curled against his chest, tears stinging her eyes. His embrace was far too soothing, his strength near intoxicating. She swallowed hard, fighting to still her suddenly shaking limbs as she realised her vulnerability. Reluctantly, she unwound her hands from his, prepared to roll away.

But he only wrapped an arm around her, holding her close. 'No. Stay.'

The deep, almost gentle tone of his voice concerned her. This closeness was dangerous. His worry, his fear for her had been dangerous enough in itself, but this—this testing of control, this open sharing, could be even more dangerous.

Especially if her fears proved true.

'Jared, please, let me go.'

He brushed a hand along her shoulder and down her trembling arm. 'What is wrong?'

Lea shuddered. It had been easier, safer, when he hated her, when he didn't care what happened to her and when he hadn't remembered how satisfying their love play could prove.

She didn't want either one of them to be hurt again. In the end, that's all that would happen. They could never wed. She would never marry a man who was warrior first, and husband last. He would never marry a woman who couldn't accept what he was.

And as sweet as the idea might be at this moment, being nothing more than lovers was unacceptable. Eventually people would discover their secret; while neither one of them would admit their shame or guilt, it would always be there.

How could she chase him back to yesterday—to when he still thought it best they stay away from each other after this? Lea hated the thought of what it would take to achieve that goal. She could see no other way than to enrage him. At least making Jared angry wouldn't endanger her life—only her heart.

She pulled his arm from around her and moved away. 'I am fine now. You performed your task for the empress successfully. Now go. Leave me be.'

'I think I performed another task successfully.' His voice was still light, bordering on playful.

'That was a mistake that never should have happened. I was frightened, upset and you sought to calm my fears.' Lea gritted her teeth, hoping it would lend a hint of steel to her tone. 'And you know full well that was not the task to which I referred.'

He rolled on to his back. 'Is that the only reason you think I helped you—because of my duty to Empress Matilda?'

'Isn't it? Honour and duty are all to you. Rest assured both are still intact.'

Jared stared at the ceiling, trying to calm his anger at her insistence this had been a mistake. He ignored that, and focused instead on her emotional tone. Lea's voice had turned cold, her words clipped. She'd gone from fulfilled to disdainful in the blink of an eye. While moodiness wasn't normal for her, it wasn't unheard of either. But this abrupt change wasn't anywhere near normal. Something was wrong and he didn't think it had anything to do with Villaire or Blackstone.

'You speak nonsense because you are upset.'

'I am not upset and I am not speaking nonsense. Your honour and duty always come first.'

He had the impression that she was only looking for an argument to avoid whatever was bothering her. He wasn't about to make it that easy for her. 'Of course they do. What sort of man would I be if they didn't?'

'Did you satisfy your honour by killing Villaire?'

He reached over and toyed with a lock of her hair. 'Would that anger you if I had?'

'You didn't?' She sounded surprised.

'Of course not. I have more self-control than to let some greedy braggart goad me into murder.' Although the idea had tempted him greatly.

'So, he's still here?'

Her choked, breathless question prompted him to ease her fears on that. 'No, Lea, I had him and Blackstone escorted to the border of Montreau.'

'They'll be back.'

'If they're foolish enough to return, then I *will* kill them.' And he'd do so without remorse.

'You'd start a war between Montreau and Stephen.'

'Then choose a side, Lea. Stop this nonsense and take a stand.'

She sat up quickly. 'No!'

Jared silently cursed himself; he should have known better than to broach that topic—even if it was how he honestly felt.

He raised his hands in mock surrender. 'I was only goading you.'

When she lay back down, he grasped her hand, stroking his thumb across the top. 'What is wrong, Lea?'

'Nothing.'

He tightened his hold when she tried to tug her hand free. 'You might get a stranger to believe that, but I am no stranger. Tell me what is wrong.'

She was silent for several minutes. Then, she softly said, 'This is too dangerous.'

He turned on his side and stroked her cheek, wanting to know what she was thinking. 'For who, Lea? How is this dangerous?'

'For me. For you.' She looked over at him. 'We share no love, no tender feelings of any kind, nothing is left except mistrust, dislike and—this.'

If he could trust what he saw in the clearness of her gaze, she believed what she said was true and he didn't disagree. But something, some niggling doubt in the back of his mind, warned him that lack of feelings wasn't the only thing bothering her.

'What do you want me to do?'

She sighed. 'You were right before. We should just stay away from each other. It was the best for both of us.'

He wasn't going to argue with her now. Not when he wasn't at all certain she was wrong. Perhaps it was for the best. He needed time to think and that would be impossible in this bed.

Jared rose and quickly dressed. He paused alongside the bed. When Lea turned her face away, he caught the glimmer of a tear and reached down to wipe it from her cheek before leaving the chamber.

Chapter Ten

Jared stared up at the ceiling of his own chamber. It was strange, but this bed hadn't seemed so large—or empty—before now.

When Matilda had first ordered him to Montreau all he could think of was the satisfying taste of revenge. He'd wanted Lea to hurt, to know the feel of pain and rejection. The idea of using her, then walking away without a backward glance had consumed him.

He'd relived her horrified reaction and his satisfaction over and over in his mind until the feelings were nearly real.

Now, the taste of vengeance was bitter; the hot rush of satisfaction had somehow turned cold.

He didn't love her. How could he? Not even in his wildest dreams could he be deluded enough to believe that could ever happen.

However, she was right—they did share one thing in common: their lust for each other.

For how many centuries had young men been told not to trust lust? It wasn't real, nor would it last. Lust was nothing upon which to build a marriage. Even his own father had warned him to be on guard for the day some beauty would turn his mind to gruel and his thoughts to stark desire.

Maybe so. But then, who was his father to talk? The man had been trapped in one night by a love spell that seemingly had woven lust into a lifetime of love.

And Jared couldn't deny the simple fact that he'd found Lea desirable from the first moment he'd seen her nearly ten years ago. The anger, the outrage, the hurt hadn't changed that attraction.

He tossed and turned on the bed, knowing there would be no sleep this night unless he figured out what to do, what he wanted, how to make this uncertainty go away.

A part of him, the embittered part of his heart that hadn't gained any wisdom through the years, still wanted her to suffer. She deserved some form of repayment, but what?

What would make her life the most miserable?

Even if he knew what that one thing was, and if by some stroke of fate he could figure out how to formulate and enact such a plan, could he go through with it? How would he live with himself afterwards?

The door to his chamber banged open. 'My lord!'

Jared's stomach clenched. Rolfe never barged into his chamber, or used that tight, worried tone of voice unless his news was something dire.

Certain the keep was under attack, he lunged from the bed, tugging on his clothes as he approached Rolfe. 'What is it?'

'One of the longships is on fire.'

'On fire?'

Jared could hardly believe that was true. It had rained for days. The wooden vessels should have been soaked through. The only way someone could have kept a fire burning would have been to use something like grease, lard or fat to keep the blaze going.

To him this was worse than Montreau being under attack. He'd made his fortune from his fleet. The longships were just as important to him and Warehaven as the cargo vessels.

The profit from cargo—transportation of humans and goods—was great, but the benefit of the longships was innumerable. They permitted him to slip in and out of enemy shores without being spotted. And they were fast enough to make a quick escape the few times they had been seen. Jared ran from the chamber, cursing.

How in God's name had someone gained access to his ships long enough for this to happen? Without pausing or turning to look at Rolfe as he raced down the stairs, Jared shouted, 'What happened? Who was on watch?'

'I don't know what happened. Timothy and Samuel are dead.'

Jared groaned. Marta would be inconsolable at the loss of both sons.

'How?'

'Arrows. Red arrows.'

Damn. How had that murdering bloodthirsty witch and her crew of harpies found him? Jared knew of only one person who took the time to make certain her weapons were easily identified. Princess Cassandra of Beille Isle had been a thorn in his side since she'd run away from her father, King Ivan, to take up piracy late last year.

He was certain there was a story behind her decision,

and he'd been curious until the first time she'd attacked him. Now, he no longer cared what caused her to leave her father's castle, or why she'd become a pirate. He'd leave the wondering and caring to someone else.

There'd been pirates roaming the seas since the first ship carrying anything of value had left its harbour. But Jared couldn't think of anything that boded more ill for every ship or boat afloat than an angry female warrior terrorising the water.

He'd be glad to put an end to the wench's activities. Unfortunately, her father wanted her back alive. Jared had thought Lea was more than he could handle at times. She was nothing compared to this wench. He didn't envy the king.

He slammed through the hall, booting sleeping guards awake, ordering, 'To arms.'

The men jumped to their feet, stumbling quickly into clothes, grabbing weapons to follow him out into the bailey.

Jared was relieved to find a handful of horses ready and waiting. An extra sword, bow and brace of arrows already secured to the saddle of his animal.

Before spurring the beast, he said, 'Rolfe, gather as many men as you can, ours and Montreau's.'

Certain his man would do as ordered and join him soon, Jared turned the horse towards the gates. He led out the men already mounted to save what he could of his longships. With any luck that pirate whore would still be around. If so, he'd try his best not to kill her, but at this moment he couldn't guarantee anything.

The horses' hooves quickly covered the clearing to reach the thin line of wooded area that rimmed the cliffs.

Tree branches tore at his face, bushes and bramble snagged at his booted feet. For the most part he ignored the minor annoyances, keeping his head down as he urged the beast beneath him faster.

Cuts and scratches could be cleaned and stitched if need be later. His ships couldn't wait. Fire would eat up his wooden vessels like a starving wolf devours an unaware deer.

The vision of his dragon prows being engulfed in flames made him ill. Over the last seven years they'd become the children he'd never thought to have. He cared for them as well as he cared for his horse and weapons.

Jared was dismounting the instant his horse broke into the open strip of land at the edge of the cliff. Before the beast ceased its frantic rearing and prancing, he pulled his extra weapons free, tossed the reins to his waiting squire and skidded down the embankment. He came to a heart-wrenching stop at the bottom of the hill.

Against a backdrop of damp, thick fog, flames engulfed his amethyst longship. 'Damn you to hell, Cassandra!' The curse tore from his throat.

In answer to his curse, a laugh, long and shrill, cut through the fog, echoing across the bay. Finally, the maniacal laughter stopped. 'Hail, Warehaven. It seems fire is eating your dragon.'

'One day you will pay!' Rage reverberated through his words, shaking him from head to toe.

She laughed again. 'You aren't my type, love.'

The splashing sound of oars hitting the water let him know that she and her crew were leaving.

Jared turned his attention back to his ships. The orange, red and yellow flames jumped from the amethyst ship, reaching for the sapphire one like a hungry predator. His men skidded to a stop behind him, their drawn swords in one hand, a bucket in the other.

'Unlash the ships,' Jared shouted his order.

Like a fool, he'd thought Montreau's neutrality would keep his vessels relatively safe. So, after dragging them across logs to the beach, they'd been lashed together as a precaution against one being easily stolen. Now it appeared that mistake would see all three ships ablaze.

Some of the men worked at the lashes, dodging flames and cursing as embers rained down on them. The others worked with Jared to push and drag the remaining two vessels to the safety of the water.

Once the oars were manned, to keep the ships in the bay, the remaining men rushed to help put out the fire.

Jared feared it was a lost cause. The ship was nearly consumed in flames. He watched the dragon prow disappear in the midst of the fire. Finally, he ordered, 'Cease.'

There was no sense in having the men continue their fruitless attempt to douse the fire. Even though he gave the men leave to return to the keep, a dozen or so remained behind on the beach.

His own men remaining was understandable since the ships were their livelihood, too. Those from Montreau surprised him a little, but he'd not question their motives. He had enough questions swimming around in his head about his own life to concern himself with another man's reasons.

Jared perched atop a boulder to stare into the fire. Too bad it couldn't show him what to do with Lea. Such a stunt had worked for his mother, or so she claimed; the flames had somehow shown her his father.

Rolfe joined him. 'I should have stayed to keep the flames under control.'

The dejected look on the man's face and the sombre tone of his voice spoke of his sincerity. This wasn't his fault and Jared would not have the man thinking such a thing.

'And who would have brought me word had you done so?' Jared picked up a stone and tossed it towards the water. 'You couldn't have done anything by yourself.'

'Maybe. But what are you going to do about Princess Cassandra? She certainly has it in for you.'

Jared ignored the underlacing of humour apparent in Rolfe's words. Especially since he agreed—Cassandra of Beille Isle did seem to enjoy targeting ships from Warehaven.

'I can't do anything right now. Not until Matilda releases us from Montreau.'

'Have you figured out why she sent you here to begin with?'

'No. Who knows what my aunt is planning behind the scenes?'

A loud crack of wood caught his attention. Jared watched the charred dragon prow fall to the beach. As he stared at the dancing flames he couldn't help but wonder if his mother had had a hand in having him sent here. As outrageous as that thought was, he wouldn't put it past her.

Brigit of Warehaven wanted her son married. More than once she'd made her feelings plain that she thought him foolish for not going after Lea. His father agreed.

Of course he'd never shown his parents the missive he'd received and still carried. He wouldn't see them hurt in such a manner. There was no need for them to know Lea couldn't bring herself to wed the son of a bastard.

Her excuse had never made any sense to him, appearing out of nowhere as it had. As far as he was concerned, that's all her reasoning was—just an excuse not to wed, not to leave her father's keep.

Had she known what her words would do? Jared was certain she had specifically chosen that excuse knowing full well how the words would sting. She had obviously wanted to ensure he would stay away.

And it had worked—until now.

He glanced towards Rolfe, not really seeing the man clearly through the smoke from the fire and the memories. 'Matilda sent us here to protect Montreau.'

'Keep telling yourself that, Jared, and maybe you'll believe it some day.'

Rolfe headed over to join the others. His parting laugh didn't surprise Jared. They'd been together too long for that to happen. The man always spoke his mind regardless of the topic.

One thing was certain, he couldn't sit around wondering what to do—that path was lined only with more questions. He was used to action and decision. This uncertainty was making him witless and disgusted with himself.

Jared walked along the beach, weaving past smaller groups of men gathered around the fire.

The men's conversations were muted, but he caught snippets of talk about Cassandra and the fire from one group. Another discussed Villaire's departure with great approval.

But hearing Lea's name mentioned by a third group slowed his steps.

'He'd be better for Lady Lea than Villaire.'

Who would be better for her?

'At least she'd have someone to finally share her bed.'

It wasn't just the suggestive comment that made Jared's chest tighten—it was the ribald laughter that followed.

One of the men spotted him nearby and elbowed the man from Montreau who'd spoken. The group quickly dispersed—too quickly.

Had they been talking about him? Did they think he would be better for Lea? Had they come to the conclusion that he and Lea were more than acquaintances? Had someone witnessed their trysts?

Apparently someone had.

What had he done? His thirst for revenge, combined with his lust, had put Lea in a precarious position. If the guards, who generally paid attention to very little, were aware of their attraction or their trysts, it was safe to assume the entire keep knew.

Through no fault of her own, Lea would look like a harlot in their eyes. She'd be the object of rumours and innuendo.

And what if she had become pregnant?

Jared resisted the urge to groan. The blame for this rested on his shoulders and it was his responsibility to see it made right.

After what had happened before, he'd long ago decided to wed without concern for feelings. Did Lea not meet that requirement?

While it was true that passion and desire were feelings, they weren't of any worth in a marriage. But their shared passion for each other could be seen as a benefit. If nothing else, it gave them something in common.

Besides, wouldn't demanding a marriage be the perfect revenge?

Jared looked up towards the top of the hill. Why hadn't he thought of this before? It was perfect. Flawless in design.

On the morrow he would inform her of his decision. He broke into a smile, imagining her shock and outrage.

Chapter Eleven

Lea rolled over and groaned against the churning of her stomach. She closed her eyes, unable to ignore the truth any longer.

Her wish had been granted.

To her surprise, her heart raced—but not with fear or dread. The simple act of admitting the truth made her suddenly happy—overjoyed to know that soon she would hold a child—her child—in her arms.

There was no longer the need to worry about *what if* she was carrying Jared's child. Instead, excitement replaced that worry. Now she could focus her concerns on all of the changes that would take place. Changes not just to her body—although she hoped this sickness would soon go away—but changes to her life, her responsibilities and her future.

The door to her chamber opened and Lea sat up, only to slap a hand over her mouth as another wave of sickness washed over her.

'Lady Lea?' Agatha shuffled to her side, a worried frown creasing her brow. 'Are you unwell?'

Lea shook her head and instantly regretted the too-fast movement. She swallowed hard in an attempt to hold the nausea at bay, then she said, 'No. Actually everything is wonderful.'

'Wonderful?' Agatha's eyebrows rose in apparent disbelief. 'You look as though you are sick to your stomach and you claim you are wonderful?' She touched Lea's cheeks. 'You don't appear to have a—'

The older woman abruptly stopped mid-sentence. Her hand hung in the air as her mouth dropped open. Finally, she exclaimed, 'You are carrying a child.'

Since no question had been asked, Lea rose and went to stand before the window. The cool pre-dawn breeze helped soothe the churning of her stomach.

She took a deep breath and frowned at the stench of burning wood. *Something was on fire.* Leaning into the window embrasure, she could see nothing aflame.

She spun around, asking, 'Agatha, where is the fire?'

'On the beach. Are you carrying a child?'

Lea ignored the question to ask one of her own. 'What is on fire at the beach?'

'Lord Jared's ship. Is the babe his?'

Lea wanted to scream. Instead she gritted her teeth a moment, then ordered, 'Tell me what's happening.'

Agatha shot her a look reserved for mothers dealing with a recalcitrant child. When Lea only returned the look, the older woman relented. 'From what I've been told, a pirate set one of Lord Jared's longships on fire. The men were ordered to the beach to help.'

'The men? Which men?'

'His own and yours.'

Certain her ears played a trick on her, Lea asked again, 'Which men?'

Agatha frowned. 'Are you sure you are feeling well?'

'Agatha!'

'The men from Warehaven and Montreau.'

Without asking her, or even telling her, Jared had ordered her men into a dangerous situation? How dare he!

'My lady?'

Lea held up a hand, wordlessly asking Agatha for silence. She needed to think. But first she needed to convince the rage burning in her chest to abate.

She was well aware he'd been ordered to Montreau to protect the keep and her. She was also aware that he'd easily assumed control because she'd done little to stop him.

Even so, these were *her* men. They owed their allegiance to Montreau and *she* was the embodiment of Montreau. She didn't blame the men—they would have naturally assumed she'd handed power over to Jared and would have obeyed his commands without a second thought.

No. She placed the blame solely on Jared's shoulders and her own weak will.

The urge to dress, march to the beach and confront him was strong. One thing gave her pause—the child she carried was his.

If, in her rage and anger, she did anything—or mistakenly said anything—to let him even so much as wonder if she carried a child, he would immediately take control of her life, too.

She'd *not* wed him. Lea didn't care what anyone

thought or would say when the truth became apparent. She would *not* wed Jared of Warehaven.

There would always be rumours, no one could stop that. But there was something she could do to keep most of the talk at bay.

She could stick to her original plan, deceitful as it might be, and claim the child was Charles's.

Her head throbbed. The thought of doing something so low was vile even in her mind. But her options were limited. She knew without a single doubt that Jared would eventually guess the truth regardless of her lies.

Once he did, he would try to force a marriage between them. Lea sat back down on the bed, fearful her shaking limbs would refuse to keep her upright.

She couldn't marry him. She wouldn't marry him. But Lea knew he would wear her will down. She feared it wouldn't take much on his part.

Far from simple-minded, Jared would quickly realise that anger would fail him. That's when he would become dangerous. She knew exactly what tactic he'd employ.

Worse—she knew she'd be unable to resist his wiles for long. Then she'd be lost. She would be chained in a loveless marriage. Wed to a warrior who would always put battle and killing above her and their child. Married to a man who would jeopardise the hard-won neutrality of Montreau.

Now that her fears had a firm grip on her heart and mind, Lea couldn't stop the swiftly forming images from appearing.

Visions of Montreau's men dead or dying on a bloody field of battle made her tremble.

More horrific than seeing the gruesome deaths of men she'd known all of her life was the mental sight of her own son perishing in the same manner.

Lea gasped. She would not permit that to happen. She wouldn't be able to live with herself if she did.

Agatha placed a hand on her shoulder. Lea jumped at the unexpected contact.

'What is wrong, Lea? It is obvious something has terrified you.'

In a shaking whisper, Lea replied, 'We must leave here. Now.'

Agatha sat on the bed next to her. 'Leave Montreau?'

'Yes.' Lea nearly lunged to her feet. 'Yes. Now. We have to leave.'

'But where will we go? Why must we leave?'

Nearly frantic, Lea asked, 'Is Jared on the beach?'

Agatha rose. Wringing her hands, she answered, 'Yes. As far as I know he is. Why? Should I send for him?'

'No!' Lea shouted, then forced her racing heart to calm. 'No, Agatha, he is the last person I wish to see.'

She opened the chest at the foot of her bed and pulled out a couple of travelling sacks. Pausing, she then reached back in the chest and pulled out the writs from Stephen and Matilda.

Where would she go?

Lea frowned. Yes, Montreau was neutral, but she didn't trust the king or the empress.

If she went running to Stephen, he might see that as a show of weakness and grant Villaire his petition for guardianship. That cur would have her wed to Blackstone before the sun set that very day.

If she went to the empress, Lea knew exactly what

would happen. Matilda cared for Jared—she would grant him permission to wed Montreau's heiress without a second thought.

So, where would she go? Who was strong enough to hold both Stephen and Matilda at bay? Whom did she know well enough that they would give her some time to determine her next move?

Relief flooded her. 'Agatha, we are going to King David.'

The older woman stuffed some clothing into one of the sacks and asked, 'Why?'

Agatha was steadfastly loyal. There was no reason to lie to her. Lea admitted, 'Because I carry Jared's child.'

Agatha sighed. 'There is no need to run. He would gladly wed you if he knew.'

'That is exactly what I don't want.'

A look of shock widened Agatha's eyes. 'Why ever not?'

'I'll not hand control of Montreau over to a warrior. And I will never have a warrior as my child's father.'

'Forgive me for saying so, but you might have thought about that before you took him to your bed.'

Lea snatched the sack from Agatha's hands and gave her the empty one. 'Gather what you need and enough food to last us a day or so. I want to be away from here before Jared and the men return.'

Agatha tossed the sack on the bed, protesting, 'Lady Lea, you can't do this.'

She could do anything she wanted to do. 'If you wish not to accompany me, so be it. But I am going.'

'Don't you want this child?'

Not want the child? From where had that idea come?

Of course she wanted the child. Confused, she asked, 'Why would you even think I didn't?'

'I thought that since it was Lord Jared's you wouldn't—'

'My God,' Lea cut her off. 'That only makes me want the babe even more.'

Agatha plopped down atop the chest. 'More?' She shook her head. 'Why would you want the babe more when you don't want the man who fathered him?'

Lea understood Agatha's confusion. Especially since she was just as confused herself. Why did conceiving Jared's child make her feel so satisfied and happy and terrified all at the same time?

And why did the idea of running away from him suddenly seem so wrong?

She tried to explain. 'It's not so much that I don't want him.' She'd wanted him for years. 'It's more that I can't accept or live with his way of life.'

'He's a man, Empress Matilda's man. How can you expect him to be other than he is?'

'I can't. I don't. That's why I'm leaving. Eventually he'll come to realise that I'm right—a marriage between us would be wrong—and he'll go back to Warehaven.'

'And if he doesn't?'

'Hopefully, he will. But if not, perhaps I'll be able to work something out while we're at King David's.'

Agatha looked at her as if she'd just declared dogs could fly. The older woman once again shook her head, but said nothing. Instead, she rose, retrieved the sack and asked, 'Are we travelling alone?'

'Heavens, no. I'll get a few of our men to travel with

us. Meet me at the stables as quickly as you can. And say nothing to anyone.'

After Agatha left the chamber, Lea donned a warm woollen gown. The sturdiness of the gown would be well suited for travelling.

She slid the writs from Stephen and Matilda into her sack. Hopefully they wouldn't be needed for anything, but one never knew what might, or might not, happen at King David's court. If she needed to be able to prove Montreau's neutrality, she wanted the documents at hand.

Hopefully David wouldn't turn her away. She knew she was taking a risk by fleeing to his court. After all, he was loosely related to Jared and might take it upon himself to force her into a marriage she wasn't at all certain she wanted.

But King David and her father had always been on the best of terms with each other. On her father's death, David had told her to come to him if ever she had need of anything. She'd not taken advantage of that offer until now.

Lea crept down the stairs as quietly as possible, praying she'd not awaken anyone who might still be sleeping in the Great Hall. She was surprised to find the hall empty. Had Jared ordered every man to attend him on the beach?

She left the keep, pulling her cloak tighter around her in the cool pre-dawn air. With any luck the sun would shine today. Rain would make the trip miserable.

Lea found three of her men in the stables. From the smell of smoke clinging to their clothing she knew they'd been on the beach.

They'd probably had little sleep this night, but that couldn't be helped. She couldn't afford to miss this opportunity, with Jared away from the keep, to leave. There was no telling if she'd get another chance.

'Simon, saddle five of the horses and make ready to leave.'

'My lady?'

She quickly made up a lie. 'King David has need of me and I wish to be on the road before the sun rises.'

'Should I summon Lord Jared?'

Why was that always the first question her people asked? 'No. His responsibility is to Montreau. He can't be in two places at once.'

Thankfully, Simon and the other two men made haste to do her bidding without any further questions.

Even though the men worked quickly, it seemed to her as if it took for ever. She kept peering out into the bailey, expecting Jared and the others to return at any moment.

If he caught her now, she'd be unable to explain why she was leaving when it was still dark. He wouldn't be as accepting of her lie as the men had been. And thinking she lied would only arouse his suspicions.

Agatha arrived at the stable at just about the same time that the men finished saddling the horses.

Thankfully, they were mounted and out of Montreau's gates before anyone else returned to the keep. To her relief, the gate guards were men from Montreau and didn't stop them to ask any questions once they saw she was in the riding party.

Lea glanced over her shoulder at the keep. She'd rarely been away from Montreau in the last few years. A part of her felt as giddy as a child setting out on a long-overdue journey.

But another part of her suffered the pangs of guilt for what she was doing, not just to Jared, but to her people.

Some time soon she would be lying to all of them. When she returned, she would have no choice but to declare the child she carried was Charles's.

She turned to face forwards. Staring out over the horse's head, Lea shivered as she silently prayed for forgiveness.

Chapter Twelve

Jared tossed the now-damp drying cloth over the bench in his chamber. He'd wanted a bath to wash the stench of the smoke from him, but there hadn't been enough hot water and he avoided cold baths as often as he could. A quick wash would have to do.

The ship had taken a lifetime to burn into embers. Each passing hour had felt like years. Like the rest of the men, exhaustion had set in long before the last crack of burning wood. They'd made their way back to the keep by the light of the dawning sun.

Now, before he took a couple of hours of sleep, he wanted to talk to Lea. She would argue with him. Vehemently. Marriage to the son of a bastard was something she couldn't bring herself to do before, and he doubted if she'd changed her mind about that. But wedding him had to be a better option for her than being seen as a whore in her own keep.

So, going into this discussion tired, and on edge, would be his wisest choice. He'd be less likely to take her logic, or complaints, into consideration and more likely to end up ordering her to wed him. If ordering her didn't work, there were other, more enjoyable ways to make her see reason.

Yes, she'd be angry. She'd get over it. And, yes, the beginning of their marriage would be tempestuous, but that would most certainly stave off boredom.

Empress Matilda might rage at him for his high-handedness, but he was willing to wager this had been part of her plan all along. So, in the end, she'd be smugly happy, claiming to all how successful she'd been at seeing her nephew wed.

Jared finished dressing and ran a comb through his wet hair, intentionally ignoring the slight tremor of his hand. The coming argument didn't bother him in the least. Lea's anger was nothing compared to his own.

What if this was a mistake? What if some day, tomorrow or even a few months, or years, from now, he met someone better suited to be his wife?

No. He shook the idea from his mind. It was nothing more than a passing thought meant to make him stop long enough to think twice about his coming action.

He'd always trusted his gut reaction before; now was not the time to change tactics. Forcing Lea's hand was the right thing to do.

He didn't want an emotional attachment and he'd not have to worry about that with Lea. He did want someone well accustomed to running a keep. Lea certainly wouldn't need any training to do that task.

He wanted a wife who didn't shy away from passion. Lea was far from being a fearful woman in the bed-chamber. In fact, she was undoubtedly as lustful as he.

He doubted if there would be any complaints from either of them on that score.

So, why did he stand here staring at the door?

Jared sneered at a nearly unheard whisper warning him that wedding Lea might prove more than he expected. He jerked open the door of his chamber and covered the slight distance to Lea's door in a matter of a few steps.

When no one answered his knock, he opened her door. 'Lea?'

Jared shut the door behind him. There was no need to let the entire keep hear their conversation. He pushed aside the curtains surrounding her bed and frowned. Where was she?

A quick check of the empty alcove deepened his frown. She hadn't been in the bailey or the Great Hall when he'd returned to the keep. Nor had she passed by his chamber while he'd washed and dressed—he'd been listening for her and wouldn't have missed hearing her.

So, where was she hiding?

Jared stormed from the chamber and down to the hall. He asked one of Montreau's guards, 'Where is your lady?'

'I don't know, my lord. Was she not in her bedchamber?'

He didn't like the man's disrespectful tone. It was proof the rumours had already started—yet another reason to see this marriage through quickly. 'No. Find her.'

When the guard left to do as ordered, Jared checked the kitchens. Not only did Lea seem to be missing, so was her maid Agatha.

Something was wrong.

She wasn't missing because of Villaire or Blackstone. Neither of them possessed enough courage to return to Montreau. He'd made it perfectly clear to both of them that they would forfeit their lives if they returned. They were devious and greedy, not witless.

'My lord, is something amiss?' Rolfe asked as he approached.

'Yes, Lady Lea and her maid are missing. Check the bailey while I finish looking inside.'

Unable to locate her, Jared's patience wore thin. *Where had she gone? Why had she left?* His curiosity had already changed to concern, but now it was simmering into frustration. What game did she seek to play?

Rolfe returned sooner than expected. Breathless, he explained, 'She, her maid and three of her men left before we returned from the beach.'

'Left? Did she say where she was going, or why?'

His man shook his head. 'No. The guards at the gate said she and her party left without any word.'

Frustration blazed into anger. Jared cursed as he headed back up the stairs. Determined to find some clue as to her whereabouts, he slammed into Lea's chamber.

On his heels, Rolfe asked, 'What are we looking to find?'

'Anything,' Jared nearly growled in response, then swiped his arm across a narrow side table, sending the contents flying in all directions. Jewellery, a polished mirror and wide-toothed comb, small vials of exotic perfume, a tray of candle stubs and an oil lamp all hit the floor. A jar of dried herbs shattered, leaving the scent of lavender in its wake.

Normally, the aroma would soothe him. Now, as he crushed it under his booted feet, it only served to anger him further.

What had she been running away from this time?
Him? Again?

Since this time her father wasn't around to deliver whatever excuse she had to offer, it only made sense that she'd taken flight.

The question was why.

No. He didn't care why. The question was where had she gone?

Her timing was far too perfect for this journey to have been planned.

Most of her clothing still hung on pegs, making it seem as if she'd packed in haste. Her personal items, the mirror, comb and perfume, remained behind.

It was doubtful if she'd gone far.

Rolfe checked the alcove, looked under the bed and in corners for anything that appeared out of place. Finding nothing, he pointed toward the wooden chest at the foot of the bed. 'What about in there?'

Jared picked up the chest and upended it, dumping the contents on the bed. A leather tube, designed to hold documents, was empty. He shook the clothing, stockings, a thin chemise and a torn gown. Nothing fell out from the fabric.

Pushing aside childhood mementos, he found two crumpled missives. He tossed the one from his aunt back on the bed; there was no need to read that one again, it would tell him nothing.

The one with King Stephen's seal surprised him. Lea hadn't mentioned receiving a message from the king. Jared took the crumpled parchment closer to the window, stepping into the light to better see what it contained.

At first the words made little sense until he realised it'd been sent after her husband had drowned.

He blinked, unable to believe Stephen's brazenness. Lea was to either produce an heir for Montreau within a few months, or wed one of the king's supporters.

That would put all of Montreau's property and wealth right into the king's coffers. He would bleed it dry, just as he had the rest of his supporters.

Matilda would have sent the majority of her army north in response, rendering the land useless—devastated.

Why hadn't Lea told him? How did she think to avoid this from happening? It would take something grander than a miracle for her to be carrying Charles Villaire's child. The man was dead.

But he'd died only a few weeks ago.

So, it could be possible that she'd become pregnant before his death.

Snatches of overheard conversations raced through his mind. Charles Villaire hadn't shared a chamber with his wife. From what he'd overheard, Jared had been led to believe that Lea and Charles rarely—if ever—shared a bed, let alone a chamber. If that were true, how could she be carrying his child?

It wasn't as if she could lie to the king for ever. Eventually he would discover she wouldn't be producing an heir. Stephen would be certain to send spies to check on her. What would she do when her body visibly proclaimed her lie? How would she fake a pregnancy?

The words of the missive blurred.

No.

She wouldn't be so deceitful.

He reached out, feeling for the bench he'd seen earlier. His foot hit the piece of furniture before his hand did and he lowered himself to the seat.

'My lord?'

Jared waved his man away, needing a few moments to digest what his heart fought to deny. Not even Lea could be that cold and calculating.

Could she?

It had been seven years since he'd last seen her. She'd been a young inexperienced woman then. Her sad attempts at subterfuge had been almost comical to watch.

But things changed. All things changed with time. Perhaps she had, too.

His stomach knotted.

He couldn't deny the fact that she'd not fought his advances. In fact, if he remembered correctly, the very night he'd arrived, she had boldly offered herself to him.

Like a fool he'd been unable to fight the desire she'd seen that night and had succumbed to the offer.

Even had she not been pregnant when her husband drowned, she could very well be carrying a child now.

But not Villaire's.

His hands trembled with rage. Jared crushed the missive in his fist.

The woman who couldn't bring herself to marry him because he was the son of a bastard, was now carrying his bastard child?

And she'd conceived the babe intentionally?

Was there no limit to the depths she would stoop?

Did she hate him, despise him so vehemently that she would use him in such a manner?

His head pounded with a rush of emotions. Pain threatened to burst behind his eyes.

Jared rose. He fought to ignore the churning of his

gut, ordering Rolfe, 'Have my horse saddled and two guards—my guards—readied to ride.'

'I can be ready to ride immediately.'

'No. I need you to stay here with the men in case anything should happen.'

Rolfe's expression darkened at being denied the opportunity to join him, but he only asked, 'Where do you go?'

Where was he going? Where would that—he couldn't even put a name to what he thought of Lea at this moment—where would *she* have gone?

Surely not to Stephen. She wouldn't risk giving the king even an inkling of an idea that Montreau required a guardian. Especially not when she knew full well that guardian would be Markam Villaire. And she wouldn't risk being forced to wed Blackstone.

Nor would she run to Matilda. If she was indeed carrying his child, going to his aunt would be the last place she'd run.

She had no family. So who did that leave?

Unable to think clearly with the incessant drumming against his temples, Jared brushed by his man on the way to his own chamber.

He pulled a leather tube holding his maps from a saddlebag and shoved the wadded missive in its place.

Unrolling the map on the bed, he stared unseeing at it. Finally, he whispered a harsh curse at himself, 'Damn you, concentrate.' Then he pinpointed Montreau on the map.

'Robert is too far away to be of any help.' The Earl of Gloucester, another one of his grandfather's bastards, was loyal to Matilda and would uphold Montreau's neutrality given Lea's previous betrothal.

'If she's only travelling with three guards, she'd never make it through York to get to Lincoln.'

The Earl of York controlled his property with an iron fist. He was king of his land and Lea would never pass through the territory without his knowledge. Lea of Montreau would be too choice a prize to leave be.

However, the distance to King David was a journey she could manage with so small a force. Plus, heading north was a safer bet for Lea.

'Where is David?'

'Last I heard he was still in Bamburgh with his son.'

He was supposed to be heading to New Castle and Roxburgh before returning to Carlisle. 'How long ago was that?'

Rolfe shrugged. 'Before we left court.'

That had been over a month ago. While David would have left Bamburgh by now, Jared didn't think the king would have returned to Carlisle yet, so that left New Castle or Roxburgh.

'I'll head for New Castle first, since it's closer. If Lea's not there, I'll cross the border and check at Roxburgh.'

'When do you leave?'

'Now. Get me two of our best men, tell them we'll sleep on the road. Find another to carry a message to my aunt.'

'The message?'

He'd had a moment of uncertainty before coming to find Lea. Now, even that slight uncertainty was gone.

'Tell her I'm marrying Lea of Montreau.'

Rolfe's mouth fell open. Quickly regaining his composure, he asked, 'Are you sure about this?'

'Yes.' He was sure of one thing—Lea was going pay

for this treachery and forcing her hand in marriage would ensure she paid for a long, long time.

And if his aunt disliked this twist, by the time she received the message it would be too late to do anything about it.

Rolfe left the chamber to see to the horses and men. Jared shoved some clothing into his saddlebag. After spending all night on the beach watching his ship burn, he wanted nothing more than to fall into bed.

Even though this journey could wait until tomorrow, he didn't like the idea of Lea travelling without stronger protection.

With the ongoing war, many of the men were with either Stephen or Matilda, leaving all manner of thieves and murderers to populate the roads. She might be carrying his child. He wasn't about to let anyone cause harm to the babe.

The last time she'd put an end to their relationship, he'd let her go. Unwilling to hear the words from her lips, he'd accepted her father's explanation and gone into battle, permitting the hurt and anger to rule him until others paid for his mistake with their lives.

Not this time.

It was possible that Lea had changed, and so had he. This time she wouldn't escape as easily. He would rule the hurt and anger, using it to make her pay.

Over his dead body would she carry and birth his child, claiming it belonged to another.

His parents had often claimed that true love was what kept their marriage strong during the hard times. Jared knew nothing about love, nor did he wish to learn.

After Lea's previous dismissal, he'd decided he

wanted no part of love. She'd proven how wise his decision had been.

Now the two of them would discover how strong a marriage based on lust and hate would prove.

Chapter Thirteen

Drenched from the rain and shivering from the accompanying wind, Lea hung her head. 'I am sorry.'

Just as she knew they would, the guards ignored her apology. They'd not complained about the miserable conditions this last day on the road. But she was sorry to have put them in this position.

Had she been capable of travelling first thing in the morning they would have arrived at King David's court the first day, or around noon the next.

Her illness upon awakening hadn't subsided. It was a few hours before she could sit a horse without being sick. And then, just about the time they were making progress, she'd been ready to stop and eat.

After three days on the road, Lea was certain the men and Agatha had had their fill of this journey—and her.

She glanced over at the older woman. Unused to riding a horse for such an extended period of time, Agatha looked tired and more than miserable.

Lea tried to reassure her. 'We'll be at New Castle today. I promise.'

When Agatha only nodded in reply, Lea sighed. This had been a mistake. She shouldn't have run like such a coward—even though that's exactly what she was.

A coward. Plain and simple.

She should have swallowed her fears and concerns and gone to Jared.

But he would have insisted on marriage. And it was doubtful that she'd have been able to convince him of how unsuited they were for each other.

Of all people, she couldn't marry him.

A warrior—a knight in service to his liege lord—would not suit her, or Montreau. She'd not see her people dragged into this war.

Lea looked at the guards riding before her. Two of the three were young—barely old enough to have noticeable facial hair.

How would she explain their deaths to their mothers should anything happen?

The third had two young sons and a pregnant wife. What would happen to his family should they lose him? How would they feed themselves? Who would protect them? How would they bear the loss?

The pain of losing her brother, Phillip, still cut her deeply. She doubted if that pain would ever subside.

No, she'd never wed a warrior.

But what did that leave? Men of Villaire's ilk? Greedy, bullying cowards who thought of nothing except themselves?

Or a pious holy man who would think only of his prayers?

Would she rather marry a weak, fearful man who hid inside the keep waiting for the worst to happen?

Lea clenched the reins between her fingers. It was little wonder parents and liege lords arranged a young girl's betrothal.

If she, a woman grown, couldn't even decide what type of man would make a good husband and lord for Montreau, how could a starry-eyed child be expected to do so?

'What concerns you so?'

Startled by Agatha's question, Lea answered without thinking, 'I need a husband. But I don't know what kind of man would suit.'

'You might have thought of that before.'

Lea slowed her horse, putting some distance between her and the guards. She'd soon be the topic of enough gossip at Montreau; there was no need to speed it along.

Once assured the distance was safe, she admitted, 'I thought I could do this alone.'

Agatha jerked back in apparent shock. 'Do what alone? Raise a child? Or live your life alone? Had you truly believed that you would never have to remarry?'

'Both, I suppose.'

'Lady Lea...' Agatha heaved a long sigh before continuing, 'Child, sometimes I think you have had your own way far too long.'

'My own way?' Lea sought a valid argument, hoping to hold off the lecture she knew was coming. 'It isn't as if I've ever been permitted to do my own choosing. If I didn't answer to my father, I answered to my husband.'

'If you remember correctly, you will admit that you chose that husband just as surely as you decided what's happening now.'

'My father chose Charles, not I.'

'Only because you had called off your marriage to Warehaven.'

Lea had no desire to argue that point. 'I can't change the past. My concern is for tomorrow.'

'I thought this is what you wanted? Now that you can fulfil King Stephen's requirement to retain control of Montreau, what concerns you?'

Lea cringed. How had she ever believed she could be that cold and calculating? Why hadn't she realised as soon as she actually conceived a child that her feelings would far outweigh her ill-contrived plans?

'Perhaps I didn't think this through enough.'

'When have you ever thought anything through?'

Sometimes her former nursemaid's bluntness stung. She was no longer a child needing firm-handed guidance.

'Lady Lea, I apologise for overstepping boundaries, but there are times your impulsiveness gets you in trouble.'

'I am not impulsive.'

'Oh?' Agatha stared at her with raised eyebrows. 'And when did you cease being so? Was it when Phillip died and your first thought was to call off your betrothal to Warehaven? Perhaps it was when you thought Villaire would be easy to control and nearly demanded a quick marriage.' The older woman frowned as if thinking, then added brightly, 'Or maybe it was when you thought having a baby you could pass off as Villaire's child would solve everything.'

Angry that Agatha would so forcefully remind her of all the things she was currently trying to forget, Lea warned, 'You go too far.'

'Do I?' Waving a hand toward the road ahead, Agatha

asked, 'And this, what is this if not an impulse given little more than a few moments of consideration?'

'Instead of berating me for things I cannot change, tell me what I can do now.'

'That's not my place. Besides, you wouldn't like my answer.'

Lea fumed. 'It's not as if you can anger me further.'

'All right.' Agatha stiffened her spine and stared over her horse's head. 'Turn around and tell Warehaven what you had planned. He will set things to right.' She turned to look at Lea. 'He won't be happy. But he will do the right thing by you.'

'Force him into marrying me is your answer? How does that solve anything?'

'How are you going to raise a child alone, retain control of Montreau and keep an eye on the ever-changing political affairs that might threaten your neutrality?'

'I don't know. But with your help—'

Agatha's bark of laughter cut her off. '*My* help? Since I can't keep an eye on political affairs, or control Montreau, that leaves me in charge of the baby. You don't think I'm a little old for that any more?'

'Old? No. Short of temper, perhaps, but not old.'

'Lady Lea, I have passed my fifty-fifth year. I happen to like sleeping through the night. If you think I am short of temper now, wait until the first time I have to walk the floors all night with a wailing babe.'

Surprised, Lea said, 'But I thought you liked children.'

'Yes. I do. When they belong to someone else.' Agatha glanced sideways at her. 'Did you think conceiving a child was the end of your responsibility?'

'No.' In truth she hadn't thought much past that part.

'Had you planned on giving birth and handing the babe over to another?'

Lea's stomach knotted, but not from her usual morning sickness. The idea of giving away the life she carried inside her made her ill. This was *her* baby. She wasn't about to give it to someone else.

Like any other woman her age she'd dreamed of having a baby. Holding her own child. Loving and caring for the small innocent life she'd been given. At times, she'd even contemplated doing things differently than her parents had.

Instead of letting a nursemaid raise the child, Lea thought it would be heaven to be the one who saw those first stumbling steps, or heard the first words spoken from such sweet lips. She wanted to be the one who bundled the baby into bed at night, with a soft kiss to their forehead and a whispered promise of undying love.

Her chest tightened with grief for what she'd never have. Without a husband at her side, Montreau would always be her first responsibility. It was their safety, their shelter. Without it, they would all be living in the woods like wild animals.

And while she saw to the running and safety of Montreau, someone else would raise her child. Someone else would hold the babe, offering comfort. Another's hands would tuck them into bed. Another's eyes would see the first steps and other ears would hear the first words.

As much as those thoughts hurt, what else could she do? There were no other options.

'No, I hadn't planned on doing that. But we have to be safe and that means seeing to Montreau.'

'A husband could help with that, Lea. You will never have the freedom to come and go as you wish. You are Montreau's lady and will always have that responsibility. But you need not do it all. Would it not be enough for you to see to the day-to-day running of the keep while another concerns himself with the safety, security and continued welfare of Montreau and the demesne lands?'

'Just like my parents did?' Even with the two of them seeing to Montreau they had had precious little time for their children.

'Bah.' Agatha made a noise that sounded suspiciously like a snort. 'Your parents hated each other. They each did whatever they could to make more work for the other. It doesn't have to be that way. There are men out there who would be honoured to be your partner in this, Lea.'

'My partner? They'd be honoured to gain possession of what I have.'

'When did you become so untrusting of others?'

'The day my brother was murdered.'

'That was years ago. Phillip was in the wrong place unknowingly. You can't hold everyone who carries a sword responsible for his death.'

'Perhaps not, but that doesn't mean I need to let a sword-wielding warrior sacrifice Montreau's men.'

The slump of Agatha's shoulders spoke of her weariness. Instead of calling an end to this discussion as Lea thought she would, the older woman asked, 'If you will not have a sword-wielding warrior, then what type of man would you have?'

'I'm not certain.' She'd just wondered that herself and still had no answer. 'No one like Charles.'

'Praise the Lord for that. You don't wish for a husband concerned with only wealth. Or one driven by only power. What are you looking for, Lea? Someone who will worship at your feet? Obey your every command, jump to your every desire?'

'Isn't there something in between all of those choices?'

'No. Even if there was, you would soon grow bored of such perfection.'

'Since it's becoming obvious I will have to remarry, I would be happy with a man who desired me first, above all else. One who could see to Montreau's safety and future. Someone not afraid to face down Stephen or Matilda if need be.'

Realising that Agatha stared at her, Lea stopped. 'What?'

The older woman shook her head. 'This pregnancy has made you daft.'

Confused, Lea asked, 'Is it so wrong to wish for those things?'

'I didn't say that. I said you were daft.'

'Why?'

Once again Agatha's grey braids swung as she shook her head. 'Child, you need to work this one out for yourself. I only hope it doesn't take you overlong.'

Only Lea could turn a one-day jaunt into a three-day journey.

Had the guard scouting ahead of him not been paying close attention, they would have run over Lea's party within hours of leaving Montreau. The act of staying far enough behind them, so as not to be seen, had become tedious. He could have walked to New Castle quicker than this, although her slow pace did make it convenient for him to spy on her. It was an easy task to leave his horse with his men, sneak up close to Lea's group to see what they were doing, then return to his own party without detection. If only spying during battle could be so simple.

At first he'd thought perhaps she was debating the wisdom of her actions and might turn around to return to the keep. But, no. He'd realised the next morning that she was ill.

About the time he'd been ready to make his presence known and order her back to Montreau, she'd started her group moving. Not for long, though. A few hours later she'd stopped to eat.

That surprised him, considering how ill she'd appeared on rising. Her seemingly sudden recovery increased his suspicions that she did indeed carry a child.

He'd been old enough to remember when his mother carried her last child. It was the same—she too would rise from bed ill, but by late morning she'd be fine. Only when his father remembered to bring her a light repast in bed did she seem able to go about her duties earlier in the day.

They used to jest about it. His mother claimed she would be willing to conceive every year if it would gain her personal service in bed every morning. His father would then feign horror at the suggestion he become her handmaiden.

Was this something Lea and Agatha didn't know? Or was it something that didn't work for every woman?

The questions gave Jared pause—what did he care if Lea was sick or not? He could only assume that she'd run away the moment she'd realised her condition— leading him to suspect the child was his.

Surely she didn't think for one heartbeat that he'd permit her to deliver a bastard child?

Since they'd taken no precautions, the blame was as much his as it was hers. In his mind it was more so his fault. He'd sworn not to ever let this happen. But lust and desire for Lea had won out over his usual common sense.

Even if she claimed the child was not his, he wasn't about to spend the rest of his life wondering if she lied. A marriage between them—whether by force or not— would alleviate any wondering on his part.

'My lord?'

Jared peered at the guard through the rain. 'Don't tell me, let me guess—she's stopped again?'

The man had no need to answer. It was plain from his dour expression and clenched, white-knuckled grip on his reins that Lea had indeed come to another halt.

Jared shrugged, trying not to let his impatience get the best of him. Then he dismissed the guard. 'See if you can find some dry shelter.'

He hoped Agatha had experience delivering a child, because at the rate Lea's group was progressing the babe would be born on the road.

Chapter Fourteen

To Lea's chagrin, King David awaited her in the bailey when she arrived. With her hopes of a luxurious hot bath and changing into clean clothing before requesting an audience dashed, she smiled as best she could.

Lea dismounted, then moved to bow, but David grasped her hand to stop her. 'I think we can do without the formalities. What brings you to New Castle, Lady Lea?'

If not today, some day soon it would indeed be a new castle. Not even when her father had rebuilt Montreau had there been so many workers seeing to the reconstruction of the keep.

She dipped her head in respect none the less before nearly shouting her answer over the din of hammering and sawing. 'My lord, I beg your protection for me and my travelling companions.'

After ordering men to see to her horses and guards, he looked down at her as he tucked her hand into the crook of his arm to escort her to the keep. 'Protection? Is someone seeking to bring you harm?'

Agatha followed them toward the keep. She said nothing aloud, but Lea heard the woman's grumbling.

'No, I'm sorry, maybe respite would be a better explanation.'

Lea gritted her teeth and glared over her shoulder at another round of muttered grumbles from her maid.

'It must be of a political nature for you to have come to me for sanctuary instead of going to the church.'

Of course King David would assume she'd seek personal respite at the church. He was said to be as pious as his mother before him. But she wasn't looking for her soul's comfort.

'Maybe a little of both.'

David patted her hand. 'With your father gone, I am glad you came to me.'

'You always had my father's trust. I would go to no other.' She'd not insult him by adding there was no other place for her to go.

Once inside the keep, Agatha followed a servant up to a chamber. King David led Lea to a couple of chairs near a warm fire. Once she was settled, he asked, 'What is so dire you needed to leave Montreau?'

She should have expected that question—wouldn't she have asked the same of someone visiting her unexpectedly? With no explanation at hand, at least not one she'd share, Lea fell back on what she knew would be a safe, acceptable answer. 'I just needed to escape Montreau for a few days, so I could think.'

The surprise on his face prompted her to add, 'Ever since Charles died, it seems I'm pulled every which way. I found that I can't determine what would be best for Montreau while trying to run a keep and fending off would-be lords at the same time.'

Thankfully, David nodded. 'I understand your brother-by-marriage felt a need to become your guardian.'

Now it was her turn to be surprised. Word travelled quicker than she'd thought. 'Yes, but luckily his mind was changed.'

'By you or Matilda's nephew?'

Lea stared at the king. Had he been spying on Montreau? Why? Was he thinking of adding her lands to his property, too?

Before she could form an answer, or her own question, he leaned closer to explain, 'Don't tell him, but my niece the empress wasn't certain there wouldn't be trouble when Warehaven sailed into your bay. She'd sent word to me asking that I be ready to defend him and Montreau should it prove necessary.'

'Ah.' Lea's worries fled. She should have guessed that Matilda would ask her uncle to assist Jared if necessary. The three of them were related through blood or marriage. 'That makes sense.'

'So, my dear, what great troubles do you need to sort out in private?'

She paused. The back of her neck tingled with the feeling that someone was watching them, listening to their conversation. But a quick glance around the Great Hall made her doubt the odd sensation.

'Marriage,' she answered, lowering her voice to add, 'Or prolonged widowhood.'

David laughed. 'I am surprised you don't already have half-a-dozen lords, or would-be lords, camped outside your keep already.'

'Villaire and his offering were enough, thank you.'

'And who did he think to offer up?'

'Blackstone—John Blackstone.'

David frowned a few minutes, then he shook his head. 'Never heard of him.'

'He was just another pawn for Villaire to control. I worry now that Markam will go running to Stephen demanding guardianship.'

'You have no need to fear that. Stephen might change his mind often enough, but I'm certain had he wanted Montreau controlled by Villaire, guardianship would already have been granted.'

Even though the idea of Stephen granting anything in regards to Montreau chafed, she hoped King David was right.

'As much as you may wish it, you do realise that you will not be able to remain a widow for long?'

Lea shivered. Once again it seemed that they were being watched. But they were alone—or so it appeared.

'Lea?'

She turned her attention back to King David, determined to ignore her unexplainable apprehension.

'They won't permit you to remain a widow.'

'I know.' She knew he was right. Whether she wanted a husband or not mattered little. The only thing that mattered was Montreau.

'Child, you could make this easier on yourself.'

'How?' Lea was certain she'd thought about this from every angle—and none of the options appeared easy to her.

'Choose.'

'What? Choose what?'

David rolled his eyes towards the ceiling as if looking

for guidance from above. 'A side, Lea. Choose a side. Then let your liege find you a decent man to wed.'

'No.' Her stomach rolled. 'I can't do that. Montreau's neutrality is all that keeps my men out of this battle and alive.'

He grasped her shoulder. 'I do not say this out of heartlessness. Lea, I know what you have lost. I know that pain well. But you keep it alive with this fear of yours.'

'I have nothing to fear as long as my keep and people stay out of this war.'

'Phillip was not in a battle when he was killed. And going into battle does not guarantee death.'

'Perhaps not.' She pulled away from his touch. 'But pitting armed men against each other only increases the likelihood of their death.'

'Your father did you no favour by loving you too much.'

That comment made little sense to her. 'How so?'

'You should have been wed to a lord—a well-seasoned warrior before you grew old enough to form such strange ideas.'

'Oh, yes, then that way I would have become used to men fighting and dying.'

'Nobody grows used to it.' He pinned her with a hard stare. 'But they soon learn it is the way of life. If you want to keep your possessions, you fight to hold them.'

'I retain possession of Montreau through our neutrality.'

'Damn it, girl. Stephen and Matilda are not going to let you do so for much longer. They are both running out of gold, they both need men and the supplies a town or field can provide.'

'No. I have writs from both of them. They—'

'Listen to me, Lea. One day—maybe one day sooner

than you think—one of them will be at your walls with an army. They will take by force what you think to hold by peace. What if it is Matilda who arrives first? What if it is my army outside your gates? What will you do then?'

He was frightening her with this talk of Montreau's fall. 'You were my father's strongest ally, why would you do such a thing?'

'You are not your father. You cannot hold your keep without a man to see to its defence.'

'How do you justify killing men with whom you've shared a table? You would attack me and mine because I don't have a husband?'

He glared at her before rubbing a hand across his forehead. 'Probably not.' David sighed. 'I would first try to talk to Matilda and you. But not every lord would be as kind-hearted. Some are just waiting for the order to take Montreau from you.'

She exhaled in relief. 'I thank you for that. My lord, I realise that even though I wish not to remarry, that Montreau has to have a strong arm in charge of our defences.'

'Have you given at least some thought to who might interest you?'

'Not yet I haven't. I was hoping to find a day or two of peace here in which to clear my head so that I might give it some thought.'

'I will be here for at least a fortnight. Take as much time as you need until then.'

Lea hoped she could come up with a solution to her situation well before then. 'Thank you.'

David motioned to a servant. 'I'm sure you would appreciate a hot bath and rest before the evening meal.'

Lea rose, eager to let a hot bath ease the stiffness from her muscles. 'That sounds heavenly.' She dipped her head. 'Until later then, my lord.'

From his hiding spot in the shadows, Jared watched her disappear up the stairs. He then stepped out of the curtained alcove behind King David. 'Interesting.'

'Interesting?' He waved toward the chair Lea had just vacated. 'Is that all you have to say?'

Jared stretched his feet towards the fire and rested his head against the high back of the chair. 'What would you prefer I say?'

'You could explain what is happening beneath my roof. Why the secrecy?'

'Lady Lea already explained. She's here to decide what she should do.'

To his surprise the king handed him a tankard of ale. He'd half-expected it to be used as a weapon for his evasive answer.

'I don't believe her either.' David took a long drink, then added, 'If I were to guess, I'd say she's escaping from...' He pinned Jared with a hard stare. 'From you, most likely.'

Jared debated his next reply. If he gave the appearance that he didn't care, David might not support his suit should he prove Lea was truly pregnant. But what would the king do with the truth? Would he seek to force an immediate wedding before Jared could be certain of her condition?

'Stop stalling, Warehaven.'

'Yes, I'm fairly certain she's trying to escape me.' He opted for the partial truth, hoping their family connection would gain him a measure of support.

'Did you attack her keep? Harm her men? Force yourself on her?'

Surprised and more than a little insulted by the questions, Jared fumed. 'What sort of man do you think I am? I do know the meaning of honour.'

'When it comes to love—or…' David slid him a narrow-eyed glance '—in this case, jilted love, honour can sometimes be forgotten.'

'Love?' Jared prayed he'd never again be foolish enough to believe in such a useless emotion. 'There is no love between us. Besides, I'd never retaliate in such a manner.'

'Then why is she running from you?'

'She might be carrying a child.'

David closed his eyes. 'Whose?'

At the forefront of his mind was the notion that Lea had come to David. She wouldn't have done so had she not been certain of his protection. There was obviously a connection between the families, one that might put his life in jeopardy.

Alert for any threat to his continued health, he carefully answered, 'I have every reason to believe it is mine.'

Instead of ordering him drawn and quartered, David only turned a hard, piercing glare on him. Thankfully the king's glare alone didn't have the power to burn him alive. 'That was your choice of retaliation?'

Well used to irate royals, Jared held his own temper in check. 'However it may have happened, be assured force was not involved.'

His answer seemed to pacify David—somewhat. The man still retained the air of an outraged father. 'What do you intend to do?'

'First I intend to make certain she is with child. And if she is, she'll become my wife.'

'You don't think she'll have something to say about that?'

'I don't care.' While he felt safe enough to tell David that much of the truth, he'd not tell him about Stephen's missive. King David was a friend to Montreau and he'd not jeopardise that relationship by making Lea appear to be a lying whore. The man didn't need to know she'd tried to get pregnant on purpose—most likely to pass the child off as Charles's in an attempt to hold Stephen at bay.

David was right about that much—Lea did need to choose. Otherwise, she would soon find herself in the middle of a pitched battle for control of Montreau.

'What do you mean, *you don't care*? That is not a good way to start a marriage.'

Jared shrugged. 'First things first. Right now, I can only assume she's pregnant. She left abruptly. When I followed her here I noticed how sick she was in the mornings. By late morning, though, she was fine. My mother reacted the same way early in her pregnancy.'

'What do you want from me?'

'I want to watch her without her knowing it until I'm certain. Then I'll approach her.'

'And if she denies it?'

'In that event, I'll make certain my aunt doesn't recall me for at least six months.'

David laughed. 'And if she admits that she is carrying your child?'

'My child will not be born a bastard.'

'You place too much weight on a word. Your father had little difficulty with the circumstance of his birth.'

Jared didn't disagree, but… 'My father was the king's bastard and grew up at court. None would have dared voice a degrading remark in King Henry's presence.'

David nodded. 'But it was not as easy for you, was it?'

'No.' It hadn't been. He'd been raised at Warehaven and at times being called the son of a bastard stung. The insult to his father bothered him more than it had Lord Warehaven.

The most painful sting had been when Lea used that as an excuse not to marry him.

'I'll not stand in your way.' David rose. 'I will do what I can for you. But if it comes down to a marriage, she has to be willing.'

Jared stared into his tankard of ale a moment before placing it on a small table beside him, then he rose, assuring David, 'Oh, trust me, she will be.'

Chapter Fifteen

Lea dreaded going down to the Great Hall. Even though four days ago King David had welcomed her, as she had hoped he would, she sensed that something wasn't quite right.

Instead of focusing on court matters, the reconstruction of the keep and the current difficulties he was having in getting his chancellor, William Comyn, appointed as Bishop of Durham, he seemed over-solicitous of her comfort.

If she didn't know better, she would think he somehow knew about her condition. Since that wasn't possible, she wondered at his kindness.

While it was true that David had been a good friend to her father and extended that same concern towards her, he was still a man. And in her experience, men didn't go out of their way to see to a woman's comfort unless they either wanted something, or were up to something.

Since she knew for a fact that David wanted nothing from her, she was left to wonder what he was up to. The nicer he was, the more she worried she'd dislike whatever he was plotting.

Lea forced herself to shake off the stomach-churning foreboding. He was simply being over-kind because of her recent loss. That had to be the explanation—it was the only one that made any sense.

And then there was the matter of her men—or rather her missing men. They'd disappeared the morning after their arrival—without so much as a by your leave.

When she'd questioned King David about the guards, he'd waved off the query as if it was of little matter. His only verbal response had been to ask if she felt unsafe in his court.

How was she supposed to answer that without offending the king? She couldn't and so she had no idea where her men were. Although it was fairly obvious the king did. She could only assume, and hope, that they had been sent back to Montreau.

Then, to top it all off, the feeling that she was being watched hadn't faded. In fact, it had grown stronger. No matter where she went inside, or outside, the keep, she felt someone behind her. Someone watching her every move.

She'd come here for some peace and solitude, some time to think. Instead, she had experienced more apprehension than she had at Montreau.

Perhaps it was time to return home.

Except Jared was mostly likely still in residence.

What amazed her more than David's kindness, her missing guards, or her sense of being shadowed, was that Jared hadn't tracked her down to force her back to Montreau.

True, he hadn't come after her when she'd called off

their marriage, but this was different. Now he was responsible for Montreau's safety and that included her. She'd half-expected him to stop her before she'd arrived at New Castle.

And a part of her—a senseless part she tried desperately to ignore—was oddly disappointed. The implication of that unwarranted emotion was too frightening to consider.

What would she have done had he tried to force her to return? No. She needn't worry about what would never happen. He wouldn't put forth that much effort or concern over her. He didn't care for her in that way. So why would he waste his time coming after her?

And it certainly wasn't as if he had any claim on her. Lea placed a hand protectively over her stomach and revised that thought. He was currently not aware of any claim he might have over her.

While he remained in the dark about her condition, he had nothing to hold over her head—nothing to force her to bend to his will.

But when that changed— Lea frowned, then she gasped. *Oh, dear Lord, what had she done?*

She quickly paced the floor, trying to calm her uneven breathing and soothe her aching head. The sudden hard pounding at her temples threatened to take away her breath. Why hadn't she thought of this before leaving Montreau?

The longer she remained at David's court, the longer Jared would remain at Montreau. If she stayed here too long, by the time she did return home her condition would be obvious to all.

She dropped down on to the bed. Her heart raced and

stomach rolled, knowing she was caught in a web of her own making.

'Lady Lea?' Agatha stuck her head into the chamber. 'They await you at the table.'

The thought of food made her ill. But she'd not eaten this morning and her stomach rebelled at the idea of going empty any longer.

She rose and fluffed out the skirt of her gown, hoping the familiar action would help still her trembling hands.

'Are you feeling unwell?'

Lea resisted the urge to groan at the oft-asked question. 'I am fine.'

Agatha glanced over her shoulder, then entered the chamber, closing the door behind her. 'I asked around about the men like you requested.'

'Good. What did you find out?'

'You were correct. They were sent back to Montreau.'

Lea frowned. 'Why would David do that without at least informing me?'

'It wasn't by King David's order.'

Impossible. 'If I didn't give them the orders and David didn't, then who did?'

The very heartbeat the words left her mouth, Lea knew the answer. 'Of course, how blind I have been. It must have been Warehaven.'

'How, my lady? He isn't here, is he?'

'No. Thank goodness he isn't.' Lea mused, 'He probably sent word to David to have the men return.'

'And leave you here alone? How are we supposed to travel back to Montreau?'

'Do you think Jared cares about that?'

'He should.'

Lea knew the older woman was still upset that she'd not told Jared about the child. She wasn't going to have that conversation again. Instead, she said, 'King David will see to it that we travel safely when the time comes.'

She didn't add that the time might be coming sooner than she'd expected.

'I suppose you're right. I just find it odd.'

Even though she agreed everything was rather odd, Lea tried to reassure the woman. 'I am certain it was Jared's doing. There's nothing at all odd about him giving orders behind my back.'

Hearing footsteps in the corridor, Agatha motioned towards the door. 'I think they grow impatient.'

Earlier today Lea had caught the aroma of apples baking. Considering how fond King David was of apple tarts, she wouldn't be surprised if he sent someone else to bring her to the table.

After one more shake of her skirt, she headed for the door. 'I think tomorrow I will approach the king about our return to Montreau.'

The relief in Agatha's long sigh followed her out of the chamber. But it was soon drowned out by the sound of loud voices and laughter drifting up the stairs from the Great Hall.

Lea paused at the top of the steps. Tiny wings fluttered in her stomach. Apprehension returned. *What awaited her below?*

'Nothing,' she whispered, seeking to still her sudden nervousness. She headed down the steep stairs, certain her unease was caused by nothing more than her overactive mind.

David rose from his seat at the head of the long table set up in the middle of the hall. 'Ah, there she is.'

He motioned to an empty spot on the bench flanking the table. 'We've been waiting for you, my dear.'

Lea dipped her head in greeting and quickened her pace. 'I apologise, my lord.'

She squeezed between the benches to take her seat next to her dining partner. He lightly grasped her hand to assist.

The touch was all too familiar. An icy chill raced through her. Numb with shock, afraid of whom she would see, Lea looked down at the man.

No! It couldn't be.

'I'm certain Lady Villaire didn't intend to hold up the meal.'

Jared tugged her down on to the bench next to him. His hip resting against hers made her thoughts flee. But when she tried to put some distance between them, he only pressed tighter against her.

'No matter how far you move away, I'll be right at your side.'

There wasn't a trace of humour in his threat. Head bowed, she stared at their shared trencher. *This couldn't be happening.* Lea hazarded a glance towards the king, but David ignored her silent plea. He only shrugged a shoulder before turning his attention to his meal.

From his reaction—or lack of reaction—it was obvious to her that he'd helped Jared arrange this little surprise.

'You will find no help from the king.'

'Help?' Lea prodded at a bite-sized piece of meat that he'd cut for her. She had to find the strength to brazen her way through this meal. 'I don't need help from anyone.'

Jared's soft laugh sent a tremor through her heart.

He leaned close enough to whisper, 'My dear, you need more help than any mortal man could provide.'

The food she was chewing stuck to the roof of her suddenly dry mouth. When she reached for a goblet of wine, Jared picked it up first.

Like a devoted lover he held the rim to her lips. His searing gaze captivated her. She vaguely heard a woman giggle. If she didn't do something to free herself from his attention, everyone would think they were lovers.

Lea turned her head and wrapped her fingers around the stem of the vessel. 'Thank you.'

Jared was slow to release his grasp, and when he did, he made a point of running a fingertip along the top of her hand.

She stared at his finger over the rim of the goblet, and then relaxed her hold, letting the cup fall from her hand. He had no choice other than to quickly grab the drinking vessel, or wear the contents.

'How clumsy of me.'

'No damage was done.' He smiled while placing the cup on the table.

'What a shame,' Lea said under her breath.

Fingers curled around her upper thigh. 'Be warned, I can make a bigger scene than you.'

She doubted that, but wasn't about to test her doubts. Lea picked up her eating knife and twirled it between her fingers. 'Remove your hand.'

'Or what?' He only tightened his hold on her leg. 'You'll stab me?'

As much as she'd like to, Lea knew she'd not be

able to carry out the act. She set down the knife. 'Just let me go.'

He did. 'Finish your food. We need to talk.'

The last thing she was about to do was hold a conversation with Jared. He didn't know how to converse. His version of talking consisted of shouting and ordering her about.

'We have no need to talk.'

'Don't make a wager on that.' Between bites of food, he asked, 'What are you doing here?'

'Looking for some peace and solitude.'

'And you couldn't wait for someone to escort you here?'

'We had escorts. Ones I assume you sent back to Montreau.'

'You call those guards escorts?' A fake smile did little to hide his foul mood.

'They've served me well thus far.'

'When was the last time you left Montreau?'

Like most women, she had little need to leave her keep. And since Charles never left to visit anywhere, she'd remained at Montreau with him. But that was none of Jared's concern. 'It's been a while.'

'A while?'

'A few years.'

'Your servants say you haven't left the demesne lands since you last visited Warehaven.'

Apparently there was little he didn't know. 'It's possible.'

'And in those years you haven't had a change of guards?'

Of course she had. After her father died, some left

because they refused to serve Charles, and some of the older ones had died. Still, she didn't understand what he meant. 'Yes, of course we have.'

'And your guards train under who, Lea? You?'

'Charles worked the men.'

Jared laughed, cutting it off by pouring wine and taking a long drink. But she could still see the disbelieving laughter in his glimmering eyes.

'Laugh all you want, Warehaven. Montreau has no need of an army.'

He set the cup down. 'No, of course not. You're neutral. Which naturally means no one will ever attack you or your keep.'

She saw the wisdom in his words, but nothing would make her agree with him to his face. 'None have thus far.'

'You and Montreau are my responsibility. From now on you will not leave the keep unless there are experienced men at your back. Am I understood?'

'Does that mean I can come and go as I please?' If that were true, some of her future troubles might be solved.

He brushed the back of his hand gently across her cheek. 'Why, dear heart, do I detect a shimmer of hope in your eyes?' He lowered his voice to warn, 'You won't get the chance to get away from me again.'

Lea jerked away from his touch. Her heart felt as if it had fallen to her stomach. *Won't get the chance to get away from him?* 'Am I your prisoner?'

'No.' He reached out to run a fingertip along her jawbone, then turned back to his food. 'Not at all.'

Unable to eat any more, Lea said, 'I'm finished.'

She made to rise, but Jared looped his foot around hers. 'Remain seated. I haven't finished yet.'

'What difference does that make? I'm finished eating. I'm going to my chamber.'

'Perhaps you misunderstood me. You aren't getting away from me again, Lea. Ever.'

'What?'

He took another drink, then addressed the king. 'Sire, I thank you for the meal.'

David's eyes widened. 'You are finished already?'

'Yes. I fear my appetite has been…lacking…of late.'

Everyone at the table laughed as if he'd told some wry joke. Lea frowned. Surely they didn't believe he was too lovesick to eat?

David nodded. 'I completely understand.'

Jared rose, reached down to take her hand and pulled her to her feet. 'By your leave, my lord?'

Already lusting after the apple tart before him, David waved them from the table.

Lea fumed silently until they reached the upper landing. Once she was certain they were out of sight, she pulled free of Jared's hold. 'Now that you've succeeded in making them all wonder if we're lovers, you can do me the honour of going away.'

He only laughed before placing his hand against the small of her back and leaning closer to remind her, 'We need to talk.'

Talk? Lea blinked at the warmth of his touch. He'd acted like an ogre at the table. She should be screaming, pushing him away, calling out for help.

So why did the semi-darkness of the corridor make her want to lean against him? And why did his touch feel so warm and inviting instead of repulsing her?

She moved away, breaking the contact along with the odd spell that had momentarily fallen over her.

'You are mistaken, Jared.' She turned to face him. 'We have nothing to talk about.'

He took a step towards her until her back was against the wall. With his lips mere inches from hers, he asked, 'No?'

Lea shook her head. 'No. Nothing.'

Jared placed the palm of his hand against her stomach. 'I think it's about time we discuss my child, don't you?'

Chapter Sixteen

How did he find out? He couldn't be certain. This was a trick. He was daring her to slip up, to admit she was carrying his child.

Lea knew that unless she admitted the truth, he would never be able to prove anything. She took a slow, steadying breath, then said, 'You have had too much wine.'

'Oh, really?'

He pulled her away from the wall, and led her by the hand into her chamber.

'What are you doing? You can't be in here.'

'Who will stop me?' He leaned against the door, barring any escape.

'I'll scream.'

He waved a hand in the air. 'If that pleases you.'

His words were light, his tone too controlled, as if every word was measured. She studied him, trying to determine his mood.

Lea gasped, then backed away from the rage evident in his returned stare.

Jared wanted to shake her until her teeth rattled. But

that would satisfy no one. If she thought for one single heartbeat that she was going to lie her way out of this, she was sadly mistaken.

He'd watched her closely these last few days. Who did she think she was fooling? Didn't she hear the whispered conversations in the hall? Didn't she see the looks when she entered a room?

'You may as well give up, Lea. I know you are carrying a child and I know that child is mine.'

She shook her head. 'You're wrong, Jared.'

'I'm wrong about what? Your pregnancy? The child being mine?' He laughed. 'You'd rather try to convince me that you're a whore than admit the truth?'

'There's no truth to admit.'

It was rather amazing how brazen she could be at times. He didn't know too many warriors who would stand there and repeatedly lie to his face. Yet this woman thought to face him down.

At another time the idea might intrigue him, but not now. The only thing he wanted from her now was the truth.

'My mother used to be sick in the morning when she carried Isabella. By mid-morning she was no longer ill.'

'I—'

'Don't.' He stormed across the chamber, stopping directly in front of her. 'You of all people have the gall to bear a bastard?'

'What are you—?'

'Cease.' He'd had enough. Jared grasped her arms. 'Listen to me and listen well. I know you're pregnant, Lea. And I know the child is mine.'

She tried to tug free of his hold, but he slid his arms

around her, pulling her close. 'You were too good to wed the son of a bastard, but you think it acceptable to bear one?'

'I never—'

'Never what, Lea? Never intended to wed me in the first place? Never meant to let it go that far?'

She struggled against him, shouting, 'What are you talking about? I loved you. I wanted to spend the rest of my life with you.'

'Yes, I could tell.' Memories of the blow she'd delivered to his heart swept over him. He couldn't have kept the sneer out of his tone had he tried. 'It was most apparent the day you called everything off.'

'I couldn't marry you. I explained that.'

'That you did. It was rather surprising to discover that after two years of courting you couldn't bring yourself to wed the son of a bastard.'

'I never—'

He cupped her cheek, stopping her denial with his thumb against her lips. 'And once again here we are, the night before our wedding. Except this time, we're both tainted. I carry a bastard's blood and you carry a bastard.'

A dozen or more angry words flitted across her mind. Countless curses were at hand, ready and willing to drip from her tongue. But something—Lea stared deeper into his gaze—something hiding behind his anger stopped her.

She whispered past his touch, 'I do not carry a bastard. His father is dead.'

Jared pulled away from her. 'You would rather lie than sully my own child with my name?'

His harsh question took her breath away. She'd once loved him—dearly. And if she wasn't seeing things, if her mind and heart weren't playing tricks on her, what she saw lurking beneath his anger was pain.

That this warrior standing before her could be hurt was unfathomable. She didn't know what to say, or what to do. Had she hurt him this badly? Had he carried this anger, this pain, all these years? Her mind was awhirl with too many questions.

When she didn't answer, he glared down at her. 'I won't let you do that. We will be wed in the morning. And this time your father isn't here to deliver your viperous missive.'

Viperous missive? She had poured her heart out in that missive, agonising over each word. She'd apologised over and over again, trying to make him see her reasons for calling off their marriage.

Lea reached towards him, pulling her arm back when he jerked away. 'Jared, I don't know what you're talking about. I never sent you anything close to a viperous missive.'

Truth be told, she'd never understood why he hadn't stormed Montreau demanding she wed him regardless of her misgivings. She'd eventually come to assume that he had never truly loved her in the way he'd so often claimed.

'What would you call it, Lea? A love letter? A fond farewell?'

She couldn't remember the exact wording any longer. But she would never forget the gist of her decision. 'Phillip had just been killed. I don't know what I was feeling other than horror and loss. Jared, I couldn't bear the thought of going through that again. And if I wed you, I knew that day would eventually come.'

His frown deepened. 'What does Phillip's death have to do with this?'

'Everything!' Shocked, Lea shouted, 'It had everything to with it. Everything. I could not bring myself to marry a warrior.' She swallowed, trying to retain a measure of calmness in this insanity. 'No matter how much I loved you, I couldn't do it, Jared. When you didn't come to demand an explanation in person, I thought you understood, and that it didn't matter.'

He rubbed his forehead. 'Come to Montreau? After you begged me to stay away?'

'No.' Lea shook her head. 'I wrote no such thing.'

Jared strode into the small alcove off the side of the chamber. She heard a rustle as if he were digging through a saddlebag, or sack.

When he came back into the main chamber, he held out a tattered missive. 'How can you lie so when I have proof? Not one word in here refers to your brother.'

She took the message from his hand and stared at the handwriting. The floor tilted beneath her, forcing Lea to reach out and blindly seek a place to sit before she fell down.

She sat on the edge of the bed. Her father's familiar handwriting swirled before her eyes. Once her disbelief faded, she read the missive again and again.

Her father hadn't delivered her missive. Jared had never seen her words, her reasoning. He didn't know how much she had loved him. Or how impossible it would have been to wed him. He'd spent all these years believing that she thought so little of him.

Her throat tightened as she tried to fight the tears wanting to escape. How could her father have done this? What had he been thinking?

She sighed. He hadn't been thinking. He had been so far lost in grief for his only son that his mind wasn't clear enough to think of anything except to make certain his only surviving child would not wed a warrior.

And she'd been too lost in her own sorrow to realise how devastated he had been, or what he'd done.

Jared frowned. Something wasn't right. Lea appeared genuinely shocked by the missive. The shimmer of tears in her eyes wasn't fabricated.

'I didn't write this.' She placed the weathered parchment on the bed, and then folded her hands on her lap. 'It came from my father, not me.'

'What difference does that make?' He'd spent too many years believing those words were hers for him to think otherwise now. 'So he wrote it for you.'

'I never needed my father to write anything for me. I did not give him this, Jared. These are not my words, not my reasoning.'

'How am I supposed to believe you?'

'I don't know.' She looked down at her clenched hands. 'Did I ever make even the smallest complaint about your father's birth? Did I ever do anything to make you think it mattered to me?'

Her voice was soft, her questions broken. Uncertain, Jared walked to the window embrasure and stared out at the darkening sky. 'You don't think that letter was enough?'

'Before then. Did I do or say anything before then?'

'No. But that doesn't mean you hadn't thought about it.'

'Jared, please, I'm not lying to you.'

A small part of him actually believed her—but his mind held fast. 'How would I know, Lea? That missive is the only thing I had. It was the only thing I could believe.'

'It was my father's lie.'

'It would be hard for me to prove that true or false, wouldn't it?'

'I never wrote that note. Those words came from a grieving father. But you are correct, there is no way to prove anything. All I have is my word, Jared.'

'Your word?' He dragged a hand through his hair before pulling another missive from inside his tunic.

'A moment ago you stated the child was Villaire's.'

When she opened her mouth to respond, he raised a hand. 'No, let me finish.'

To his amazement Lea closed her mouth and nodded.

He crossed the chamber to stand before her. Jared wanted to see every nuance of her response. 'You were willing to lie to me and the world about the baby's father. Why? If what you say is true, and your father's missive was a lie, why would you think to deny me my child?'

'I can't marry you.'

He detected no subterfuge in her simple answer. Whatever her mistaken reasoning, she honestly believed it was true.

'You've forfeited the choice, but that isn't what I asked you. How am I supposed to trust your word, if you're so willing to let our child live a lie?'

Lea wanted to lie down on the bed and sob. How was

she going to answer him? Whatever she said would
sound crass, or witless. What did that matter now?

'Can't you think of an answer?' He dropped another
missive on her lap. 'You don't need to, I know why.'

It took one glance to know what damning evidence
she held in her hand. Lea closed her eyes and let King
Stephen's note flutter to the floor.

She stared up at him. 'Yes. I had planned on using
you to keep Montreau.'

'Only planned?' The expression of disbelief and
disgust on his face made her look away in shame. 'It's
obvious you did more than plan.'

'No. You're wrong. I had changed my mind. I'd
hoped the empress would call you away soon, giving me
time to find someone to father my child.'

'And claim it was Villaire's?'

'Yes.'

Jared shook his head. 'I don't believe you. It makes
no sense. Why would you sleep with a stranger you
didn't know and risk physical danger, rather than
someone you knew wouldn't harm you?'

He had no idea how much harm he could do to her.
Not physically—she knew he'd never seek to hurt her
body. But the pain this man could cause her would hurt
more than any physical injury.

'Will you answer me?'

His clipped tone let her know that his patience was
growing thin. Lea rose and skirted around him to pace
before the window. She couldn't just sit there on the bed
and willingly tear out her own heart with her hands.

'I had always dreamed of having your child. Always.'

She paused to look out at the stars. 'A baby born of love, one who would bind us as a family.'

Lea turned to glance at him before once again pacing. Oddly enough, he didn't appear surprised by her admission.

'Your family, your parents, were proof that not all marriages were like my mother and father's. I wanted what your family had, for our marriage to be like theirs.'

To her relief, Jared remained silent.

'But I knew that was never going to happen.' She raised her hand. 'My fault, I know that. But when I received Stephen's threat, I knew the only way to retain Montreau, without being forced into a marriage that would only end up a repeat of what I had with Charles, would be to have a child. At first I was certain I could dupe you to get what I needed.'

'And it worked, didn't it, Lea?'

'No. Once you were there, I knew I couldn't go through with it.'

'But you did.'

'No, Jared, I didn't.' She stopped pacing to look at him. 'Touching you, kissing you, made me realise that what I had planned was wrong. I couldn't conceive a child with you—not that way. Not without love.'

He raised one eyebrow. 'I don't remember you worrying about conception at the time.'

'Nor did you.' Her face flamed, but she ploughed ahead. 'Blame that on lust.'

'It matters not what we blame it on, you are pregnant.' He grasped her wrist and pulled her close. 'With my child. You will marry me, Lea.'

'No.' She buried her face against his chest. 'Don't you understand? I can't marry you.'

'You were willing to whore yourself to retain possession of a keep—a pile of stone—but you refuse to make an honest woman of yourself—for a child.' He tugged her hair, forcing her to look up at him. 'When did you become so coarse and vulgar, Lea?'

'Montreau is all I have.'

'Is that what you planned to tell our child about his father one day? That Montreau was so important that you spread your legs for the first available man?'

Lea gasped. She'd been right. This man could hurt her more with words than another could with his fists. She pushed against his chest. 'Let me go.'

Jared released her immediately. 'Does the truth make you feel guilty? Perhaps ashamed of yourself?' He paused long enough for her to respond. When she didn't, he added, 'It should.'

'How dare you! You know nothing about my life, or about me.'

'I would dare much when it comes to the mother of my child.'

'*Your* child? I'm fairly certain you aren't the one carrying a child.'

'So you finally admit that you are pregnant.'

He hadn't phrased his statement as a question, so she didn't respond. He hadn't asked why she couldn't marry him. Apparently, her reasoning didn't matter. 'And I'm positive you aren't my husband, or my guardian.'

'I will be.'

Jared pulled a ring off his finger and grabbed her wrist. When she couldn't pull free, Lea curled her fingers into a fist. The useless act didn't stop him from having his way. She had not the strength to prevent him from uncurling the ring finger on her left hand.

'No, Jared, don't. I am not going to wed you.'

He ignored her and slid the Warehaven signet ring on to her finger. 'I will be your husband in the morning.'

Before she could voice her indignation at his high-handed actions, he warned, 'You have no choice in this. You can wed me. Or, once the babe is born, I will take the child and throw you out of Montreau by force.'

Speechless that he would even consider something that cruel, she mutely stared up at him.

Still holding her wrist, he pulled her closer and leaned forwards, to brush his lips against hers, whispering, 'I am certain the life of a whore will suit you quite well.'

Lea jerked out of Jared's hold, tore his ring from her finger and threw it at him. 'Get out of my chamber!'

He crossed his arms against his chest and shook his head. '*Our* chamber.'

A blaze of anger clouded her vision. 'If you don't leave, I will.'

When he didn't move, Lea rushed for the door. 'I am not staying in here with you.'

Chapter Seventeen

Lea flung open the chamber door, prepared to storm out, but instead she walked into King David.

'Going somewhere?'

'Yes. I am going home—to Montreau.'

He grasped her shoulders to turn her around, then gently pushed her back inside the chamber. 'You'll return to Montreau when your husband gives you leave to do so.'

Had he lost the ability to reason also? 'I am *not* married.'

'You will be on the morrow.'

She stepped away to spin round and face him. 'Have the two of you been in some type of accident that caused you both to lose your common sense at the same time?'

David reached behind him to slam the door closed before replying. When he focused his attention back on her, Lea forced herself not to back away from the anger evident in his scowling expression.

He could be as angry at her insolence as he wished. She wasn't changing her mind on this matter.

She could not—she *would not* jeopardise Montreau's safety by wedding a warrior, no matter the reason.

If they wished to call her a whore for seeking to protect her keep and her people, so be it.

'This wouldn't be an argument if your father were still alive.' The king didn't wait for her response. 'If he knew you were carrying a child outside of marriage, he'd be more than enraged, he'd be ashamed of you.'

Perhaps, but she wasn't a little girl still under her father's thumb.

'He'd also make certain you wed the man regardless of your wishes on the matter. Since he isn't here, I am obligated to step in.' David's scowl deepened as if he could frown her into submission.

'Forgive my bluntness, but you seem to have forgotten something, my lord. The church requires that I come willingly into this union.' Lea returned his glare. 'And I will never agree.'

'Then you will never leave this chamber.'

'You can't keep me prisoner here.'

'Now you've forgotten something, Lea. I am the king here. I can do as I please, when I please.'

David turned to Jared. 'Until she agrees to this union, neither of you will leave this room.'

If the look on Jared's face was any indication, he wasn't pleased with that decision. But he didn't argue. Instead, he nodded. 'She'll be ready to agree by morning.'

As the king headed for the door, he told her, 'Don't try to leave. My men will be at either end of the corridor.' He paused with the door partway open. 'You brought this on yourself, Lea. You may as well make the best of it.'

Jared watched as emotions of anger, confusion and horror played across Lea's face as she stared mutely at the closed door.

Certain it was going to be a long night, he saw no point in being uncomfortable. He sat on the edge of the bed to remove his boots. 'Give up, Lea, you've lost this battle.'

She turned to glare at him, stating, 'I am not sleeping with you.'

I am not were her favourite words of late. She was so certain she wasn't going to do a lot of things. In the end, she had no choice. Eventually she'd come to realise that for herself.

For now, however, he was tired of arguing and had every intention of going to bed. 'Sleep where you wish, Lea. Just don't leave this chamber.'

Jared circled the room, feeling her gaze on his back as he doused the candles and moved the oil lamp to the bedside table before disrobing. He smothered a laugh when she turned her head away as his last garment hit the floor.

She'd been married—how could she still become embarrassed so easily?

Once he'd climbed beneath the covers and stretched out on the bed, he patted the space next to him. 'Come to bed, Lea.'

She huffed away from the bed to push a bench into the far corner of the chamber. He watched as she sat down with her back propped up against the wall and her legs outstretched along the bench.

'You aren't going to sleep like that.'

For an answer, she crossed her arms against her stomach and closed her eyes.

This woman was far more than just impossible. If he had the leisure of time, he'd leave her right there. She could sit in her corner and pout for days on end as far as he was concerned.

But he didn't have the leisure of time. He couldn't be away from Montreau for any length of time.

With a curse he threw back the covers. 'Damn it, woman. I've had enough of your pigheadedness this night.'

Her eyes flew open and she nearly lunged from the bench. Jared crossed the chamber before she could put anything between them.

Without pausing, he swept her into his arms, carried her to the bed and dumped her on the mattress.

'If you touch me, I'll scream.'

'You do that.'

'Jared, I mean it. Don't you dare touch me.'

He crawled over her to the other side of the bed and pulled the covers up to his chest. But instead of stretching out on his back, he rolled on to his side, facing her.

'What do you think will happen if you scream? Do you think any of David's men will come to your rescue?'

She shuffled as close to the far edge of the bed as she could and kept her arms wrapped tightly across her chest. 'Is that why you sent my men back to Montreau?'

'To keep them from protecting you? No. That should be their duty. Unfortunately, it's one they are still ill equipped to perform. They had no business escorting you on this harebrained journey. Especially not without my permission.'

'*Your* permission?'

'Now we're going to argue that point? You don't think we've covered enough topics already?'

'They *are* my men.'

'And they always will be. But when it comes to your protection, they will answer to me and me alone.'

The line of her jaw tightened, but she remained silent—too silent. He saw her throat work and heard the unevenness of her breath. He remembered enough to know she was fighting to keep from crying. He also remembered how quickly she would lose her battle.

Jared caught the first tear with the tip of his finger. 'Lea, don't.'

Ignoring her feeble protest, he pulled her against him. As he stroked her cheek, he asked, 'Why do you fight me so? Why have you been so difficult, so damned unreasonable of late?'

'I could have loved you so.'

Her hoarsely whispered admission sucked the breath from his chest. His heart ached with a pain he couldn't identify. Nor did he wish to at this moment.

Tomorrow she would be his wife and while she wasn't his enemy, as far as he was concerned the same rules still applied—he could not risk showing weakness. To do so now would be a mistake he might never be able to correct.

He tore off the covers and moved over her. Cupping her face between his hands, he reminded her, 'You threw that chance away, not me.' He lowered his head to brush his lips against hers. 'What do you want me to do, Lea? It was not my fault, so what do you want me to say?'

She pushed against his shoulders. 'Leave me alone, Jared. Please, just leave me alone.'

He realised that if he did as she asked, it would only be harder to break through this barrier between them later. He didn't understand her reasoning. To be honest, he wasn't certain he cared.

'No, I will never leave you alone. You will be my wife just as surely as the sun will rise in the morning.'

'I can't marry you. I can't. I won't.'

Strong-headed, opinionated women didn't bother him. In fact, he'd rather argue with a passionate, resolute woman than suffer even a moment of quiet in the company of a meek and virtuous maiden.

He'd spent his entire life surrounded by strong women, who never hesitated to stand up for what they believed was right. But Lea had far surpassed even his aunt's level of demanding arrogance. She'd gone from being strong-willed to callous and selfish, regardless of the cost.

When had she become so insistent on getting her own way and so spiteful? What had changed her once-thoughtful patience into unreasonable anger? She used to be willing to listen and consider both sides of an argument. Now, *her side* was the only one to receive consideration.

'You are not some landless and penniless peasant, Lea.' He brushed at her tears with his thumbs. 'Your life does not belong to you. It never has.'

Flickering light from the oil lamp shimmered in her eyes. Jared saw resentment flare to life and knew she'd heard his words.

'You will do as you're ordered and you will do so with the honour and dignity befitting the Lady of Montreau and Warehaven.'

'Do not talk to me like you would a child.'

'Then stop acting like one.'

Her eyes widened. Apparently no one had dared to order her about in some time.

'Why, you—'

Jared cut off her words with a kiss. The taste of lingering salty tears gave him a pang of guilt. But the softness of the curves and swells beneath him quickly turned guilt to nothing but a distant memory.

Unable to summon the will to fight him any more this night, Lea slid her arms around him and surrendered on a broken sob.

What was she going to do? He was right. No matter how much the knowledge pained her, she no longer had a choice in this marriage.

She would wed her childhood beloved. She would bear his son, or daughter. And one day her heart would shatter with the news that he had perished on some far-flung battlefield.

They would tell her that he'd died a hero and describe his final moments as some great victory. Eventually, some lack-witted troubadour would compose a ballad in honour of Jared's valour.

There would be no body to bury, nothing tangible to mourn. Only an unbearable emptiness that would slowly, but surely, suck the life from her.

She had called off their previous wedding to avoid the terrible pain that would come with loss. But fate was a cruel taskmaster and from this night on she would live in fear of that day. For it would come.

When Phillip had been killed, she'd spent years wrapped in sorrow. The only thing that had kept the abject terror at bay was Montreau's neutrality.

Now, even that would be denied her.

The coming losses wouldn't be just hers. The women and children of Montreau would suffer just as horribly. She had a small army at her beck and call. Losing her husband would not put her life in grave danger—only her soul.

But for a villager, losing the man of the family would mean they were prey to any who chose to harm them. They would lose not only their protection, but also their ability to make enough money to eat, and to live.

And it would be her duty to carry the desperate news to their door.

Lea's breath caught in her throat as she tried to stop a threatening sob. She couldn't breathe, she couldn't think. She couldn't see past the cold, dark shroud of fear swirling around her.

Jared broke their kiss. He rolled on to his side, pulling her along. 'Dear God, Lea, tell me what is wrong.'

'What will I do when you die?' Her voice broke, but she couldn't stop the question from choking past her lips. 'I can't bear that pain again.'

He sighed, then tightened his embrace, holding her close, her cheek resting against his chest, his chin atop her head. 'Is that what all of this has been about?'

Unable to speak, she only nodded.

'I am not your brother, Lea. I was not raised to be a lord of the land. From the time I could hold a sword, I was raised to be a fighter, to be a leader of soldiers. I have trained hard, without pause, for years. You have to trust me on this. You have to believe that I will be successful in all of my endeavours.'

'How can you ask me to believe in something you can't know for certain?'

'So now you are telling me that I am not strong enough, or experienced enough, or intelligent enough to protect myself and my men?'

That wasn't what she meant. 'An arrow can come from nowhere.'

'And it will play hell getting through double-linked maille.'

'You can't see in every direction at once. You can't defend yourself if you are outnumbered.'

'Which is why I make certain that doesn't happen.'

Lea didn't need to see his face to know his patience was nearing an end. It was evident in the clipped tone of his voice and the rapid pounding of his heart beneath her ear.

'There may be no logic to my fear. But I am sorely afraid.'

'In all the years of your marriage did Villaire never face an enemy?'

Lea stiffened at the mention of Charles. That cur wouldn't have been able to fend off a kitchenmaid had she been inclined to attack him. 'My father chose him because it was apparent from the beginning that Charles would never bring battle to Montreau.'

He absently stroked her hair. 'Is that your way of saying your dearly departed husband was a coward?'

'More bully than coward.'

'And what is the difference?'

'A bully has no qualms sending in someone else to exact any form of physical revenge.'

Jared's embrace fell away. He pushed her on to her back and stared down at her. 'What are you saying?'

Lea shrugged. 'There are some at Montreau who did not mourn Charles's death. I am sure the scars on their backs, or their now useless limbs, ache a little less from his passing.'

For a moment, Jared said nothing. His frown deepened with each passing heartbeat. Finally, he asked, 'Did you mourn his death?'

'No. But not for the reason you are thinking. He never caused me physical harm—only threatened. I think he feared I would slip into his chamber and gut him in his sleep.'

'Why did you never say anything? Why did you never ask for help? Did you think I would leave you to suffer under that monster's whims?'

Lea glanced away a moment, seeking words that wouldn't start yet another argument. Unable to find them, she caressed his cheek and said, 'I feared you more than I ever feared him.'

Chapter Eighteen

Jared jerked his face away from her touch. 'Perhaps you should fear me more now than you did then.'

But fear wasn't the emotion he wanted from her. Not even when his need for revenge drove him to the brink of insanity did he thirst for her fear.

'You are twisting my words.'

'Am I?' He rested his elbows on the bed. Looming over her, he threaded a hand through her hair. 'You have told a warrior to his face that he can't be trusted to defend or protect himself and his men. You have just admitted that you would rather be the victim of a bullying lout than suffer my presence.'

To know she'd been willing to live with Villaire's constant belittling and bullying rather than ask him for help grated. He'd never witnessed her husband in action, but he doubted if the man behaved any better than Markam.

'You misunderstood—'

If that were true, it was her fault. He tugged on her hair. The light pressure was enough to bring her explanation to an instant halt. 'I don't care what you meant.

I heard what you said. If you wish not to be misunder-stood, perhaps in the future you will choose your words with more care.'

He wearied of all this talking. Jared tugged again on her hair, easing her head to one side, and took advantage of the expanse of pale flesh along her neck. There were more interesting things to do in a bed. The skin was soft beneath his lips. Her pulse raced beneath his tongue.

'I am done with your words,' he whispered against her ear. 'You can be fearful for me, or of me. It doesn't matter. In the morning you will be my wife.'

She said nothing, only sighed softly as he traced his mouth across her collarbone. He paused a breath away from her lips. 'Do you understand me?'

'Yes.' Her breathless response filled the slight distance between them with warmth.

'Our marriage may never be easy. We may never discover love. But, Lea, we do share this.'

When she surrendered to his kiss this time, there was no choked sob, and thankfully no tears. She reached up to wind her arms around him with a throaty moan, and he released his hold on her hair.

Jared knew that years from now, when her greying hair thinned and wrinkles lined her eyes, he would still find her as desirable as he did now. She was a wanton madness in his blood—one he never wished to cure.

He unlaced her gown. Impatient to be rid of the fabric between their bodies, he made quick work of removing her garments and tossing them to the floor.

Between heated kisses, Lea complained, 'That is the only gown I have to be married in tomorrow.'

'I'll find you another.'

He loved the way she shivered when he stroked the side of her neck.

'But that one is mine.'

Her barely perceptible gasps when he discovered a sensitive spot beneath her ear acted like a siren's song to his senses. He longed to lose himself in her passion, wanted her to share the fire rushing through him.

'The marriage isn't one you desire.' He followed the faint, lingering scent of lavender between her breasts. 'What does the gown matter?'

Jared caressed her breast, and teased the pebbled tip, while trying to focus on her concern.

'I wouldn't want all to think you wed a beggar in a torn and filthy gown.'

Her breathless reply deserved a response. He traced a line down her torso with his fingertip, before following with his lips. Her skin was so pale, so soft to his touch.

'You could attend naked. I wouldn't mind.'

Jared rested his cheek against her belly, wondering when, or if, he'd be able to detect his child inside.

'You might not, but I'm sure David would.'

He caressed her hipbones, suddenly wishing she weren't so thin. It was rumoured that women with wider hips had less trouble during childbirth.

'You aren't really listening to me, are you?'

Training five men at once was child's play. Defending himself against four men could make him yawn. But carrying on a conversation while his mind and body were muddled with lust wasn't an easy task to master.

Jared dropped a kiss along one side of her hips, then the other, stopping to give her a heated stare. 'Would you rather we talk?'

'Talk?'

'Obviously I'm doing something wrong.' He slid his hand lower to caress the heat at her core. 'Perhaps a discussion of the weather might be more exciting.'

She arched into his touch. 'Perhaps.'

He nearly growled as he came over her to capture her impertinent mouth beneath his. She instantly hooked her legs over his thighs, inviting—demanding—more than just a commanding kiss. A demand he instantly fulfilled.

It was hard to tell whose groan of satisfaction was louder. And it was near impossible to tell whose desire was hotter, whose lust more desperate as they clung to each other.

Lea tore free of his kiss, frantically pleading, 'Jared, please.'

He shifted his weight, slid his hands beneath her, tilting her tighter against him until she curled her fingernails against his back as she found her release.

His own followed, leaving him satiated and winded. Jared gathered her into his arms, laughing weakly against her hair. 'Now, what were you saying about your gown?'

Lea's chest trembled beneath him. Trying to talk between broken laughter, she asked, 'What gown?'

He rolled off her and retrieved the bedcovers. Lea curled halfway across his chest. 'Maybe this whole marriage concept won't be so bad.'

Jared pulled the covers up to her shoulders, reminding her, 'Unfortunately I won't be in your bed every night.'

'No.' She reached up and covered his mouth with her hand. 'Jared, don't ruin this moment. Just go to sleep and let me pretend.'

He kissed the top of her head and held her until her gentle even breathing let him know she was asleep.

'I wish it could be that simple, Lea.'

Through the fog of sleep, Lea heard something—someone—moving about the chamber. She groaned, throwing off the covers with her eyes still closed. It couldn't be morning already.

'Stay there.' The bed dipped as Jared sat on the edge and put something in her hand. 'Eat this before you sit up.'

She lifted her hand to her face and opened one eye. 'Bread crust?'

'Just eat it.'

When she was done, he suggested, 'Now sit up and drink this.'

She took the cup from him and sniffed. Ginger. Lea shook her head. Why hadn't she thought of that? She sipped the hot infusion that would calm her queasiness. 'Thank you.'

Jared nodded, then rose from the bed, handing her a gown and stockings. 'When you are dressed, David is waiting.'

She studied the brilliant emerald gown. Intricate needlework, interspersed with gemstones, decorated the hem, neck and cuffs. The detailed craftsmanship of the leaves and flowers was beautiful and far more delicate and time-consuming than anything she would ever attempt. 'This isn't mine.'

'Yes, it is.'

'Where did you—?'

He waved off her obvious question. 'It doesn't matter. Rest assured the gown is yours.'

If she didn't fear the motion would make her ill, she would throw herself into his arms. 'It is beautiful, Jared. Thank you.'

He shrugged, looking more than a little sheepish. 'I couldn't have you saying your vows naked. No matter how much I would enjoy the sight.'

Lea smiled. The lout had been listening to her. She blinked back surprised tears. 'Still, it is the most gorgeous gown I have owned. Thank you.'

'Are you crying?'

She laughed at the sudden harshness of his voice, then laughed lightly, hoping to dispel the gloom. 'Doesn't every woman cry on their wedding day?'

'I wouldn't know, would I?'

Lea sucked in her breath at her unthinking question and studied him intently. Something was wrong, that much was evident in his tightly drawn features. 'Jared, I…'

She paused. No. He wasn't truly *angry*. He was a moody, nervous groom on his wedding day. She was fairly certain that standing here doing nothing was only making him more frustrated. 'Tell the king I'll be down directly.'

Jared shook his head. 'No. There is no rush. Take your time.' He pointed towards a tray on the bedside table. 'If there is something else you'd rather have to eat, let me know.'

Lea stared at the over-laden tray. Bread, cheese, fruit, a pottage, meat pie… 'Am I expecting company?'

At her question, Jared's sullen mood appeared to lift. He headed toward the door, laughing. 'No. I wasn't certain what you'd want, so I chose a little of everything that didn't look as if it might make you ill.'

Speechless, Lea stared at him as he bent to pick up

something from the floor and then left the chamber. She turned her attention back to the tray and down at the gown still in her hands.

Never in her entire life had she ever received such attentive care. Not only had he found her the most beautiful gown ever created, he'd brought her morning repast to her in bed. He'd tried—and succeeded—in fending off her morning sickness with food and drink he'd chosen himself.

What had she done to deserve such attentive and kind consideration?

Nothing.

She wasn't going to cry. Lea held her breath. No. She would not cry.

Not for the unexpected kindness he'd shown her this morning, and most definitely not for the things that might have been, or could have been.

Nor would she shed tears for how much she could have loved him.

And, oh, how she could have once loved him.

But now?

Lea stared down at the gown through a watery gaze. Her chest constricted. She greatly feared she was already lost.

'Surely you aren't wearing that to your wedding?'

Jared nodded at Rolfe as his captain entered the chamber. 'Apparently I am.' He pulled an emerald-coloured tunic over his chain maille. 'I didn't think you'd make it.'

'I arrived as soon as I could. It's not like you couldn't have sent word sooner.'

'I sent word as soon as I knew I'd have need of you. Besides, you had plenty of time.'

Rolfe snickered. 'You gave me a day to make a two-day journey.'

'And you whine like an old woman.' Jared glanced over his shoulder. 'Thank you for coming.'

'Nothing could keep me from seeing you finally exchange vows with a woman—especially this one.'

'Bunk. You feared my parents adorning Warehaven's gates with your head if you didn't witness this event.'

Rolfe nodded. 'Well, yes, there is always that.'

He handed Jared his sword belt. 'I suppose you'll go armed, too?'

'That depends. Did you find Montreau's ring and sword?'

Rolfe handed Jared the crested signet ring, then retrieved the sword from the pile he'd dumped near the door. 'Found this buried in the weapons room beneath the keep. Cleaned it. And carried it here like a precious child. As you ordered.'

Ignoring his man, Jared glanced at the sword. The hilt alone, while ornate, made the blade more toy than weapon. Glittering gems fully adorned the guard. The leather and gold thread wrapping the grip would be uncomfortable to grasp for long. It was doubtful that a solid gold ball as the pommel would be of any use as a counterweight.

With unsharpened edges, the ceremonial sword would be useless in self-defence. Jared tested the weight in his hand and shook his head. He was right—the blade end was heavier than the grip.

'The scabbard?'

Rolfe's eyes widened. 'You wanted the scabbard, too?'

'No. I thought I'd carry it down your throat.'

His man rolled his eyes and retrieved the scabbard from the same pile. He handed it to Jared. 'Aren't you in a fine mood this morning?'

'I'm pledging my entire future to a woman who fears war and warriors. What sort of mood should I have?'

'So you choose to attend the ceremony wearing—full armour?' Rolfe scratched his head. 'You sure you don't want to reconsider?'

Jared threaded the belt through the scabbard before securing the wide leather low on his hips. 'No. She needs to get used to the accoutrements of war.'

'So you'll train her like you would one of the pages.'

When put in those terms, the idea suddenly seemed rather…crass. 'I tried talking. That didn't work. Lea isn't going to have her mind changed with words.'

'You'll frighten the poor little thing half to death.'

'She needs to get used to being afraid, otherwise she'll never work out how to come to terms with the fear. Besides, she isn't a *poor little thing*. She's just irrational when it comes to anything connected to battle.'

'I would think—'

Jared cursed. 'It doesn't matter what you think. I don't have time to ease her into this. There's no way to know when Matilda will call us away. Should I leave my wife witless with fear while I attend to my duty?'

'With no family to bolster her, she's going to be witless with fear the first few times no matter what you do.'

'Then what the hell do you suggest I do?' Jared resisted the urge to throw up his hands in frustration. 'Either you help me in this, or you can stay with her the first few times.'

Rolfe reached for the mailled coif he'd removed upon entering the chamber. 'I think spurs would be a nice addition. They'll clink against the stone floor of the chapel with a memorable echo.'

Jared tapped his heel against the floor. 'Already thought of that.'

Lea paced outside David's private chapel. As much as she wished not to go through with this marriage, Jared had been right—what other choice did she have?

None whatsoever.

She'd gone over all the possible things that could, and probably would, happen to him in her mind more times than she could remember. Not one of the scenarios ended with them growing old together.

All of them ended with their child becoming father-less before she, or he, reached adulthood.

And she was supposed to live with this fear, day in and day out?

How?

The only way she could think of was to first make sure Montreau didn't get dragged into Matilda and Stephen's war because of this marriage. And then somehow ensure Jared remained at Montreau.

But Lea knew the likelihood of that happening was slim at best. Jared had said himself that he'd not been raised to oversee the land. He'd been raised and trained for battle. How much time would pass before he grew bored at Montreau?

Their days together could be few. She knew the choices before her. She could willingly give him her heart, knowing that some day soon it would be shredded beyond repair by his death. Or she could hold on to her heart, set aside the chance for love and not risk the pain this marriage would surely bring.

Neither option appealed to her.

But she had to choose one.

'Lady Lea, they are coming.'

Startled, Lea stared at Agatha. 'Who?'

The older woman rolled her eyes toward the ceiling. 'And where has your mind gone? The men are coming.'

'Oh.' Of course they were. Jared wanted this ceremony over and done with as quickly as possible.

'Are you ready?'

'Not that it matters, but, no.'

Agatha fussed over Lea's hair, readjusting the green ribbons through the braids. At the sound of voices coming from inside the chapel, she peered through the doorway. 'People are gathering.'

'This was supposed to be private.' It wasn't as if they were going to make a grand show of exchanging their vows.

'You didn't think King David was going to permit you to skip the blessing of this union, did you?'

The church's blessing was not required, but Lea knew that David's close relationship with the church would make it mandatory in his keep. So she shouldn't have been surprised that he'd sent for his priest and ensured the chapel would be filled with witnesses.

What had been surprising, however, was when he didn't put up more of a fuss when she and Jared had signed the nuptial document a short time ago in David's chambers.

Jared had scrawled his name to the brief document

without so much as reading a word. She, on the other hand, had made a point to read and reread each line before adding her signature and the Montreau seal below his.

It was odd to be the one agreeing to this union. Her father had taken care of all the details when she'd wed Charles.

While that had been a long, drawn-out process with days of haggling and more haggling, the agreement between her and Jared had been simple.

Since she had no need to essentially purchase a groom, the dowry was waved. In return, Jared had no need to pay for taking her virginity, so the bride price was also set aside.

He would retain possession of Warehaven and she of Montreau.

In truth, Lea was rather surprised Jared had consented to such an unorthodox agreement. But he had, saying only that it made little difference to him if they exchanged gold or property in writing when in reality nothing would change—they would both still be responsible for Montreau and Warehaven.

She knew her father would have balked. And even though King David urged her to think carefully of her future, she agreed with Jared. What difference would it make?

Thankfully neither property was entailed to a ruler, so she and Jared had the right to settle as they pleased.

Of course, a sizeable contribution would need to be given to the church for this hasty blessing. She left that decision in Jared's hands.

The jingle of chain maille caught her attention. Lea frowned. Had David ordered troops to this ceremony?

If so, why? It wasn't as if she intended to run away again. She'd tried that before with little success.

And Jared certainly wasn't going to change his mind at the last minute. He'd made that perfectly clear. Besides, he now considered the child his responsibility. He would never dishonour himself by turning his back on his duty.

Nor had there been enough time for anyone to discover their pending vows and take offence. The only person who might protest their union was Villaire. And he wouldn't have had the courage to come to King David's court prepared to fight.

Men's voices drifted down the corridor leading to the chapel. She turned to see who was coming to this ceremony prepared for battle.

When three men in full armour rounded the corner, Lea's breath caught. She heard Agatha's whoosh of breathy approval.

While, yes, Jared, King David, and Rolfe created a feast for the eyes, this was her wedding, not a mêlée. What did he think he was doing?

She directed her glare towards Jared, prepared to demand an explanation. But his hard, dark stare from behind his nasal helm seemed to dare her to complain.

An unspoken threat glinted from his gaze, effectively chasing away her chastisement. He stopped before her, took her hands in his and graced her with a seductive half-smile.

Lea's heart somersaulted. A sudden shocking warmth low in her belly sent a heated flush of longing and embarrassment to her cheeks.

She was marrying a lout.

One who obviously knew he could so easily take her breath away with nothing more than a look.

She smiled weakly at her loss of coherent thought. 'You did this on purpose.'

Jared only nodded.

Lea looked down and caught sight of her grandsire's sword hanging from Jared's belt. She closed her eyes, knowing that every time in the future when she thought of their wedding she would see a man dressed for battle.

Oh, yes, he'd most certainly done this on purpose. Nothing else would have emphasised the fact she was about to willingly swear an oath vowing to take this man—this warrior—as her husband.

Her future complaints and fears would be useless. There would be no doubting that she'd known exactly who and what she'd sworn to accept.

Lea scraped her teeth across her lower lip. Then, squaring her shoulders, she took a breath before returning her gaze to his. 'Jared…'

He backed her away from the small gathering at the chapel door. 'You left me little choice, Lea.' His voice was soft and steady.

She stared down at their hands, unable to think of what she'd wanted to say.

Jared slid the edge of his hand beneath her chin, forcing her to look back up at him. 'Lea of Montreau, I will not force you. Will you wed me? Will you accept who and what I am?'

'I…' Why did her voice tremble? Why did her chest constrict at the mere thought of saying no?

He remained silent, waiting for her to decide.

The simple act of finally giving her the right to decide

chased away her will to decline his offer. Their days together wouldn't be easy. But the nights she didn't spend alone, shaking with abject fear, would be pure bliss.

Lea sighed. 'You'll pay for this one day, Warehaven.'

She was fairly certain her low, seductive tone of voice wiped away any hint of threat.

Jared cupped her cheek and smiled. 'I will count the hours until then.'

A collective sigh from behind Jared's back made Lea laugh. Had the king, Rolfe and Agatha been holding their breath, waiting for her to say no?

She brushed her cheek against his palm. 'Could you do one thing for me?'

'That depends.'

'When I'm old and feeble I would like to think back on this day and remember a face, not some warrior demon seeking to haunt my dreams. Could you at least remove your helmet?'

He stepped back and for a long moment she feared he would say no. To her relief, he unlaced his helmet and beckoned Rolfe forwards to assist him with the coif.

Once the armour was removed, the heat returned to her belly and cheeks. Just looking at him made her shiver with need. She would never voice it aloud—his self-worth was large enough as it was—but she was marrying a very fine specimen of a man.

Lea reached up to brush her fingers through his hair before slowly lowering herself to one knee before him. 'Yes, I will exchange my vows with you willingly, Jared of Warehaven.'

Chapter Nineteen

Jared knew his concerns that she'd not uphold the honour of Montreau and Warehaven had been unjustified. It was a lack of faith that he'd make certain to amend…later.

He assisted her to her feet, tucked her hand into the crook of his arm and led her back to the chapel door.

Still outside of the chapel, with their chosen witnesses—David, Rolfe and Agatha—behind them, they stopped before the priest.

'Do you both come willing to this blessing?'

Lea's voice mingled with his as they gave their affirmative answers.

The priest stepped back, leaving the two of them to attend to the man-made part of this ceremony.

Jared took a steadying breath. To his amazement his hands trembled like those of an old man. Lea smiled, obviously aware of his unusual reaction, and placed her hand on his chest.

The slight touch, her gentle smile, calmed his riotous pulse, giving him the power to speak without embarrassing himself.

They'd never exchanged official vows of the future, so he said, 'I, Jared of Warehaven, do so swear to receive you as mine, so that you become my wife and I your husband.'

To his relief, his words were steady.

Lea lowered her hand and stared up at him. 'I, Lea of Montreau, do so swear to receive you as mine, so that you become my husband and I your wife.'

The priest asked, 'Are there any known impediments to this union?'

King David and Rolfe answered in unison, 'Nay.' The strength of their reply would have given anyone with an objection pause.

When the priest nodded, Jared recited the vow he'd thought never to speak to her. 'I, Jared, take thee, Lea, to my wedded wife, to have and to hold from this day forward, for better, for worse, for richer, for poorer, in sickness and in health 'til death do us part. Thereto I plight thee my troth.'

Softly, with a suspicious shimmer in her eyes, Lea repeated, 'I, Lea, take thee, Jared, to my wedded husband, to have and to hold from this day forward, for better, for worse, for richer, for poorer, in sickness and in health 'til death do us part. Thereto I plight thee my troth.'

King David and Rolfe each handed a ring to the priest, who blessed the tokens before giving them to him and Lea.

Jared slipped his family signet ring on her shaking finger. 'With this ring I thee wed.'

Lea turned her father's signet ring over on her palm before sliding it on to Jared's finger, vowing, 'With this ring I thee wed.'

They faced the priest, who with raised arms led the

party to the chapel's altar where they knelt to receive the church's blessing on their union.

Once the blessing was given, Jared rose and swept Lea up into his arms. She gave her lips to him willingly, as greedy as he for a taste of passion.

Those gathered in the chapel noisily shouted their approval. King David granted them a few moments before he loudly cleared his throat, reminding them that they stood before a holy altar.

Jared reluctantly released her from his embrace and took her hand. He kissed her fingers, asking, 'Will you be upset if this celebration David has arranged for us is cut short?'

'Why?'

He glanced at the altar, and then led her from the chapel before explaining in a whisper so only she could hear. 'When we share our first bed as man and wife, I want it to be our bed.'

Lea's eyes widened briefly as her cheeks flamed. 'We could leave now.'

Jared laughed, asking, 'Do you think perhaps we could at least eat before taking to the road?'

Lea sighed, then turned her lips into a pout. 'I suppose so.'

Knowing full well that this light-hearted mood of hers would last only until the first time he had to draw a sword, or someone foolishly mentioned war, Jared played along.

'On the other hand, I'm not at all certain I want to wait until we reach Montreau.' He nodded toward a dark corner, then lowered his lips to her ear. 'We could always hide away for a few moments.'

David walked past them, commenting, 'There are chambers a-plenty above stairs.'

Lea stroked the line of his jaw. 'They wouldn't even miss us.'

As delightful as that sounded, Jared shook his head. 'I was serious about our marriage bed. I want to return to Montreau.' He paused to tease her tongue with his own, then growled low against her lips, 'Quickly.'

She sighed and leaned against his chest. 'Then I need to pack and change my gown.'

He pulled her into his embrace, brushing his cheek across the top of her head. 'Right after we eat.'

Lea stroked the needlework on the edge of his tunic. 'I like the way you dressed nearly the same as I.'

'Well, not completely.'

'True. But then I did leave my chain maille back at Montreau.'

He chuckled. 'Now there's a vision.'

'Perhaps, but I could never be as beautiful as you are in armour.'

'Beautiful?'

'Oh, yes, you are a beauteous sight to behold today.'

'I'm sure that's what every big strong man wants to hear—that his wife thinks he's beautiful.'

He felt her laughter against his chest. He remembered other times when she had laughed against him in just this way. He wished he could somehow hold this moment for ever.

'So, you think you are a big strong man?'

'No, Lea, I know I am.' He lifted her from the floor and held her against the wall.

Lea threaded her fingers through his hair and feathered light kisses across his mouth and cheeks. 'Thank God for that. But you need to put me down.'

'Oh?' He nuzzled the side of her neck. 'Why is that?'

'Because, Jared, I want you so badly it's all I can do not to wrap my legs around your waist and beg you to take me here and now.'

He ceased his teasing to stare at her. The flash of fire in her lidded gaze and flushed cheeks let him know that her brazen talk wasn't in jest.

The mental image of them naked like this, against a wall, with her legs wrapped tightly around his waist, while she begged him to take her, sent a rush of blood to his groin.

Jared swallowed. 'How fast can you eat?'

She dropped her forehead to his shoulder. 'Since I don't hunger for food, it will take me no time at all.'

He stepped away from the wall still holding her, then lowered her slowly to her feet. 'I'll take that as your word.'

At her nod, he led her quickly toward the celebration in the Great Hall.

Seated between Jared and Rolfe, Lea picked at the food before her. She pushed it around idly as her attention kept drifting back to the man seated next to her.

When had she forgotten how devastating his deep voice was to her senses? Or how just a piercing glance from his green eyes made her weak with desire?

Back when she'd first wed Charles and he'd rejected her so thoroughly, she used to wonder if her memories of Jared had remained true. He'd become her fantasy then, her dream. When she had lain in bed at night, alone and lonely, she'd wrap herself in memories of him.

After a while she'd begun to wonder if, in her loneliness, her mind had somehow enhanced her memories, making them appear more than what they'd been in real life.

Lea sighed. No. If anything, time had served to lessen…weaken…the effect Jared had on her.

In her mind's eye, she hadn't become inflamed with lust until after he'd kissed her, or after he'd stroked her flesh.

In reality, it took nothing more than the sound of his voice, the scent of his rosemary soap, or just simply the thought of him, to send her soaring with need.

What would happen now that they were wed? Would he still find her as desirable when they no longer had to steal precious moments for each other? Would the thought of bedding her be as exciting once they'd shared a bed night after night?

And what about her? Would his kisses still make her heart race when they became something she expected? Would the sight of him naked over her, trailing sensuous touches down her body, make the earth beneath her spin madly out of control?

'Where have your thoughts flown, Lea?'

She realised he'd asked her a question, but wasn't certain what. She turned to look up at him. 'Hmm?'

Jared slid his hand behind her neck. His palm was warm against her skin. His stroking touch beneath her ear set tremors to ripple down her back.

'Your flush gives you away.' He leaned closer. 'And that smouldering stare should be reserved strictly for a bedchamber.'

She blinked, trying to free herself from the haze of desire swirling round her. But his breath against her cheek and the rumble of his voice did little to help clear her mind. 'What?'

He trailed a fingertip along her cheek. 'I'm almost afraid to ask what you were thinking about.'

'Now that we don't have to sneak around any more, will you still want me in your bed?'

Rolfe choked. Jared stared at his man, daring him to say a word. But the man was too intent on swallowing enough wine and water to dislodge the food caught in his throat.

Lea's cheeks reddened more, but this time with embarrassment. She placed her hand on his forearm. 'I'm sorry, that wasn't a very dignified question for a lady to ask in public.'

He covered her hand. 'My fault entirely. You only answered my question.'

When she turned her head to stare down at their food, he drew her back with a finger on her chin. 'Does this have anything to do with Charles?' He'd heard the rumours and wanted them out of their life now.

She shrugged before admitting, 'In a way, yes.'

'Lea, I can't promise you many things, but I can ease your concerns on this.' He leaned a little closer, not wanting anyone else to overhear. 'Charles of Villaire was an ass.'

'I don't disagree.'

Jared placed a brief kiss against the corner of her mouth. 'But I am grateful to him.'

She leaned back to stare at him as if he'd lost the ability to reason, before leaning closer once again. 'Grateful? For what?'

'For leaving what was mine, to me.'

Her blush returned, as she realised what he'd meant.

'And in answer to your question—I will never be able to get enough of you.'

A seductive smile curved her lips. 'Or I, you.'

The desire and lust that had been roiling in his gut jumped to life. Jared rose with his goblet of wine in his hand and faced King David. 'I want to thank you for your assistance and hospitality. But I fear we need to make ready to leave for Montreau.'

While others at the table snickered and laughed, obviously guessing at what the newlyweds had in mind, King David smiled. 'I was honoured to be of help. Increasing our family is never a bad thing. I wish you well.'

The king motioned one of his men forwards, asking Jared, 'How many guards do you require?'

Had he been travelling back to Montreau alone, he'd have turned down David's offer. But he wanted as much protection for his wife and child as possible.

'Four will do.'

'Six will do better.'

'Thank you.' Jared dipped his head. 'By your leave, my lord.'

Once David waved him away, Jared assisted Lea to her feet. Knowing what they planned, it was all he could do not to drag her across the Great Hall towards the stairs.

Lea ignored the ribald laughter and comments as she and Jared raced up the stairs hand in hand.

One man, she wasn't certain who, offered to come to witness the bedding.

Over his shoulder Jared shouted, 'Feel free to try. I am armed.'

He kicked open the partly ajar door to her chamber. Agatha jumped, screaming at the abrupt intrusion.

'Get out.' Jared pointed at the door.

Agatha swung her wide-eyed stare to Lea.

'It's all right, Agatha. Please, leave us.'

The older woman shook her head. 'And the two of you can't wait?'

Jared was already pulling his tunic over his head. 'Out.'

The instant the door shut behind the woman, he dropped the bars across the top and bottom. If anyone thought to witness this bedding they'd have to have an army to break down the thick, solid door.

'Sit.' Lea pushed Jared down on to a bench and knelt to unlace his chausses. While she made quick work of the leather lacings holding the mailled leg coverings in place, he tugged and freed the laces of her gown.

He grasped the hem of her gown as she rose and pulled it over her head. He folded the garment and placed it on a nearby chest. Lea laid the chausses out across the bed, then returned to the bench. 'Lean forwards.'

While she'd done this often enough for visitors to her father's keep, she didn't remember her hands shaking, or her heart pounding so hard in her chest. Their short meal had given her mind enough time to make her anticipation nearly unbearable.

Jared rose slightly and pulled his hauberk from beneath him before leaning forwards. Lea lifted the shoulders of the protective maille and tugged hard, pulling it over his head and outstretched arms.

She hadn't expected the weight of the armour and staggered toward the bed to drop it on the mattress. By the time she finished straightening it out and turned back to Jared, he was naked.

Her breath caught. Oh, yes, a very, very fine specimen.

With a feral gleam in his eyes he came towards her, stalking her slowly, like a beast stalks its prey.

He wanted to play? Lea laughed and raced around to the other side of the bed. She paused to prop one foot up on the mattress and casually unroll her stocking. 'I'm not ready yet. You'll have to wait.'

Before he could capture her, she ran to the other side of the room, dragging a table between them.

To her shock, he barely swatted at the table, yet it crashed against the wall, splintering into firewood.

The surprise kept her immobile just long enough for Jared to grab her and pull her against him. 'I'm done waiting.' He jerked her chemise over her head and tossed it to the floor.

She trailed the tip of her tongue down his chest before asking, 'Am I supposed to be afraid of you?'

'You should be just for calling me beautiful.'

Lea boldly ran her palm down his stomach, then more slowly over the length of his erection. 'Ah, but you are beautiful.'

Holding his shimmering stare, she slowly eased down his body, letting her lips trail the path she'd blazed with her hand.

He blinked as if awakening from a dream and grabbed her beneath her arms to drag her back to her feet. 'No.'

Lea wound her arms around his neck; burying her face against his shoulder, she said, 'Jared, don't make me wait.'

Without further urging, he lifted her in his arms, swung around and backed her against the wall.

'What were you saying earlier?'

His question brushed against her ear, sending shivers

down the length of her spine. Knowing what he expected, she wrapped her legs tightly around his waist.

His touch along the backs of her legs made her gasp with surprise at the way her body quivered in response to such a slow, gentle stroke.

But when he captured her lips beneath his, there was nothing gentle about his kiss. The desire for more than a touch, more than a kiss, drew a moan from her throat.

Lea felt him smile slightly against her mouth and knew he wasn't yet ready to ease her frustration. Instead, he moved his hips just enough to tease, silently promising to fulfil her needs, then drawing back, leaving her wanting more.

She relaxed her legs, hoping to slide down enough to take what she wanted. But Jared's strong hands beneath her held her firmly in place.

He moved again, this time barely stroking her heat with the tips of his fingers.

As her heart seemed to slam against the inside of her chest, she realised then what he wanted from her. She'd made a promise and he was obviously not going to let her take it back.

Lea turned her head, breaking their kiss. She buried her face against his neck, oddly embarrassed, but needing him desperately. 'Jared, please. I beg you, take—'

Before she could finish her sentence, he answered her plea.

Fulfilment at his driving pace came quickly, leaving her breathless and limp against his chest. While long heated nights on a bed were heavenly, and stolen kisses in a darkened alcove were thrilling, this was…was so sinfully, breathtakingly wonderful.

Jared's ragged groan drew a shaky, but completely understanding laugh from her. He staggered a few steps to the bench and sat down, holding her on his lap.

She wiped the sweat from his forehead and dragged her fingers through his damp hair. 'Are you certain you wish to leave today? We could wait until morning.'

'No.' He shook his head. 'We can be halfway to Montreau before the sun sets tonight and at the keep before the noon meal tomorrow.'

He tightened his embrace, hugging her tightly to his chest and added, 'And in our bed tomorrow night.'

Chapter Twenty

Jared glanced back at the women riding in the middle of a ring of guards. Agatha's downcast expression made her displeasure with travelling known.

But Lea's excitement at being on the road heading for Montreau was obvious. She chatted lightly with the men, all the while paying close attention to their surroundings.

She was like a youngster on her first outing. Everything seemed new to her, from the birds or clouds overhead to the plants lining the road.

But every now and then she'd grow quiet and he'd feel her stare burn hot against his back. He'd made the mistake of turning to look at her once.

The direction of her thoughts had been more than obvious in her liquid gaze and the sensual tilt of her lips. He quickly learned that riding a horse, in full armour, while his blood pounded through his body wasn't the most comfortable thing he'd ever done.

Thankfully distracting himself proved easy. Even though ten men—counting himself, the two guards he'd brought with him, Rolfe, and the six men David had lent him—guarded Lea on this journey, Jared knew better than to let down his guard.

No matter where one travelled, the roads weren't safe. With Stephen and Matilda pitting the majority of their troops against each other, security on the byways was slim. The time was ripe for an enterprising knave to seek his fortune from attacking others.

More times than not, Jared had run across unfortunate travellers who'd been robbed of not just their possessions, but their very lives.

To ensure their safety on this relatively short trip, he'd sent two men ahead to make certain the way was clear of danger and two other men followed behind in case any thought to attack from the rear.

He, Rolfe and the remaining four men formed a ring of arms and armour around the women.

To his relief, Lea hadn't voiced a complaint, or concern about the weapons or men protecting her. He'd half-expected her to make some inane comment about the safety of the men. Perhaps the show of strength had unknowingly made her feel secure enough not to worry, although he wouldn't stake his life on it.

It didn't matter. He wasn't about to question her, because he knew that her reaction would be much different when Matilda called him back to service.

The sound of a horse's hooves pounding the dirt-packed road ahead alerted him to possible danger. Jared raised his hand, signalling the others to stop, and brought his own mount to a halt.

Swords hissed from scabbards, sounding eerily like a nest of vipers. Rolfe ordered the men to tighten the circle around the women.

'Jared, what's wrong?' Lea's voice shook.

Not knowing what was ahead, he didn't have the time or the necessary information to ease her fears.

'My lord!' One of David's men headed towards them at a breakneck pace, his shield dangling uselessly at his side. 'Surrounded! We're sur—'

The shouted ended abruptly on a strangled choke. He fell from his horse, an arrow lodged in his neck.

Agatha's scream startled the horses. Jared cursed the man's carelessness and death in one breath, as he fought to bring the animal beneath him under control while swinging his shield free of his shoulder.

He joined the circle around Lea and her maid, lifting his shield before him to provide an additional ring of safety, then gave what he hoped would prove an unnecessary order, 'Protect the women.'

Without having to look, he knew that Rolfe had fallen into position facing the road behind them. His man would always be at his back.

Lea touched his shoulder. Before she could say anything, he shrugged her hand off of him. He knew she was afraid, but he also knew that he'd do her no favour if he treated her gently now. It would only increase her anxiety. And he had not the time, nor the desire, to be distracted by her fear.

She'd be better served with anger, no matter where it was directed. Her anger could be soothed later. But her fear now could get them all killed.

Without turning his head, he nearly growled at her, 'Do as I say and keep quiet.'

She said nothing, but he heard the movement of her horse as she moved back alongside Agatha.

Six men charged toward them from ahead, just as Rolfe called out, 'Six at the rear.'

A quick glance to his left, then to the right, assured him that for now, there were no others.

Twelve against six of his own men wouldn't be bad enough odds to make him wonder about the outcome. But three of the men in his circle were from David's force. They were men he didn't know. Nor did he know if the two men he'd sent to guard the rear of their party were alive or dead.

The two enemy groups stopped within hailing distance. The set of men ahead of him parted, letting another rider come through to approach.

The man coming closer was either completely void of wit, or foolishly certain of his safety. He wore no armour, nor did he carry a weapon.

When he was near enough to identify, Lea hissed. Jared shook his head. 'What is the meaning of this, Villaire?'

'Send the woman out to me and no one else will be harmed.'

The cur was brazenly arrogant when backed by a dozen armed men. Didn't he realise he was close enough for Jared to throw a dagger straight into his heart? If it wasn't for Lea and Agatha, he would have already done so.

'No. I will not send my wife out to you.'

'Your wife?' Villaire laughed. 'Not likely.' He reached inside his cloak to retrieve a scroll and waved it in the air. 'She is my ward. I gave her no permission to wed anyone, most especially you.'

Jared knew the answer, but wanted it spoken aloud. 'By whose authority are you her guardian?'

'King Stephen's.'

'Montreau doesn't answer to a usurper of the throne.'

Lea's gasp was audible. Jared didn't turn to look at her, but he spoke low enough so Villaire wouldn't hear. 'You either do this my way, or feel free to join him.'

'But—'

Villaire shouted, 'Stephen is the true king!'

'Choose right now, Lea. Matilda or Stephen.' Jared added more harshness to his voice, trying to convey the seriousness of their situation.

For a long moment, she said nothing. Finally, she whispered brokenly, 'Warehaven.'

Her answer took him by surprise. She would go where he chose?

He turned his full attention back to Villaire. 'Stephen is naught but a liar and a thief.'

'He is our king!'

Jared countered, 'I and every other noble swore allegiance to Henry's daughter.'

"No God-fearing man would follow a woman—especially that one.'

Weary of sparring with words he'd heard countless times from countless dishonourable cowards in the past, Jared pointed his sword at Villaire. He twisted his wrist slightly, letting the sunlight shimmer off the double-edged blade.

'Stand aside, or find a sword, Villaire.'

Jared grimaced at Villaire's high-pitched laugh. 'You are outnumbered, Warehaven. Give me the woman, or die.'

From behind him, Lea pleaded, 'Too many men have already died for my safety. I am not worth the loss of more. Just let me go.'

He'd been expecting her to issue some witless comment sooner or later. 'You are my wife. You will go nowhere.'

When she made a move to push her horse past him, Jared ordered, 'Hold that beast or I'll tie it to my saddle. You aren't going anywhere.'

'He isn't going to harm me, just humiliate me.'

'And wed you to another.'

'He wants control of Montreau too much for him to wed me to someone who will take away his lordship of the keep.'

'You are going nowhere.'

Lea sighed. 'I'll not risk your life. Let me go.'

Her imitation of a long-suffering sigh had angered him. But her words enraged him.

She didn't think him capable of claiming victory in this skirmish? What sort of man did she think she'd wed?

A coward?

An inexperienced fool?

Some weak, fearful man who would hide behind the skirts of her gown?

She didn't trust him to keep her and their unborn baby safe?

When he heard her horse's hooves move once again, Jared turned his horse sideways in front of her, blocking her path. 'I said no.'

'Jared…'

He flinched as something sharp laced his arm.

Lea's words choked in her throat at the sight of an arrow protruding from Jared's arm.

She opened her mouth to scream, only to seal her lips closed at his blazing glare. He jerked the arrow from his arm and tossed it to the ground. 'Stay behind me.'

She nodded, barely recognising his hard, unforgiving voice.

He turned to face the approaching men while ordering, 'Take the archer.'

Before Villaire's force came more than two or three steps closer, Rolfe had dispatched the archer with his own arrows sent flying into the man's throat. Lea turned her head away from the gruesome sight.

But found one more fearful. Another group of men came at them from the rear.

Both groups of men were upon them before she could scream. Certain this would be the day she died, Lea made herself as small as possible on the saddle, tucking her head and shoulders down towards the horse's neck and waited, with eyes closed, for her untimely death.

Not seeing the battle did nothing to shield her from the sounds.

The clang of sword meeting sword sent shivers down her back. She cringed at the shouts of pain and anger coming from the men. And when the thud of a body hit the ground it was all she could do not to cry out.

Dear Lord, she wasn't ready to die. Not yet. Lea covered her stomach with one hand. Did her child not deserve a chance to live?

Jared cursed, making her fear he'd been injured yet again. Lea gasped at the pain lacing her chest and throat. She leaned forwards over the low, hard pommel of the saddle to bury her face in the horse's mane and hung on tightly.

Her horse skittered back and forth, bumped in all directions from the horses and men surrounding her. Through the din of battle she caught the sound of Agatha's cries.

The older woman's fear fed her own. Like some oddly contagious disease, each of Agatha's wails sent Lea's heart to pound harder as a cold, sick dread filled her veins, making her limbs near useless.

She couldn't think. All of the sounds bled into each other, until one horrific buzz filled her mind with terror, chasing away any rational thought.

Lea gasped, fighting to withstand this overwhelming sense of defeat threatening to consume her.

She teetered on the brink of surrender when as suddenly as it'd begun the buzzing ceased.

Horses pawed the ground, snorting. And while the shouts of men still rushed around her, they weren't as angry, or desperate.

Lea straightened slightly and cautiously opened her eyes. The battle appeared to be over. She took a breath, fortifying herself to face Villaire, and sat up.

Except the angry visage trained on her wasn't Villaire's. The pinpoint pupils and sneering lip beneath the nasal helm didn't belong to Villaire.

Relief nearly knocked her from her horse. 'Jared,' she whispered his name.

His eyes narrowed with an anger directed at her. He said nothing before spinning his horse around to issue orders to the men.

Needing to know, she asked, 'Villaire?'

Jared pointed towards an obviously lifeless body without stopping and without comment.

Lea swallowed hard. The sick feeling in the pit of her stomach didn't come from the babe inside.

Never had she seen him this angry. Never had he appeared so cold and remote. Even his manner towards his men seemed distant. He barked orders to gather the dead and see to the wounded.

His men didn't appear concerned. Perhaps this was nothing more than his usual manner after a battle.

Certain that was the case and noticing that Jared ignored his own wound from the arrow, Lea urged her horse forwards to his side. When she reached out to check his injured arm, he swung away, asking, 'What are you doing?'

'You were hurt, I only thought to—'

'It's nothing but a scratch.'

'And could be your death if it gets infected.'

'It will wait.'

Lea lowered her arm and stared at the ground.

'Damn it, Lea. Don't.'

His tone, his expression, his obvious lack of concern for his own well-being, not to mention hers, sent a new type of tremor down her spine.

'What?' It was all she could do not to scream at him. She'd not given herself over to Villaire. She'd swallowed her fear the best she could while weapons clashed all around her.

And even though she wanted to run, to hide from the sounds of death, hadn't she done as he'd ordered and stayed behind him?

Then she'd offered help, only to have it turned away. And now he was snarling at her like some rabid dog.

'I'm not doing anything.' Her own anger built. She tossed the reins of her horse at him and dismounted. He might not need her help, but from the looks of things, others did. Besides, staying busy was always the best distraction against fear or worry.

'Get back on this horse.'

'Go to hell, Warehaven.' She'd had enough of him this day. He'd ordered that the wounded be attended and that's what she was going to do whether he liked it or not.

'Lea, I'm warning you.'

She ignored the darkly sinister undercurrent in his voice and looked instead at Agatha. She told her maid, 'Have his *lordship* get me some water and yarrow.'

Lea headed to Rolfe. Jared's man held his arm as he directed the men. She stopped next to him. 'Sit down.'

He looked down at her as if she were some three-headed beast, before he glanced toward Jared.

'I said sit down, Sir Rolfe. You are bleeding.'

When he made no move to do as she'd requested, Lea spun around with her hands on her hips to address Jared. 'I am the Lady of Montreau and Warehaven. Tell them to obey me.'

Even though his expression didn't change, he nodded at Rolfe. 'She is your lady.'

Rolfe sat on the ground and permitted her, with Agatha's help, to remove his helmet, coif and hauberk. The older woman staggered under the weight before finally just dropping it in a pile alongside the man.

Jared's captain grimaced at the hasty treatment of his armour, but said nothing as Agatha left to see if any of the other men required their care.

Lea ripped the bloody sleeve of Rolfe's shirt and shook her head at the gash on his arm. 'You'll live, but it appears your maille isn't as impervious to penetration as your lord claims.'

Rolfe just grunted, sitting stoically as she poked and

prodded at the injury. 'I don't suppose needle and thread are available?'

A pouch landed at her feet. 'In there.'

Lea watched Jared ride away before commenting, 'He must be a joy to follow into battle day after day.'

'We live.'

Determined to keep him talking while she knit the edges of his wound together, she said, 'Yes, I can tell by your scars that you live.'

'I don't need to be pretty.'

Actually, Rolfe was an attractive man, not as ruggedly handsome as her husband, of course, but she didn't know him well enough to tell him that. Instead, she teased, 'No, I can see where being *pretty* might lead to trouble.'

Jared's man blushed from his neck to the tips of his ears. But he said nothing.

'I need your knife, Sir Rolfe.'

She used the weapon to cut the thread. 'Jared may very well keep you alive, but there is no need for him to act so surly about it afterwards.'

'Would you rather he celebrated the deaths we cause?'

Lea frowned. She hadn't thought of it like that before. 'No. I wouldn't.' She cut a slash into her chemise and tore off a strip to wrap around his arm. Knowing how her father and brother used to ignore their injuries, she suggested, 'Try not to tear the stitches too soon.'

She handed him back his knife and reached for his hauberk.

He snatched it from her grasp. 'I can get that, my lady. Thank you.'

Lea rose and turned to stare at Jared. He'd ridden

ahead just a little ways, stopping at a small copse of trees to dismount. With his back against the trunk of the largest tree, he watched her.

Something in the intensity of his stance, the tilt of his head, sent a wave of desire washing over her. She flushed, wishing they were alone and not out in the open surrounded by men.

Without taking her gaze from Jared's, she called out to Agatha, 'Do you need help?'

'No, my lady, these are nothing more than a few scratches and bruises.'

'Call out if you need me.'

Lea slowly headed towards her husband. She wanted to see his expression. Did his eyes blaze with rage or hunger? Were his lips hiked into a sneer or tipped into the seductive half-smile that set her heart to racing?

She wanted to stroke his face, to feel his lips brush against her palm before he dipped his head to steal a kiss.

And she wanted to feel his arms around her, holding her tight against his chest. The strong, steady beat of his heart pounding against hers would assure her they were indeed safe for now.

Halfway across the distance his eyes widened. The sound of pounding hooves drawing closer pulled her out of the fog of desire.

'Lea!'

She turned to see who rode down on her, only to be swept from her feet to land face down across a hard, un-yielding saddle.

Jared threw himself on to his horse and raced after the brigand who'd just captured his wife.

What had coaxed him to let down his guard in such

a manner? Yes, Villaire was dead, but that didn't mean all danger to Lea had passed. Blackstone still lived.

Certain that's who had taken his wife, he cursed.

Rolfe quickly caught up to him. 'I should have been paying closer attention.'

'We both should have.'

He couldn't very well blame his man for something he should have seen to himself.

The man ahead of them veered off toward the east, wringing another round of curses from Jared. 'He's headed toward York.'

Jared urged his horse to pick up the pace. He couldn't let the man take his wife into enemy territory. He wouldn't be there to stop York from marrying her off to someone else just for his own amusement.

The man would do anything to thumb his nose at the church and Matilda. Having the means to do both at once would be far too tempting a treat for the earl to ignore.

Once within shouting distance, Jared yelled, 'Halt!'

The kidnapper only leaned lower over Lea and put his spurs to the horse.

Rolfe pulled his dagger free and took aim.

'No!' Jared stopped him. 'If he drops Lea, she could be trampled beneath the horse.'

Somehow he had to get the man to stop, then wrest his wife free. At this moment, anything was worth trying.

Knowing the kidnapper's main goal was to get possession of Lea's keep, Jared shouted, 'I will raze Montreau and torch the land.'

It was only an assumption, but he doubted if Blackstone was any more ambitious than Villaire when it came to physical labour. And there was little that was more labour intensive, not to mention expensive, than rebuilding a keep.

To his relief, the threat served to slow the man. Jared kept advancing as he added, 'There is no income without the land.'

He had no idea how true that was any more. Once, Montreau's lands reaped great profit from sheep, crops and fishing. That was what had brought Lea's father to Warehaven in the first place—he'd wanted transportation for his wool.

But with Charles Villaire in command for all these years, there was no way for him to know if that remained true or not.

If not, hopefully, Lea wouldn't think to correct his statement.

Whether she did or not mattered little as the man once again slowed his pace enough for Jared to catch up.

'You wouldn't be that brazen.'

Jared slid his dagger out of the scabbard, tightened his thighs against his horse and snagged the reins beneath his sword belt.

'You have no idea how brazen I would be if forced.'

Catching Blackstone off guard, Jared grabbed the back of Lea's gown, while he rammed his dagger through the man's side, aiming straight towards his black heart, then pushed Blackstone from the horse. 'You were warned to stay away.'

Lea flailed, her arms flying and legs kicking as she sought solid purchase.

Jared tightened his hold on her gown and grabbed the

dangling reins of Blackstone's horse as he relaxed his legs and sat harder on to his saddle, slowing his own horse.

Once both animals stopped, he grabbed Lea around her waist and dragged her up over the high pommel of Blackstone's horse.

She slid her feet into the stirrups and leaned back against the cantle, shaking from head to toe.

'Are you injured?'

She shook her head and stared at him. Her blue eyes were brilliant against the paleness of her face.

'You sure you're all right?'

Again she shook her head.

Since she wasn't screaming or crying, he could only assume she was scared witless.

Jared sheathed his dagger and dismounted. After motioning for Rolfe to give them some distance, he reached up to her, softly ordering, 'Come here.'

She nearly flew into his arms.

He pulled her tight against his chest and soothed a hand down her hair. 'Shh, Lea, you're safe now.'

She shook harder. His words seemed to upset her even more. At a loss as to how to calm her fears, he relaxed his embrace.

'No.' Lea clung to him, as if she couldn't get close enough. 'Don't go.'

'I'm going nowhere.' He rested his chin atop her head and swayed back and forth. 'I'm sorry. This shouldn't have happened.'

When she didn't respond, he asked again, 'Are you sure you aren't hurt?'

'No. Yes. Just hold me.'

'I am holding you.'

She lifted her face away from his chest. 'I want to go home.'

'That makes two of us.' He dropped a kiss on her forehead, then helped her mount Blackstone's horse.

'Jared?'

He paused, his hand resting on her thigh. 'What?'

'No more. Promise me, there will be no more of this killing and dying.'

He squeezed her thigh, then reluctantly stepped away. 'You know I can't promise that.'

'But…'

'No.' He paused, trying to find a way to force the harshness from his voice. 'Lea. This is who I am. This is what I do. You wed me knowing full well who I was. How can I be other than what you see before you now?'

'Take me home.' She looked away, whispering, 'And don't make me love you.'

Chapter Twenty-One

Lea stared out across the bailey. In the two weeks since returning to Montreau, she'd seen Jared rarely. And on those few occasions, he'd kept their meetings brief and impersonal.

She turned away from the window. They couldn't continue in this manner. Something had to change.

But what?

There was little hope that Jared would change his mind and leave his aunt's service. And she wasn't about to change her opinion of this war.

Nor was she willing to send her men into Matilda's service. It was hard enough knowing she'd eventually lose her husband in some battle far from Montreau.

How was she supposed to accept this as her way of life? Yes, she'd knowingly wed a warrior. That didn't mean he couldn't change.

There had to be something else besides duty and honour to the oaths he swore to Empress Matilda.

What about the vows he'd exchanged with her?

Would there ever come a time when those vows held any meaning or importance in his life?

Lea took a long shuddering breath, wondering when this heaviness in her heart would ease.

'My lady?' Agatha entered the chamber. 'Lord Jared wishes a moment of your time.'

Lea shook her head. He was so formal of late—asking for an audience instead of just coming to their chamber himself.

'Where?'

'He and some of the men are in the Great Hall.'

Some of the men? What was this about? The last time some of the men had gathered for an audience it had been to argue over a small plot of land in the village.

'Tell them I'll be right down.'

She ran a comb through her unbound hair, then quickly plaited it into a braid before heading out of the chamber and down the stairs.

To her surprise she heard no arguing from the men. No voices were raised in anger. In fact, except for Jared, there were no *men* present. Instead, five of Montreau's older boys were seated at one of the tables.

Lea approached and saw the missive in front of Jared. The moment he looked up at her, she froze, knowing what the missive contained.

It took a few deep breaths and a hard swallow before she could get the question out of her mouth. 'When?'

'Tomorrow.' Jared waved at the boys gathered around the table. 'They wish a word with you.'

Tomorrow. He was leaving tomorrow. Lea bit the inside of her mouth to keep from crying aloud. There wasn't enough time. She needed at least a few days.

She needed time to drink her fill of the sight of him. Time to hold him.

Time to touch him.

Time to etch him into her mind so she would never forget the feel of his hands, the taste of his lips, the sound of his voice.

'Lea.'

She fought the misery swirling about her, settling as a twisting pain in her gut and as a heaviness in her chest that threatened to take her breath away.

She turned toward the boys with an odd feeling of other-worldliness, as if her body responded, but her mind, her soul, were someplace else.

'My lady.'

Frank, one of the cook's sons, rose and doffed his cap. He twisted it in his hands and stared down at the table. 'My lady, I…we…' He motioned to the other four young men at the table. 'We want to go with Lord Jared.'

'No.'

Jared was at her side instantly. 'Come, sit down.' He gently grasped her arm and pushed her down into the chair he'd just vacated.

When she found her voice, she asked, 'Did you put them up to this?'

'No. This was their idea.'

'I am not sending Montreau's boys into battle.'

'My lady, please.' John, the cook's other son, addressed her. 'We are no longer boys. None of us is married. We have no children. And to be honest, there is nothing for us here.'

'Nothing for you here? There is life here.'

'Without any purpose, this is not a life,' John disagreed. 'I would rather take my chances on a battlefield than die of old age in my mother's hut.'

'Old age? You have seen what—maybe sixteen years? And you speak of old age?'

'Eighteen years and I refuse to spend another year wondering if there is anything outside this land. I want to see something besides these walls, these fields.'

'John, think of your mother.'

'He has already spoken with me, my lady. They both have.' Hawise approached the table and stood behind her sons. 'I gave both of them my blessing, but told them they had to obtain your permission.'

She stared at the woman, unable to believe what she'd heard. 'You are willing to send them away?'

'They are men now, my lady. It is their choice.'

Lea frowned. Grasping for excuses, she said, 'They have no armour, no weapons.'

'That is our responsibility.' Jared grasped her shoulder. 'I will provide for them.'

'You will take them into battle without training?'

'We have been training with Lord Jared's men these past many weeks, my lady.' Frank's eagerness was evident by the excitement in his voice.

'I would never put an untrained man where he didn't belong, Lea.'

She looked at Hawise. 'Both of your sons?'

The cook rested a hand on the top of each chestnut-covered head. 'They will take better care of each other if they are together.' She curled her fingers into their hair and gave a tug. 'Because if they don't, they know what awaits them at home.'

'Please, my lady.' Frank glanced at the others, then looked at her. 'Please, let us have the chance to be men.'

How could she say no to that? She leaned back in her chair and stared up at Jared. 'You will see to their safety?'

'I hadn't planned on feeding them to the lions or anything, Lea.'

She looked back at the expectant faces of the young men. 'You will stay together.'

They nodded in unison.

'You will swear to obey Lord Jared on everything.'

A chorus of ayes and yeses filled the hall.

'You will send word to your mothers about your well-being on a regular basis.' She narrowed her eyes. 'And that doesn't mean once a year.'

When they all just looked at each other, Jared stepped in. 'I will make certain word is sent to Montreau on a regular basis.'

'Then I suggest you go spend some time with your families tonight and pack.'

They all rose and dipped their heads to her before racing out of the hall.

Hawise stepped forward and took her hand. 'Thank you, Lady Lea.'

Did the woman not realise that one day she might not be so grateful for this decision? 'Be sure to let me know if they aren't sending word home.'

Hawise laughed. 'Since you'll have to read their missives for me, you'll know before I will.'

After the cook headed back for the kitchens, Jared released her shoulder and turned away.

She couldn't let him leave. Not like this. 'No one dismissed you.'

He turned around, one eyebrow cocked at an arrogant angle. 'Oh?'

'Jared, please.'

'Don't start, Lea. I have too many things to see to before we leave in the morning.'

'What about your wife? Don't you need to see to her before you leave?'

He stepped closer and stroked her cheek. 'I have every intention of seeing to my wife. I've no doubt she wishes to rail at me before I go.'

'Yes. As a matter of fact, she does.'

'Good. Then I will meet you…' He paused. From the intent look on his face, she guessed he was mentally running through the tasks requiring his attention. 'I will meet you at the gates just before the evening meal.'

'Fine.' She placed her hand over his and leaned her cheek into his palm. 'Is there anything you need me to do?'

'No. Not this time.' He leaned down to kiss her forehead. 'Just rest and try not to make yourself sick with worry.'

Unable to speak, she nodded, and then watched him leave the hall before lowering her head to the table.

Lea pulled her cloak tighter around her shoulders. Where was he? Everyone was already gathering for the evening meal in the Great Hall.

She'd spent most of the day torn between fear of what tomorrow would bring and anticipation of what tonight might hold. Now, she stood at the gates like some eager, besotted young girl waiting to catch a glimpse of her beloved.

Just as she'd done countless times many years ago. 'Waiting for someone?'

She spun around. 'You are late.'

Jared threaded his fingers through hers and headed toward the bay. 'I wanted to offer a toast in the hall before joining you.'

'That was thoughtful.'

'It should have been offered by the two of us together.'

His rebuke stung. When she tried to pull away, he only squeezed her hand. 'How was I supposed to know that?'

'You weren't. I'm just telling you now for future reference.'

Future reference. It would be a miracle if they had a future. Her breath hitched. It would be more than a miracle if they had more than just this one last night together.

'Say it.'

'Say what?'

'I can guess your thoughts, Lea. I know what's on your mind. I'd have those fears spoken, now.'

She shook her head, unwilling to burden him with her terror.

'I might die. I might never see you again.'

Every fear, every horrific nightmare burst in her mind. She whispered in a voice choked with tears she didn't want to shed. 'Don't. Jared, don't.'

'I might never hold my baby in my arms, never see him or her grow into a child, take those first steps or speak the first words.'

'Why are you doing this?' Her question came out as a sob.

He stopped and pulled her hard against his chest. 'Because I won't be here tomorrow. I won't be able to hold you and order you to trust me. This is all we have. This night. I can't ease your fears if you won't speak them aloud. I can't help you conquer them if I don't know what they are.'

She pushed against his chest, crying, 'Don't go. Stay with me.'

'I can't and you know that.'

'Jared, please.' Her knees threatened to buckle beneath her. She curled her fingers into his tunic. 'Please.'

Jared had known this wouldn't be easy. And he'd been well aware that it would be harder on her. But he hadn't expected to share her pain.

He lifted her in his arms and resumed their hike to the beach. When she struggled, he tightened his hold. 'Stop, Lea. I'm not letting you go.'

She circled her arms around his neck and cried against his shoulder. He brushed his cheek against her hair, wishing he could take away her fear, dissolve her pain.

Dear Lord, he hoped this would be their worst parting. He wasn't certain he could do this each and every time.

Not without his heart breaking into pieces a little more with every parting.

Once on the beach he dismissed the men loading the longships with a nod. They could finish later—even tomorrow morning. He wasn't leaving the beach until he knew his wife would be able to stand on her own. And he had only one night to make it so.

He'd arranged things earlier. There was a roaring fire nearby. They had covers to keep them warm, food if they got hungry and enough wine to dull even the deepest pain.

It was imperative that she be able to hold this keep

without him at her side. Jared closed his eyes and cursed her father. The man had had no right to let his only surviving child live like this.

It had been his responsibility, his duty, to ensure the keep and people residing at Montreau thrived. How could they do so if every move they made, every breath they took, was shrouded in fear?

He sat down on a cover, holding Lea on his lap. 'Talk to me, Lea.' He pulled another cover over them and tucked it around her, whispering against her ear, 'Tell me of your fears.'

'I can't.'

She tried to sit up, but he held her head against his shoulder. Stroking his thumb across her cheek, he coaxed, 'Yes, you can. Try.'

She took a long shaking breath, then finally asked, 'What will I do if you never return?'

The last thing he wanted to think about was dying in battle—especially the night before returning to Matilda's service.

'What choice do you have, Lea? You will go on. You will take each day as it comes and then the next and the next one after that. People depend on you. Our child depends on you.'

'When Phillip was killed it was impossible to drag myself out of bed. How am I to manage alone?'

'In a keep full of people you aren't alone. Besides, nobody was prepared for Phillip's death. It was an accident, a mishap of war.'

'And you think I'm prepared for yours?'

'You will be.' He reached into a nearby pouch and pulled out a piece of parchment. 'This will help.'

She took it, asking between sniffles, 'What is it?'

'It's a list of things you need to see to should anything happen.'

Lea let the list fall from her fingers. But he picked it up and put it back in her hand. 'No. Keep it. Put it away where you'll be able to find it should you have need of it.'

She looked at him in amazement. 'You made a *list* of what to do after your death?'

'I'm used to lists.' Jared shrugged. 'Cargo isn't loaded into the hold without an accounting of each item. My ships don't leave the dock without a course charted. I thought it might be of use to you.'

'You have lost your wits.'

'That should be obvious to all. I wed you, didn't I?'

'*What?*'

He flinched at Lea's shriek. But at least he knew for certain that somewhere beneath her worry, there was still a spark of anger ready to be flamed.

'We must face the facts, Lea. I am and always will be a warrior at my liege lord's call. While you—you are content to hide yourself and those who serve you behind the walls of Montreau.'

'I am not content to hide. And I don't force anyone to stay at Montreau.'

'Oh? Then why was John, Frank and their companions joining me such an ordeal?'

'They are just boys.'

'Boys? They haven't been boys for many years now. The only reason they haven't yet become men is because you denied them the opportunity to do so.'

'Going off to fight a battle that is not theirs will make them men?'

'No. Making their own decision to do so and seeing it through is what will make them men.'

He felt her shudder against him, but to her credit, she didn't cry. 'They are so inexperienced.'

'That fault belongs to your father and Charles.' He slid his hand up her back and caressed her neck. 'And you.'

'I was supposed to put a weapon in their hand?'

'Since the men of Montreau didn't see fit to see to their training, then, yes, you should have.'

Her eyes widened. Light from the fire flickered in her gaze. 'What if our child is a boy?'

'He will carry a sword from the moment he can walk without falling.'

Lea tried to launch herself from his lap, but he merely tightened his hand around the back of her neck to keep her in place. 'It will be wooden at first. Then an unsharpened, blunted blade. Only when I deem him ready will I give him a true weapon—one of my choosing.'

'Jared, no.'

'It is the world in which we live, Lea. He needs to be able to defend himself and those who serve him.' He pulled her across his lap so he could gaze down into her eyes. 'And he will need to know his mother trusts him enough to see to his own safety.'

Jared stroked her cheek with the back of his fingers. Her face was cool against his touch. 'You can't let your uncertainty, your fear, give him second thoughts.'

He grabbed another cover and pulled it around both of them. 'The slightest hesitation, a mere second of doubt, could be his death.'

She gasped. 'Jared, I...'

'Shh. And I need you to trust me, Lea. I am no longer a callow youth who trips over his own big feet as he walks across the bailey. I can reach across a table without knocking over everything in my path.'

She smiled softly and he knew she remembered his gawky, less-than-graceful youth.

'Even if I hid with you behind our walls, I could die in my sleep, fall from a horse or be felled by some unnamed disease.'

He traced the seam of her lips with his thumb, savouring her tremor of desire. 'Or, I could live and die the man I was meant to be with dignity, with honour, when and as God wills it.'

Lea understood what he was saying. It did little to ease her fears, but she'd not send him away with her doubts filling his mind.

'I understand you, Jared.' She laced her fingers through his hair and tugged him closer. 'Now hear me. Do nothing foolish. Leave the heroics for another and come home to me.'

He leaned forwards, gently pushing her down on to the cover beneath them. 'No heroics, I have far too much to live for.'

Jared unlaced her gown. The brush of his fingertips against her flesh chased shivers and heat into her blood. 'I swear to you, Lea, I will be home when your time comes. We will hear our babe's first cry together.'

She didn't know if it was the reverence of his gentle, lingering touch, or the surety of his voice, but she believed him.

The breeze coming off the water was cold against her skin, but Jared chased away the chills. Slowly, surely he caressed her body as if committing each curve, every inch to memory.

His lips followed where his hands led until Lea thought she'd die from his touch. 'Jared, please.'

He pushed her arms aside. 'We have all night. I want to carry you in my heart, see you in my mind.'

She moaned at what seemed a wickedly wanton way to perish.

He held her fast as she found fulfilment, crying out his name, begging him for more than just his touch. Then he'd temper his teasing torment, giving her heart a chance to beat more normally, and her breath to slow before once again taking her over the edge of desire.

Finally, when she thought for certain she would faint from pleasure, he came over her, filling her slowly as he held her gaze captive with his own.

'Remember me, Lea.' He lifted her, bringing her tighter against him, as he deepened his thrusts. 'When the nights are long and your arms are empty. Remember me.'

His words were ragged, his breathing harsh, but his intent gaze was steady.

She reached up for him, wanting to hold him against her, promising, 'I will. Oh, Jared, I will.'

He came into her embrace, holding her tightly as they found their release together.

Lea's throat tightened and she fought the building tears.

Jared pulled the covers over them and rolled on to his side, taking her with him. He threaded his fingers through her hair, gently caressing her as he held her face to his shoulder. 'Cry now. I'll have no tears in the morning.'

She instantly lost her battle and gave up to the sorrow knifing through her heart. 'I will miss you so.'

'I hope so.' He stroked the rim of her ear. 'I will miss you, too.'

When her tears lessened, she wanted to beg him to stay, but knew it would only anger and upset him, so she held her tongue on that score. Instead she asked, 'You swear you'll keep your promises?'

'Of course I will.' He wrapped both arms around her and rolled on to his back. 'I don't want you coming down here in the morning.'

'You don't want me to see you off?'

'I'll see you in our chamber before I leave. I don't want you down here on the beach.'

'I won't cry.'

She felt his chest tremble beneath her. 'Yes, you will.'

'So will the other women.'

'True, but if they see the lady of the keep in agony, it will only serve to build their fears.'

'But—'

'No, Lea. Not this time. This time I want to remember you naked in our bed. You can cry there all you want— just don't do so in front of Montreau's people.'

Not at all certain that would be possible, she nodded. 'I'll try.'

'Go to sleep.'

Lea stretched and froze at the feel of her bed beneath her. How'd she get here? She sat up quickly. Had he left? Without waking her up? Without saying farewell?

She swung around and rose from the bed, pulling on a chemise and gown as she headed for the door. Jerking it open, she stared up at Jared.

'Going somewhere?'

Relief washed over her. 'I thought you'd left already.'

He backed her into the room. 'I wouldn't leave without bidding you farewell.'

She wasn't certain what to say, or what to do. 'Jared…I…'

He lifted her in his arms, crossed the chamber and dumped her on to the bed. 'Get undressed and go back to sleep.'

'But…' She knew that nothing she said would change what was going to happen, so she removed her gown and slid back beneath the covers.

Jared tucked the covers around her, and then sat on the edge of the bed. 'Another ship of my men will be here within a day or two. They know they are to answer to you. Use them to keep Montreau safe until I return. Can you do that?'

She nodded. 'Yes. My father's old captain still lives in the village. I'll call on him if I need help.'

'You do that.' He brushed her hair back from her face. 'Take care of yourself and our baby, Lea.'

'I will.'

She stared at him. Dressed in chain maille, his sword already at his side, he was a frightening vision. One she realised she loved dearly. She'd tried not to. She'd sworn never to give her heart to a warrior. But staring up at him, she knew she had.

Lea cupped his cheek. 'And you take care of yourself, too.'

'I will.' He kissed her palm, then tucked her arm beneath the covers. 'Stay here. Go back to sleep.'

Jared rose and Lea swallowed the lump building in

her throat. He leaned down and kissed her. 'I will return in time, Lea.'

Without another word he headed for the door. When he grasped the handle, Lea panicked. She didn't want him to leave without knowing how she felt. She called out, 'Jared.'

He turned to face her. 'Lea.' His voice held a warning that he'd not tolerate any hysterics.

'Jared, I love you.'

He showed no trace of surprise. Instead, he closed his eyes and nodded. 'I know.'

When the door closed behind him, Lea gripped the covers in her hands, refusing to break down. She might not go down to the beach, but she couldn't just lie in this bed.

She rose and donned her gown once again. The missive he'd given her last night, the one that detailed what to do should he not return, lay on the bench by the window.

Lea went to stand before the window and flicked her fingernail beneath the wax seal. She read the list, her heart breaking with each gruesome order.

Her eyes filled with tears at the thought of telling his family about his death. Her knees grew weak at the idea of gathering them together here at Montreau for a memorial service should his body not be found.

She leaned against the wall next to window and read the last line. Her heart stopped as she read his words over and over again.

Lea clutched the note to her chest and raced from the chamber. Her feet barely touched the stairs as she headed for the Great Hall and out into the bailey.

Frantic, she searched for him. 'Jared!' Spotting him, she shouted again, 'Jared!'

He pulled up on his reins and turned his horse around.

Lea held up the note and ran to his side. 'I will. I swear, I will.'

One eyebrow winged up. 'You weren't supposed to read that yet.'

She smiled up at him. 'You knew I would.'

He reached down and grasped her beneath her arms to haul her up and hold her close. 'I'd hoped you would read it last night.'

She cupped his cheeks between her hands. 'Doesn't matter.' Lea kissed him, whispering, 'I swear, I will always love you, Jared. Always.'

'I'll take that with me, and I leave my love with you.' He kissed her until the sounds in the bailey faded away and there was nothing except his lips on hers and their hearts pounding in unison.

Jared lowered her to the ground. 'Now go.'

'No.' She shook her head. 'This is my keep and I will take my place on the wall until you are gone.'

'So be it.' He reached down to trace a fingertip along her nose. 'You keep my baby and my love safe, do you hear me?'

When she nodded, he pointed toward the gate towers. 'Go.'

Chapter Twenty-Two

Silent as North Sea raiders of old, the three longships slipped on to the sandy beach of Montreau's bay.

Jared, Lord of Warehaven and Montreau, leapt from the centre boat, his booted feet splashing in the shallow water. Heart pounding, he rushed forwards, leaving his men behind as he raced for the keep.

At the top of the hill, he turned to spare a glance toward the beach, his mind flying back to a night that had kept him constant company these last long months.

Jared turned to the task at hand. Had he arrived on time? Was he late? They'd run into a storm two days ago, delaying their arrival at Montreau. Anticipation rippled through his muscles and curved his lips into a smile.

After six long months of a seemingly never-ending war for the crown, his aunt, the Empress Matilda, had granted him leave to return home. She had issued only one order, and that was to invite her to his child's christening when the time came.

He patted the documents secured to the inside of his mantle, a gift for the lady of this keep.

Halfway across the field, a group of men rode towards him, leading a spare horse. 'My lord, you need hurry.'

He grabbed the reins, mounted and urged the beast toward Montreau. He flew between the twin gate towers, barely hearing the shouts and cheers of the men on the walls and brought the horse to a prancing stop.

Hawise, the keep's cook, met him in the bailey. She twisted her apron in her hands, staring at him expectantly. Jared spared a moment to assure her, 'Frank and John are behind me.'

Once inside the keep, Jared slowed his pace, hoping to catch his breath before mounting the stairs to his chamber. But the men and women gathered at a table in the Great Hall pointed in unison toward the steps.

'Noooo! Not yet!'

Lea's pain-laced voice sailed down from the chamber, prodding him to hasten his pace.

'Where is he?'

Agatha paced the corridor in front of the doorway to their chamber. When she saw him, she turned and rushed back inside. 'He is here, Lea.'

Jared swung into the room and came to a rocking stop. His blood roared in his ears as he took in the scene before him.

A broken birthing chair lay in pieces in the far corner. A dishevelled older woman—the midwife, perhaps— glared at Lea, scolding, 'See, here he is. Now, get on with this.'

Agatha wrung her hands together as she paced the floor alongside the bed.

His wife turned to look at him. Sweat dampened her hair. Her eyes were red, her cheeks flushed.

He couldn't remember a time when she'd looked more beautiful.

Jared crossed the room and knelt on the edge of the bed to take Lea's hand. 'Are you giving these poor women trouble?'

She grasped his hand. 'They said you'd not make it in time.'

Her voice was weak. Concerned, he looked at the midwife. The woman rolled her eyes towards the ceiling before bringing her attention back to him. 'She would be fine if she'd just do as she's told.'

Relief that the only thing wrong was Lea's temper swept through him, leaving him light-headed and silencing the roar in his ears. 'Are you saying my sweet wife isn't obeying you?'

Lea's laugh was ragged. 'Impossible to believe, isn't it?'

'No.' He dropped a kiss on top her head and asked the midwife, 'What can I do?'

'Since she broke the chair, perhaps you could get behind her and give her enough support to push this baby free.'

Lea broke the chair? That should prove an interesting story to tell their child some day.

He slid behind her and straddled his legs around her. With his lips against her ear, he asked, 'Don't you have something you should be doing?'

'No.' She shook her head. 'I thought I'd relax a while and let you take over from here.'

Before he could respond to her cheeky response, her stomach visibly contracted. Lea went stiff. Screaming, she leaned into the contraction.

Jared closed his eyes, certain the chamber had some-how begun spinning around him.

He vaguely heard the midwife mutter something about men. Agatha slapped a cold, damp cloth over his face. 'It's nearly over, my lord.'

Lea slumped back against him; a string of ribald curses left her lips.

Where had she learned such foul language? He didn't get the chance to ask. Another contraction washed over her.

By the fourth time, he was cursing with her, swearing silently that the next time she was with child, he'd stay for the pregnancy and leave right before the delivery.

Lea reached up and grasped his arm. Panting, she asked, 'How many children do you want?'

He'd be content with one. But she might change her mind tomorrow. Instead of giving her a specific number, he suggested, 'Let's get through this one first.'

'I want—' Her response was cut short by her own scream.

The midwife's voice rose. 'That's it. Come, my lady, this is the last one.'

Agatha rushed to the foot of the bed, holding a sheet in her hands.

'It's a girl!' The midwife handed the baby off to Agatha and turned her attention back to his wife.

Lea reached up and stroked his cheek. 'Oh, I'm so sorry, Jared.'.

He grabbed her hand and kissed her palm. 'Sorry? For what?'

'I wanted to give you a son.'

A tear slipped down her cheek and Jared thought in

that moment he would die. His chest tightened along with his throat. He couldn't find the words to express his gratitude for the daughter she'd just given him.

Across the chamber their daughter wailed. Her first cry seemed to echo off the walls of the chamber.

Unable to speak, Jared swallowed hard and motioned toward Agatha. The maid brought the baby to him and placed it in his arms.

She was so tiny, and so utterly perfect. 'Lea, look at her.' He put the baby in her arms and wrapped his own around both of them. 'You could not have given me a more precious gift.'

Lea stared down at their daughter in amazement. She lightly stroked the soft cheek and traced a finger over the dark hair covering the baby's head.

'She's perfect.'

A solitary tear splashed on to the baby's forehead from above. Lea wiped it away, then reached up behind her to caress Jared's cheek.

She felt the dampness on his face, but said nothing to embarrass him in front of the other women. It was enough to know that he was as moved by their tiny miracle as she.

He kissed her hand. 'She's perfect, just like her mother.'

She chuckled. 'I will remind you of that the next time we disagree on something.'

The midwife stood and stretched. 'My lord, if you would but give us a few minutes, Agatha and I can set things to right here and then perhaps you could see that your wife gets some rest?'

Lea felt him hesitate behind her. She nudged his leg with her elbow. 'Go. Get something to eat, to drink, then come back and tell me about your time away.'

He untangled his legs from around her and rose. But instead of leaving, he reached down for the baby. 'We'll go sit in the alcove.'

She watched him walk slowly into the small room off the side of their chamber. He held the baby gingerly in his arms, whispering to her as he disappeared into the shadows.

If she'd had any doubts that her battle-hardened husband would shy away from their child until it was older, his actions vanquished them.

The women completed their ministrations quickly as promised. Once the bed linens were changed and she was cleaned and dressed in a fresh chemise, Agatha called for Jared.

When he came back into the chamber, the maid took the child from him. 'We've called in a wet nurse for tonight.' She nodded towards Lea. 'See that she gets some rest.'

Lea wanted to argue, but she realised her maid was most likely right. She was exhausted and desperately wanted a few stolen moments alone with her husband.

Besides, from the weakness of her limbs and the succession of yawns, she was fairly certain the tea Agatha had given her had been laced with something to make her sleep.

On her way out of the door, the midwife stopped to ask, 'How were you so certain he'd arrive in time?'

Lea slid down beneath the covers. 'Because he promised he would be here.'

Once the door closed behind the women, Jared stretched out beside her. 'I kept my promises—both of them.'

She couldn't argue with him on that. He had kept them—he'd returned home safely, and in time to hear their baby's first cry together.

He reached down alongside the bed and fumbled with something on the floor. 'I have something for you.'

She rested her hand on his chest. 'I have all I need.'

'I think you might want this.' He handed her a rolled document.

Lea read the contents and gasped. 'How did you do this?'

'It wasn't easy. But there are benefits to being related to both Matilda and Stephen.'

'So you don't have to go back into battle for the empress?'

'No.'

'And Montreau doesn't have to defend either side? We won't have to battle for or against either of them?'

'No.'

Lea frowned. 'But what will you do?'

Jared laughed. 'I have a fleet of ships, remember? I'm going to make us enough gold to support our children.'

'And that will be enough for you?'

'Enough?' He eased her into his arms. 'Love, you are enough for me. There is a whole world out there. Places neither of us have ever seen.'

He settled more comfortably in the bed. 'We can go anywhere we want. I can make love to you all over the world.'

'I might like that.' Lea grimaced. 'Although, maybe not tonight.'

'Or we can stay here at Montreau and, when you're ready, we can make love on the beach.'

A shiver caught her by surprise. 'I know I'll like that.'

She trailed a finger down his arm. 'You never answered me before. How many children do you want?'

Jared leaned over to kiss her slowly, deeply, before saying, 'One or a dozen matters not to me, Lea. As long as I have your love I am content.'

She brushed her hand over his stubble-covered cheek. 'I keep my promises, too. I will always, always love you.'

* * * * *

"AREN'T YOU GOING TO SAY 'Fly me' or at least 'Welcome aboard'?"

Amanda Bauer didn't. The softly muttered word that actually came out of her mouth was a lot less welcoming. And had fewer letters. Four, to be exact.

The man shook his head and tsked. "Not exactly the friendly skies. Haven't caught the spirit yet this morning?"

"Make one more airline-slogan crack and you'll be walking to Chicago," she said.

He nodded once, then pushed his sunglasses onto the top of his tousled hair. The move revealed blue eyes that matched the sky above. And yeah. They were twinkling. Damn it.

"Understood. Just, uh, promise me you'll say 'Coffee, tea or me' at least once, okay? Please?"

Amanda tried to glare, but that twinkle sucked the annoyance right out of her. She could only draw in a slow breath as he climbed into the plane. As she watched her passenger disappear into the small jet, she had to wonder about the trip she was about to take.

Coffee and tea they had, and he was welcome to them.

But her? Well, she'd never even considered making a move on a customer before. Talk about unprofessional.

And yet…

Something inside her suddenly wanted to take a chance, to be a little outrageous.

How long since she had done indecent things—or decent ones, for that matter—with a sexy man? Not since before they'd thrown all their energies into expanding Clear-Blue Air, at the very least. She hadn't had time for a lunch date, much less the kind of lust-fest she'd enjoyed in her younger years. The kind that lasted for entire weekends and involved not leaving a bed except to grab the kind of sensuous food that could be smeared onto—and eaten off—someone else's hot, naked, sweat-tinged body.

She closed her eyes, her hand clenching tight on the railing. Her heart fluttered in her chest and she tried to make herself move. But she couldn't—not climbing up, but not backing away, either. Not physically, and not in her head.

Was she really considering this? God, she hadn't even looked at the stranger's left hand to make sure he was available. She had no idea if he was actually attracted to her or just an irrepressible flirt. Yet something inside was telling her to take a shot with this man.

It was crazy. Something she'd never considered. Yet right now, at this moment, she was definitely considering it. If he was available…could she do it? Seduce a stranger. Have an anonymous fling, like something out of a blue movie on late-night cable?

She didn't know. All she knew was that the flight to Chicago was a short one so she had to decide quickly.

And as she put her foot on the bottom step and began to climb up, Amanda suddenly had to wonder if she was about to embark on the ride of her life.

Whirlwind Secrets
DEBRA COWAN

HE *WILL* UNCOVER THE TRUTH!

Russ Baldwin has learned from harsh experience
to look twice at people. When his business partner,
Miss Lydia Kent, moves into town, he goes
on high alert....

Russ's watchful eyes rattle Lydia. She must keep
her noble, yet underground, activities—and
her emotions—tightly under wraps. When Russ
realizes his curvy, sweet-talkin' co-owner has
hidden depths, he's determined to uncover them!

*Available February
wherever you buy books.*

HARLEQUIN® HISTORICAL:
Where love is timeless

The Viscount's Betrothal
LOUISE ALLEN

SWEPT OFF HER FEET!

Decima knows her family regularly remind
themselves to "marry off poor dear Dessy." But who
would ever want a graceless, freckled beanpole like
herself? Then she encounters Adam Grantham,
Viscount Weston—the first man she's met
who's tall enough to sweep her off her feet...
literally! Could such a handsome rake really
find *her* attractive?

*Available February
wherever you buy books.*

HARLEQUIN® HISTORICAL:
Where love is timeless

The Gentleman's Quest
DEBORAH SIMMONS

HE WILL PROTECT HER, BUT AT WHAT COST?

When lightning illuminates a stranded beauty
Christopher Marchant must do as any gentleman would.
Although, once rescued, she must be on her way.

But if Hero Ingram leaves empty-handed her uncle will
punish her. As a gentleman he must protect her and make
Hero's quest his own. But as a red-blooded male…?
She has awoken him from his slumber!

*Available February
wherever you buy books.*

HARLEQUIN® *Blaze*™

*It all started
with a few naughty books....*

As a member of the Red Tote Book Club,
Carol Snow has been studying works of
classic erotic literature...but Carol doesn't
believe in love...or marriage. It's going to take
another kind of classic—Charles Dickens's
A Christmas Carol—and a little otherworldly
persuasion to convince her to go after her
own sexily ever after.

Cuddle up with

Her Sexy Valentine

by STEPHANIE BOND

Available February 2010

red-hot reads

REQUEST YOUR FREE BOOKS!

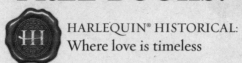

HARLEQUIN® HISTORICAL:
Where love is timeless

2 FREE NOVELS PLUS 2 FREE GIFTS!

YES! Please send me 2 FREE Harlequin® Historical novels and my 2 FREE gifts (gifts are worth about $10). After receiving them, if I don't wish to receive any more books, I can return the shipping statement marked "cancel." If I don't cancel, I will receive 6 brand-new novels every month and be billed just $4.94 per book in the U.S. or $5.49 per book in Canada. That's a saving of 20% off the cover price! It's quite a bargain! Shipping and handling is just 50¢ per book in the U.S. and 75¢ per book in Canada.* I understand that accepting the 2 free books and gifts places me under no obligation to buy anything. I can always return a shipment and cancel at any time. Even if I never buy another book from Harlequin, the two free books and gifts are mine to keep forever.

246 HDN E4DN   349 HDN E4DY

Name	(PLEASE PRINT)

Address	Apt. #

City	State/Prov.	Zip/Postal Code

Signature (if under 18, a parent or guardian must sign)

Mail to the **Harlequin Reader Service:**
IN U.S.A.: P.O. Box 1867, Buffalo, NY 14240-1867
IN CANADA: P.O. Box 609, Fort Erie, Ontario L2A 5X3

Not valid for current subscribers to Harlequin Historical books.

Want to try two free books from another line?
Call 1-800-873-8635 or visit www.morefreebooks.com.

* Terms and prices subject to change without notice. Prices do not include applicable taxes. N.Y. residents add applicable sales tax. Canadian residents will be charged applicable provincial taxes and GST. Offer not valid in Quebec. This offer is limited to one order per household. All orders subject to approval. Credit or debit balances in a customer's account(s) may be offset by any other outstanding balance owed by or to the customer. Please allow 4 to 6 weeks for delivery. Offer available while quantities last.

Your Privacy: Harlequin Books is committed to protecting your privacy. Our Privacy Policy is available online at www.eHarlequin.com or upon request from the Reader Service. From time to time we make our lists of customers available to reputable third parties who may have a product or service of interest to you. If you would prefer we not share your name and address, please check here. ☐

Help us get it right—We strive for accurate, respectful and relevant communications. To clarify or modify your communication preferences, visit us at www.ReaderService.com/consumerchoice.

HHI0

The Accidental Countess
MICHELLE WILLINGHAM

Stephen Chesterfield cannot recall the past three
months of his life, never mind having a wife!
What's more, someone is trying to silence him
before his memory returns....

Emily Chesterfield is trapped in a marriage of
convenience with a man who doesn't remember her.
Stephen clearly thinks she is the most unsuitable
countess.... Can they find trust and love before
it is too late?

*Available February
wherever you buy books.*